The Twelve Cataclysms

Book 1: Protasis

Rob Queen

The Twelve Cataclysms: Protasis

Cover by Gilberto Salas

Cover type by HdE

ISBN: 1499528442

ISBN-13: 978-1499528442

Dedicated to my parents,

Douglas Murray Queen

Jeannie Maclane Worthington Queen

Writers and teachers

From art and heart lands unfound

Individual

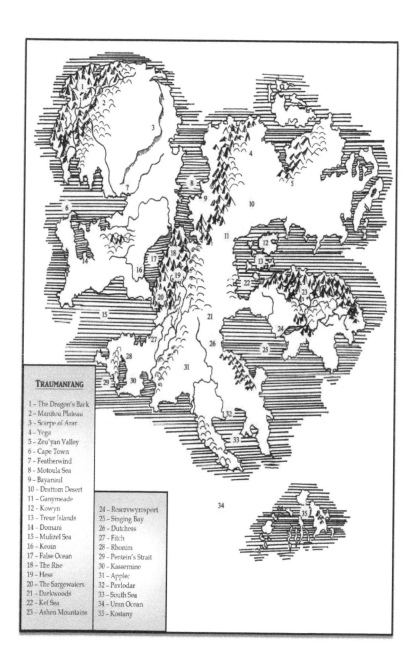

TRAUMANFANG

1 – The Dragon's Back
2 – Manitou Plateau
3 – Scarpe of Arar
4 – Yega
5 – Zeu'yan Valley
6 – Cape Town
7 – Featherwind
8 – Motoula Sea
9 – Bayanaul
10 – Drattum Desert
11 – Ganymeade
12 – Kowyn
13 – Treur Islands
14 – Domani
15 – Mulizel Sea
16 – Keoin
17 – False Ocean
18 – The Rise
19 – Hess
20 – The Sargewaters
21 – Darkwoods
22 – Kef Sea
23 – Ashen Mountains

24 – Reservwyresport
25 – Singing Bay
26 – Dutchess
27 – Fitch
28 – Rhonim
29 – Pentein's Strait
30 – Kassernine
31 – Applec
32 – Pavlodar
33 – South Sea
34 – Uran Ocean
35 – Kostany

Acknowledgements

It will take a while for the reality of this adventure to kick in but, until that happens, let me say my bit about this ride and the people who helped make it happen.

First and foremost, I owe my wife, Bia, a tremendous amount of gratitude for her willingness to try out life in such a strange part of the world. Honestly, I can't even begin to thank you for humoring me in this.

Secondly, I want to thank my beta and gamma readers: Peter Michaud, Charla Arabie, Emily Baum (who technically was neither a beta nor gamma, but was still really helpful!), Jeannie Queen, Clyde Brown, and Jessica Arnold (shout out to your daughter, Olivia Ann Moral-Arnold, who was born during this creative ride!). I also want to thank my editor, Thomas Hill, who suggested many late-minute changes, and darned if he wasn't right about them.

To help make this happen, I went through Indiego-go.com's crowdfunding and, from there, I was on the receiving end of some of the greatest generosity I have ever encountered. People from all walks of life—from my connections in the horse world, to my students, to friends new and old, family, and even some potential readers!—came together and provided me with a tremendous show of support.

I honestly do not know what I did to deserve the love you all gave me, but I can only pray that this novel does not disappoint. Without you all, this could not have happened, and I will be eternally grateful to you for this. So, before I start tearing up in appreciation, let me give special mention to a few of you for the overwhelming generosity you showed: Rafael O. Morales, Derrick B. Queen, Sophia Freire and Kurt Katala, and Deborah Johansen-Harris.

But most of all, I just want to thank you, the reader, for getting this far.

Chapter 1

"COME ON, LASS, NOT MUCH FURTHER," SAID THE OLD, TOOTH-less man on Vie's right.

"Hold on... dizzy," Vie said as the motion of the hall-way took a sudden spin for the worse. A moment ago, she was feeling a bit better but, with each step, the pounding on her skull increased. She now felt as drunk as if she had bathed in gin. She wondered if she would vomit again.

"We haven't got time for you to get your bearings," the man to her left said, not unkindly. "You have been summoned to the Keyhall and figuring how to block the wards has taken enough time."

"Give 'er a momen' more, Dane Wunds," the tooth-less man said. "Even you said yourself that this was nothin' you experienced before. Push her now an' we'll never get her side o' dis mess."

"The wards were set up as a barrier to prevent extra-dimensional intrusion into the Innervein. It should not smack a mere girl like this. But, with me as a conduit, she should be stabilized."

"An' how are you holdin' out?"

Dane Wunds tapped his chest. "It's a strain."

Vie's attention to her escorts drifted away. Regardless of Dane Wunds's plea to continue, he had not forced her on. Expecting this respite to be short, she made the most of it, focusing all her attention on a single dark knot in the polished, soft pine flooring. Feeling a swelling of bile building up deep in her belly, she gritted her teeth and pushed at the spinning world. Slowly, the swirling vortex diminished into a slow ebbing on the edges of her headache. She was panting now, and doubled over with her hands on the rough cloth of her traveling pants. A slash of personal vanity unfavorably compared her own cheap clothing to those of these two wizards.

"Magi," she corrected herself as Dane Wunds had done not too long ago, when she accidentally called them wizards. "Six hundred years and the public still hasn't forgotten. I'd love to bring Thermon the Tool back to life just so that I could strangle him. No way should we ever be called anything as lame as a wizard. Damned fools at conjuration, that's what your 'wizards' are. It's like calling a king 'friend.'"

Her two escorts were still in the midst of their discussion and were oblivious to her imminent recovery from this vertigo that had hit her. Squite, the more familiar to her of the pair, was as old and tall as any man she had ever seen, hunched with age yet still casting a very tall silhouette in his feathered cloak. His lack of teeth created a cold irony with his caustic bite of words, yet despite this, he had showed her nothing but kindness since their meeting. Dane Wunds, on the other hand, showed himself as a meticulously kept master of order. Not a hair of his greying head was out of place, and he wore a perfectly white long jacket tied at the waist with a back-tying cinch. Under the long sleeve of his jacket, his left hand was a tapestry of peculiar lines and symbols, reminding Vie of art found in the Great Sept.

Indeed, men like these, she had seen only once before this horrendously unfortunate night. It had been one of the many nights where helping dear Yue at her pleasure house, The Released Stout, was the far easier route toward comfort and coin than a night of burglary. A magus, wanting to double his pleasure, was brought before the pair. It took only a glance to know him for an arcana user of the Order of the Vein. He wore a loose-fitting robe of exquisite silks and, later on, once he had removed his clothing, she saw the tree tattooed on his right shoulder. He was clean-shaven and portly, thin of limb, and smelled pleasantly of exotic smoke and warmth. When he spoke at all, it was quiet and both self-conscious and commanding.

He was not what she had expected. The stories from her youth had stirred her imagination into images of magi freezing water and scorching air. It was said that they could control fire, move around the world in a moment, and enter people's minds. These were dangerous men. (It was always men, never women. The women were called Hearts, those who battled tiger-oxen and chased storms and could create food from an open palm.) They were smart and learned and they were powerful in skill, politics, and wealth. Being so close to that first magus had been so disconcerting for the younger Vie that despite all Yue's considerable efforts, Vie had not been able to relax properly enough to take him without feeling her insides tearing. Even after his exhaustion, when, at his word, she and Yue entertained him by spreading pleasures upon one another, it was impossible to concentrate on Yue's knowledgeable touch. She had faked pleasure well enough, but throughout she kept imagining he would recognize her deception and rain acid upon her face. When their time together concluded, he grunted a simple compliment, paid his money like a regular man, and departed, seemingly oblivious to Vie's terror.

"They are regular people," Yue had said after he had left. "Such as regular is." It failed to quiet Vie's concern. Over the night, however, filled by an atypical feast of a half chicken and rutabaga pie bought with the not-un-generous money the magus had paid, Vie was better able to consider Yue's words. She ran her fingertips across the thin golden velvet that coated Yue's body and considered how varied "regular" was. Some, like Yue, had the obvious physical oddities of the Blessed: fur, or horns, maybe wings or claws, that one man she had seen with the lower body of a horse. Others, like Vie herself, had been blessed with an ability. She had even once heard that magi, as with the Sisters of the Heart, were among the blessed who were able to play with the very arcana that created their gifts. To be perfectly honest with herself, it was why she was so terrified of these two men.

Now Vie was in their home, the Innervein—the place where they came to study and do their magicking and experiments and who knows what else. Since Squite had brought her here, the place had been beating her over the head with its protective wards. It was constant and chronic and struck her in waves, like bleeding cramps but in her head and gut and in her bones. Through her ringing ears, she could hear shuffling and muttering. A crowd of young men in magi robes were clustered nearby. Some were grinning at her with a certain degree of lechery, some glanced about nervously, but most stared at her in innocent curiosity. Wanting to be out from under their questing eyes, Vie straightened herself. A wave of nausea hit with the motion but Squite was right there with a hand around her upper arm to support her.

"Yah, good," he said. "Righ' up this hallway, lass. Easy there. One foot in front'a d'other. That's it."

They stopped before a pair of mighty wooden doors bearing intricately detailed carvings of a spreading oak. Massive and lined with silver steel, they seemed to glow of their own power.

"When you go in through these doors, you will be judged for your crimes. Do you understand this?" Dane Wunds asked.

Her crime. To Vie, her crime was no more than getting caught in the act of burglarizing the silver tower. There was nothing for what she wanted; she had had to take a risk. Was it her fault her agent's information had been inaccurate: that the tower had not, in fact, been deserted tonight?

"What will they do with me?"

The two magi looked at one another, concern and insecurity plain in their faces. Neither spoke.

"Am I going to be locked up? Will I... will they—" Vie swallowed. "Will I be killed? Tortured? Please, I need to know."

Dane Wunds sighed. "I don't even know what you

did. Squite brought you to me so that you could make it here to the Keyhall. There are certain... protocols that are required in this type of situation."

"Ha!" Squite snorted. "Wimmen are never allowed here. Dis isn't no 'type' a situation. We can tell ya dat you're our guest, so we'll treat you as such until y'give us reason otherwise. Ya'll be charged for breakin' into de tower—that's nothin' he'll let go. But..."

The two magi looked at one another again.

"What happened..."

"We all felt it."

"Something dat big..."

"I was suffering a headache of my own when Squite brought you in," Dane Wunds said. "I was hoping to rest it out. Something big like that will pull our brothers home from all over the world. I hate crowds. But you came in. It was an order to get you to the Keyhall. I had to heal you."

"Never felt anything like dat. Dese crowds are all de proof we need," Squite said, gesturing to the mob growing behind them. These were no mere boys as Vie had seen before. These were men and boys of all ages, some of whom had thick beards and scars of experience etched across their faces. Fear was mixing with shock at finding her here, and it would not be long before the slit-tongued mistress of gossip slipped from their mouths. "Dis is bigger dan you, me, Wunds, and whatever you thought you were doing."

It was hard to consider that right here, not with all of these cold eyes staring into her, burning her with accusation and haughty insolence. Such attitudes were not unknown to Vie, but the pressure of these mystical men in addition to the pressures of the wards were all the motivation she needed to straighten her back and look at each of her escorts in the eyes. "Whatever happens, promise me that you will take me back to Sludge before my punishment is filled."

"We don't know—" Dane Wunds began, but Vie cut him off.

"You will promise this to me."

Squite gaped at her for a moment, his mouth bobbing open and close, a fish wondering at food. Then he flashed her a grin that exposed his fleshy gums. "Yah, I'll promise ya dat, little missy. Why not?"

She squeezed his hand in thanks then turned toward the door.

With a wave from Dane Wunds, the mighty doors groaned away from them. The domed room beyond was enormous, circular, and quite dark compared to the arcanic illumination of the hallways. A strip of lights circled around at a level twice Vie's height. Beneath this glowing ring, there were shadowed heads of two score people seated or standing on an elevated dais. The circular quality of the room guided her eyes toward the center, where the image of Reservwyresport glowed. Off at the southwest end of the phantom city, wedged between the seedier piers of the wharves and the roiling hills set before the Western Gate, plain as day, was Sludge, the slum she had just cajoled Squite to return her to before her final fate be passed. She was distracted from this almost at once by the screaming ruckus of shouts and japes of the men assembled.

Vie backed off from the tempestuous clamor and directly into her escorts. She heard a small protest come from her lips, their hands tight against her upper arms. They compelled her forward but she refused, struggling against their strength to escape. She could feel their fingers digging into her skin, knew that there would be fresh bruises there tomorrow. Yet still she resisted.

As she was beginning to gain ground toward the door, a voice cut though her efforts and caught her at her throat, where a thin choker of arcana had been bound. "Behave." The voice resonated with the choker and stripped her body of her control. With her arms now limp at her sides, Dane Wunds and Squite guided her easily into the room. Though she could feel her face and body as limp as a dead pigeon, inside she was seething. This was the second time tonight this had happened— it was how her captor had brought her here to the Innervein in the first place. If she were being turned into a walking puppet again, that meant that he was somewhere in the room as well. Since her outside was placid already, she forced her fury down into her heart, where she kept it in wait until a better time.

The magi brought her into the center of the room, beneath a pale golden light that rose up from a detailed mural of an oak on the floor. Her guided progress through the chamber brought the arguments to an end. Stopping dead over the branches of the mural triggered them to rise up menacingly toward her. As she backed away from the pale blue limbs, her foot bumped against the light and a blast of color rippled away from the contact. Within a moment, the limbs had created a fine mesh around her so bright that she could scarcely see through. Just as she feared she had been judged before the trial could even begin, the dark limbs began to crack, releasing a tower of heatless light around her. In this spotlight, Vie could feel every one of the two score eyes boring into her, carving into her soul to excavate the secrets from within. She closed her eyes and took a deep breath. This was happening. Come what may, she would be brave.

"Hello," a smoky voice called to her from across the hall. There sat a massive wooden chair whose tall back had been shaped to resemble the pervading motif of the Innervein. Its canopy was dotted with small lights that played like fireflies in darkness on the figure seated. From the shadowy half-light, the figure spoke again in a voice as dark and murky as the room. He spoke softly, yet it felt to have come from directly next to her. "I am Hamza, 714th Skeleton Key to sit the High Seat of the Keyhall, Master of the Order of the Vein, and Protector of the Arcana. You may call me Skeleton Hamza." It was as he tilted his head to the side that some of the light fell over his face. Where his eyes would have been, empty sockets stared off away from Vie. By tilting his head like this, he moved one of his ears toward her—a human adaptation of what dogs and horses do to better hear. "What is your name?"

"Vie."

"Is that all?"

"I am Vie... Skeleton Hamza?"

Someone snorted.

"Indeed," Skeleton Key Hamza replied, tilting his head the other way. "Dane Wunds. If my sources are correct, upon her arrival to the Innervein, this young woman was struck by our defensive wards. I was under the impression that your skill would be ample enough to prepare her for this inquiry. Based on your learned opinion, does this woman, in fact, have the lucidity to go ahead?"

"If it please you, Skeleton," Dane Wunds replied. He stepped forward just a bit to address the master. "In my opinion, a mere girl should not even feel the wards, let alone suffer them as she is. Because they are crushing her, I have taken it upon myself to ease the bulk of the pressures upon her. Short of dematerializing all the wards we have present, there is nothing we can do to totally alleviate her assault, but can I assume that is a route we choose not to take?"

"Indeed it is not."

"So far, this has proven to be of help to her. While I am here, she should be strong enough for this. A conduit may be required to share this pressure if this inquiry takes too long, however."

"Good. I think all here are interested in learning just what this... Vie has to say about tonight's events."

"If it please you, Skeleton," Squite called out. "Ya may not know what it's like to be out and about in de world outside de Veins, but I'm from Reservwyresport, an' I know de peoples who live dere, from de rich who live out on de Twin Hills, to de merchants out on Mercant Way, Hobknob Knob, an' Foxglove Road, to de farmers across de river in Milltown, and even de sailors what come in offa de Singing Bay. I seen dem a' coming and going. And dis girl, I know girls like her from de rest of dem. She's Sludge, through and through." Squite nodded proudly at his own wisdom.

"What is your point, Master Ventagist?" Skeleton Hamza asked.

"Dat in Sludge, dere are no titles, nor names oder dan what deir mudders give 'em—if even dey get dat far. Everything you have in Sludge is what you kill for; people from Sludge aren't given nothing. If de place gives you anything, it's a swift kick in the arse and maybe a cuff upon de ear. What I'm saying is dat girls like dis aren't at fault for dat which dey been forced to do. Dey are only de result of a system that don't care about dem. More importantly, dey aren't idiots to be insulted or laughed at just because dey haven't had de education we've been fortunate to have. I'm an old man and prone to ramble, so excuse me and let me put it simply: keep your opinions outta dis and let's just find out what happened tonight without prejudice."

Vie looked over at the man beside her, the age-swelled nose, the enormous ears, balding head with long white wisps hanging loose from the spotted dome. Crooked and bent as he was, he radiated strength. With his brown-and-white–feathered cloak she beheld not a wizened corpse, but a fresh eagle, sharp beaked and deadly. In that moment, she loved the old man both for coming to her defense and for his ability to drive this audience to utter silence.

"Despite the insult to my person, you speak well, Master Ventagist," Hamza conceded with a tilt of his head. "Perhaps we of the Order have grown a tad accustomed to the titles we dispense to one another. I suppose that is the nature of a brotherhood such as ours. We reward accomplishment and assume that all in the world do so in similar fashion. Perhaps this is a question best addressed to our guest. Vie, do you feel capable of answering the questions that we have to ask tonight?"

"Yes," she said, feeling a bit bolder from Squite's words.

"Good. As far as our purposes are concerned, we only need you to confirm a few details from today. Because we are only interested in the facts, we must have you be honest as possible. We need these details to be as forthcoming as possible. We opt not to use threats or coercion, but you would do well to keep in mind that if you do not provide us with an accurate detail of tonight's activities, our hand will be forced. Will you present your description of this evening to this august assembly?"

Vie glanced at Squite. He nodded back, his large watery green eyes encouraging and threatening at once. Unlike Hamza's threat this was more preventative, like he was telling her that she did not want the less cooperative form of inquiry. "I will gladly do that."

"Excellent. Allow me to formally welcome you to the Keyhall, where we, the Order of the Vein, conduct our most important and pressing business. Not many women have stood within its walls. Sadly, tonight, I must confess that this is no honor."

"And just what did happen tonight, Skeleton Hamza?" a gruff voice called out from the assembled magi. "I was twenty leagues from the closest Vein, yet I felt it ripple."

"It took weeks to get that whore's time," complained another.

"—sleeping soundly!"

"—could even cause such a thing to happen?"

"—jam and toast—"

"Brothers!" a short man with a bald head and tattoos down his cheeks roared, bringing the assembly to order. What had been discord and clamor became silence. The man, who was standing like a guard to Skeleton Hamza's right, then nodded at the Skeleton.

"If you will still your tongues, perhaps one who was

at the source could teach us how the Veins came to ripple in the first place. My girl, do you know what the Veins are?"

"They are giant pools of energy that are all over Traumanfang. They are also the things inside people's bodies. They store blood."

"Just as the Veins of Traumanfang store Arcana," Hamza said, nodding, his eyeless face creepily menacing in the cold dancing light of the oak-shaped chair, "tonight, there was a rippling of the Veins. I don't know if you can understand what that is, but any who embrace the Veins would have felt it, just as every single magi in this room have done. Some might describe it as an earthquake but done so through the aether rather than the ground. Just like an earthquake, it is extremely devastating. Indeed, some of our brothers are confirmed dead or missing. We have many questions for you. The first and most important, results from our knowledge of you being where you do not belong. What were you doing in the Apocryptein tonight?"

It had all come down to this, Vie realized. The pounding in her head worsened as she looked out of the branches of light at the assembly around her. She stood before a gathering of legends. A former street urchin from the slums of Sludge was being weighed by men with the power of gods. What was she to them? More importantly, how could she have let this happen? She yearned to leave these shadowy men to their enormous room and return home to Sludge, where she could sleep and forget this entire affair.

"To the Hells with that," she mumbled.

"Could you repeat that, please?"

Vie stared up at the dark holes in Skeleton Hamza's face. "Squite's right. I'm from Sludge. I've lived there my whole life. An orphan with nothing going in my favor but what I picked up on the streets. I did what I did to get by. I've done things you couldn't imagine, but I'm still here. I survived that pit."

"Your history is noted and acknowledged," Hamza's guardsman said. "So why bother telling us this?"

Vie sighed. "Because I'm sick of it. I'm sick of the men and their sick smiles, the smell, the filth. I'm sick of the tribunals who don't give a damn. And the greedy clerks who only want to feed their faces. I'm sick of the poverty and the jealousy of the rich and being forced to whore or to steal to get a night's sleep or a bite to eat. I was told there was a treasure in the tower. I would have made a lot—magi things sell for a whole lot on the markets. And then my tail would be to the city. And once I got out of that dungheap, I'd never look back."

In response, she heard a single snort. It was a moment before she realized it was a stifled laugh. She looked up into the assembly. The shadows over the magi played with her eyes; there was no way she could identify the one who had spoken. Nonetheless, Skeleton Hamza knew him at once for he had no need of eyes.

"Do you have something to say, Lord Haphenasis?"

A globe of light glided down toward one of the shadowy men. As its light fell on him, Vie saw the well-fed form of a man dressed in a navy silken robe trimmed in pale orange. The close-cropped beard matched the close-cropped blonde hair of his head. He looked down his round nose at her through piggy little eyes that burned a colder teal than the ocean. Rage swirled in Vie's head as the lord scrutinized her.

"My pardons, Skeleton Hamza, my esteemed brothers," he said in a voice tinged with aristocratic whine, "but I was merely chortling at the notion that the scrubs of society could elevate themselves beyond the limitations of their own minds, as this thief had hoped to do."

"Yet this 'limited mind' managed to get into your precious tower!" Vie's outburst took herself by surprise. It could not be helped. The aristocratic sod was deserving of all the choler she could dredge up.

"Indeed," Hamza said, holding up a hand to Lord Haphenasis. Though he did not turn his head, Vie knew he was talking to her. "That is a point well raised. The Apocryptein is a fortress in and of itself. How was it that you managed to penetrate its defenses?"

It was not that she wanted to show them, to show off what little magic she could do, but there was a sense that so long as they were all watching her anyway, doing anything less than show them would just not work. They had asked, after all.

Vie sucked in a breath and imagined herself small, compact, a tinier aspect of herself. There, in her mind was the shape and size she desired. Reaching for it, she felt the change happening. Her body pulled itself not uncomfortably into itself—shrinking and consolidating, while spreading the dark hair on her head over the entirety of her body.

When all was done, Vie had disappeared. In her stead was a small grey mouse.

Chapter 2

"IT'S A MOUSE!"

"Is that a mouse?"

"Is it dead?"

"*Maketh-el!* A Morph!"

"Why isn't it moving?"

"Where did the girl go?"

"—time for breakfast yet?"

The Keyhall came alive with the assorted observations and questions of the assembled magi, but Vie heard none of them. She had collapsed to her small furry side, breath laboring from her tiny buck-toothed mouth. In her natural form, she could barely endure the brutality of the Innervein's protective wards. But, in this form, her body was far too brittle, too fragile, too light to endure it. Darkness threatened her as she stared blankly at the room, insensitive to everything around herself.

Dane Wunds lurched forward into the glittering lights surrounding Vie. From a small glass vial that he pulled from a pocket of his sky blue robe, he dribbled several drops of colorless liquid into Vie's panting mouth. This done, he pressed—gently for fear of crushing the small animal—the palm of his left hand to soft fur of Vie's side. This was the hand, Vie had noticed earlier, that had been crisscrossed with strange markings and sigils whose meanings were far beyond her limited knowledge of arcana. Warmth spread through her, followed by a tingling joining his hand to the liquid burning within her. With contact between these two elements made, a thrumming of relief began to trickle throughout her body. Heavy drops of sweat began spattering on the tiles around her. The effort of easing the pressure from the wards were starting to crush the magus.

"I need a conduit!" Dane Wunds shouted at the assemblage. At first none responded. Then a single magus came to his side. With a motion much like stretching, beads of colorful light appeared and drifted from the volunteer to the healer. The new magus grunted once as he took on the bulk of the pressure assaulting Vie.

"If you can change back, it would be most appreciated," Dane Wunds said through clenched teeth.

The healer's voice had a muffled quality, as if he was talking from under a pillow. It was unnecessary instruction, for she was already busying herself with the struggle to remember herself. While the transformations had become easier as she had gotten older and more practiced at it, the sense of having her skeleton ripped out of her mouth and crushed beneath the feet of a giant made breathing difficult. The act of thinking, of putting one thought after another, or to conjure an image that was not blind horror or incomprehensible suffering? That was a challenge far more complicated than the transformation usually was. Through the efforts of the two magi, breathing was becoming less difficult—she would live, if she could only change back—so she conjured the image of home and her whole reason for the damned theft that brought her to the silver tower in the first place.

Dry heaves wracked her full frame—she had vomited up everything in her belly when she first arrived at the Innervein—but as she curled up on the floor, she noticed her hands, real human hands. She sighed, accepting the pounding headache with relief. Compared to the sensation of several seconds ago, this was bliss, like the dull cramping that came after a particularly bad bleeding period.

"Can you stand?" someone above her asked.

Vie opened her eyes to see the man who had come to Dane Wunds's aid. Tied back was dark hair dipped in the night's sky and glistening like the coat of a well-groomed horse. This hair framed a chiseled face as strong and welcome as a bitter cup of coffee after a long night of exhausting work. The cool eyes staring down at her were limned by the trials of life, yet in their sadness there was genuine concern for her. His broad shoulders were the kind that she liked in her clients, which could wrap themselves about her and envelop her. She wondered if it was simply the relief that he and Dane Wunds had brought her, but she could not help the flood of emotion.

"Please tell me you're not married."

The magus smiled sadly and looped his large hands under her armpits. She felt herself pulled upright and, for a brief moment, considered letting this big strong man hold her like this. Yet Sludge had created in her a stubborn pride in what little she had, so while she would have liked to make this man do all her work for her, she put her weight on her unsteady legs and looked up at the assembly.

"What was that?" Skeleton Hamza asked. He was no longer seated and was taller than Vie had thought. She realized the deception was due to the enormity of the tree chair surrounding him.

"The Wards, Skeleton," Dane Wunds replied, pulling a small ramekin from another pocket. Into this he dribbled some more of his liquid. Then, he circled his hands in the air and when he made a specific shape, a simple metallic teapot appeared in it. From this, he poured a steaming red tea scented of jasmine, rose hips, and—was that pomegranate? Vic took the ramekin in unsteady hands and sipped it despite the near-scalding heat. "We have a number of extremely powerful wards that protect the Innervein from multidimensional threats. Well, more human threats, too, considering what happened after the so-called Wizard's Cleanse. Squite proposed that one of her parents be not from Traumanfang, and I am inclined to agree. We have had guests to the Innervein before, but never have I seen a reaction as severe as this. Nor are these the simple effects of what we have against our own people. Most people who come here are blasted with a personal Thunderclap and then bound in the Threads of Ignity. This, however, is visceral, affecting her entire system. It is only a matter of time until it destroys her. I've been acting as shelter for her, but in her mouse form, there was naught I could do. Ishtower's aid was nothing short of a life-saver."

"Ishtower?"

The big handsome man shrugged. "I can support her for the rest of this. I'm way too curious about what this is all about to let something like a little ward problem keep me from it."

"Hold, brothers!" a wiry man from the audience said, interrupting. "Dane Wunds, is this your learned analysis or mere speculation? Skeleton Key, our humble Order has survived this past twelve hundred years not for ignoring the barriers and wards that surround us. I motion we return to Traumanfang for inquiry. If she poses a threat to what we've created here, each moment that we spend with her here could put us all at greater risk."

"Your point about the potential danger to the Innervein is a valid one, Secretary of Practicality Safa, but your motion is denied. Based on what Lord Haphenasis has mentioned to me earlier, this present situation can bear no further delay."

"Then, by all means, let us inquire of the peon what has happened this evening," Lord Haphenasis suggested with a sneer.

Skeleton Hamza resumed his seat.

"Vie of Sludge, you stand before us to provide your side of events from this evening. The sooner we get your testimony, the sooner we can take the necessary actions in dealing with the repercussions of it."

Repercussions? Vie thought. *Like beheading me? Like maybe locking me up in a dungeon here, where the four hells that is this place will smother me constantly?* Despite her misgivings, Hamza was right: the sooner this was over the sooner she could get out of here.

"In my mouse form, the Apocryptein was easy to get into..."

Chapter 3

"OLD BUILDINGS ARE LIKE THAT. WOOD ROTS, UNLESS, LIKE the wharves down by the bay, they're painted each year in tar. Stone and brick are stronger, but even those aren't perfect. Look at the eastern wall of the Temple of the Mother up Crescent Street, and you'll know what I'm talking about. That was what? Fire? Place looks like it's melted. Stone's tougher, yes, but it's not perfect.

"I'm a burglar. My job's to find ways to get in. When I was a kid, I said 'to the four hells with people' and went mouse. It lasted almost a year, until a really scary run-in with a pelican-hawk. I scared the shit out of that prick when I became myself again. Made a tasty roast, too. In my time as a mouse, I learned how mice work, what they look for, how they find it. In wood, it's the knots and poorly cut wood planks. In stone, it's the caulking and drill holes. When rope rots and crumbles, what's left? Holes just big enough for us—for me. When the caulking crumbles and the rains wash them clear, it's the same thing.

"Places where there's lots of water get it bad. And when I got in the Apocryptein, there was lots of water. A big pool of it, water dripping down from a big metal spigot, the huge basins—I can only guess they were for bathing, but I've never seen none that big before. But it smelled of fire, wildflowers, and street filth. Never seen no toilet that fancy before.

"Didn't pay much thought to that room, really. All I cared about was that I was in. Off this room was the big room—the entering hall, or whatever it's called. *Fooyay* or something. Nice place. I liked the mural in the middle of the floor. It looks a lot like this thing here," Vie said, tapping the mural of the oak under her feet. "Pretty as the floor was, I liked the sculpture under the twin stairs more. You know the one, with the big fight, the wizards... sorry, *magi*, going up against the others. Fancy work there. There was a little light shining down on it from the glow balls above it, but I didn't spend much time looking at it, as there's no way I could pack that up in my little gift bag.

"I scaled the stone handrail going up to the bannister. Stone and my claws are good friends, you know. On the second floor, there were easy chairs and a sofa. Some nice vases were set out with flowers—by the way, the blue ones? Yeah. Those are stinging bluebells. Any idiot knows that not only do they sting to the touch but, after a couple days, they reek of a latrine. They're the worst flowers to have in a house. Anyway, though there was a silver tray with crystal glasses and those fancy bottles for liquor on them, it was no place for treasure.

"I should'a just grabbed these and run, but there's

no way to pay for a life away from Sludge with just this."

Vie's mouth was horribly dry after this long stretch of speaking. She would have loved to have had a chair to sit in, wanted to ask about one, but asking for one here felt wrong. What were the protocols for talking with the magi? Could you ask for a chair to sit in? To steady her wobbling legs, she took a deep sip of the ramekin. *Yup, pomegranate.* It was nice and hot and it filled her throat and belly with a comfortable burn.

"So I went up. And up. And up. Seven more levels of this place and nothing but dust, mice—"

"There are no mice in the Apocryptein!" Lord Haphenasis snapped, interrupting Vie.

She arched an eyebrow at him. "Did you spend a year with mice? Do you know what to look for? I doubt it. I know from mice, and there were others there, you mark my words."

She took quiet satisfaction in seeing a couple of the assembly whispering to one another behind their hands. The chubby lord's affected smugness did not touch the seething cauldron of irritability in his eyes.

"The tenth floor. That's where I found lights again. These were bright. The place smelled clean, of use, of people. Here, *Lord Halfass-ness*, you are right that there were no mice. I did smell you, though. I smelt you on the stairs, on the big wooden door that was the only thing beside the lights. The whole thing was a big entryway to the door. Trust me: you make something like that, and you're telling thieves *Come here for treasure!*

"Most people would leave the place locked, though."

Vie paused to let this idea sink in with the other magi. Petty prodding though this was, it felt good for the misery she was feeling. The political battles that came with insults and doubt were easier to win than those based on merit alone.

"It was locked!" Lord Haphenasis snapped. *I'm getting to him,* Vie thought, quite happily. If she were to be killed for her trespass, she would at least make sure that she was not the only one going down. Sludge had taught her that any fight where both parties lost was still a victory for the loser.

"Oh, that's right, it was," Vie said, tapping her lip in remembrance. She reached up to the coil of black hair that sat high on her head and extracted one of the two silvery chopsticks holding it in place. The stick danced in her fingers as she pulled it down. With a practiced flick, it returned where it was, holding up her braid. "You know, I'd heard that the rich don't ever think that anyone'd be crazy enough to steal from them. That's why they don't lock their front doors. Anyone who's ever had to struggle knows better. Softness is no blessing. It's only an invite to lose everything—and, trust me, the more you have, the more people want from you.

"Behind the door...." She drifted away at the memory of that immense room. "Wow."

With the abuse the Innervein had been stacking on her and the quickness of the night's events, there had been no time to consider what she had seen, but now it all came back to her. Crystal figures, miniature chairs; ceramic drinking glasses, brightly colored vases, fancy coats of arms. Impressive jackets and robes filled one big part of this place. There were weapons on display on walls, and shelves of books and doodads and knick-knacks of precious metals and gems sat off along the far back wall. "It was amazing. I knew I've never seen nothing like that. I know a guy. He's a collector, but everything he has would only take up a small part of this room. I knew then that I'd found what I was looking for.

"I felt like a virgin in a pleasure house, where there's more than I could even stand. I wanted to stay there forever, to touch every pretty sculpture, to run my fingers through the fabrics and wrap myself in the coats and wear the jewelry, and maybe, for a little while, to feel as beautiful as those snobs from Hope Lane."

Bidden by her thought, those *ladies* from Hope Lane, in their wide dresses covered in ribbons, with lace collars that climbed up their perfect necks, nearly to their chins, shuffled forth. They always walked in pairs, a parasol in silken gloves, their faces done up in pale powder, their red cheeks wide with smiles. Pearls and gold at their throats or hanging from their ears. They were beautiful in a way Vie had never felt. She envied their easy lives, and while she had been chiding the magi for their carelessness, she would have killed for the chance to live that carelessly.

"I knew valuable when I saw it," she continued, after taking a deep sip from the still-hot ramekin of tea. *Yes, I know valuable. And knowledge is most valuable of all.* She looked at the men around her, their faces dark in the dull cold light of the Keyhall. There was only so much she could mention on this subject, so she buried the truth of her objective, and distracted them from it with the facts that she felt they needed. "It was a crystal dragon. Coiled in on itself like a cat, with its nose tucked under a wing. It was a beautiful mix of purples, blacks, and greens. I was drawn to it. No, I *wanted* it. But when I got close... I wasn't expecting *that*.

"It slid its head out from its wing and looked at me with its tiny, shiny eyes. Its little wings unfolded and flapped twice and it opened its mouth. I've known babies that could scream like the hordes of the four hells were hot on their heels, but this was something else."

It was only now, thinking about it, that the sound was not just a meaningless sound. It was almost as if there was a message in that roar. A greeting? Or was it a plea?

"A burglar needs silence and speed. But, after that roar, I knew my time was done. I didn't want the damned dragon thing roaring again, so I made for a far wall, where most of the smaller things were. Having gone to the trouble of going in there, I had to get something. I couldn't let it all be a complete waste of time. The crystal dragon kept babbling to me the whole time I was there. Wagging its tail, flapping its wings—it was almost like a little puppy. But I didn't have time for it. And no way was I going to try jamming that thing in my sack."

She finished the last of the tea. To her everlasting joy Dane Wunds automatically topped it off with both the strange liquid and the tea. This new cup was just as hot as the last one had been. But this one she just sipped at, momentarily becoming distracted by how empty her bladder felt. With her arrival here, had she pissed herself? The tea was too strong to smell, but she hoped she hadn't. That was the last thing she needed—meet a whole lot of the magi, only to puke and piss all over them. She smirked into her cup.

"And then I was out of time altogether," she almost whispered to herself as the smile departed.

"'What is this now?'"

"*What is this now?*" Hamza repeated for clarification,

but not, she knew, for her sake. It was for the sake of the others gathered in the Keyhall.

"Yes, that's exactly what he said. Those were exactly his first words to me. If you don't know who I'm talking about already, you'll know your blonde *brother* for the piggy-like face and barrel of a body. He was standing in the doorway of the..." she fiddled about for a good word that described the room. She went with her gut. "...*treasure* room with a glass in hand. Sure, I had disturbed whatever he had been doing, but so was he disturbing what I was doing.

"I didn't know what one of you wi—*magi* would do to me if you caught me, so I went mouse, thinking that he'd never find me, or that if he did, he'd think I was just another rodent that needed to be thrown out. All I wanted was to get out of there. My plan was to stay behind the pedestals and table legs and dash out through the door while he was looking for me.

"He said something arrogant and high and mighty about liking the fact I can change into a mouse but that I couldn't get out. Then there was a big boom, like thunder. I heard nothing after that for a while; my ears were ringing painfully. I thought I would puke it hurt so much. Then I was blinded by a big white light. While *Lord Halfass-ness* might not know how to keep someone *out* of the tower, he sure knows how to hurt people that come in. I could barely run, let alone think. Blind, deaf, I knew that was about it. I cowered where I was, sure I was going to die.

"Then something grabbed my legs and wrapped them up. Whatever it was—ropes?—felt like needles going in my leg. Where the ropes touched me it stung like mad. I could feel it all throughout my body, and where it touched felt like it was swelling up. It burned and I whimpered out in pain. I knew I was changing, being jerked back human again. I felt my body moving in itself. That..." Vie paused. A chill had ridden up her spine and she hugged her arms across her chest, took another sip of tea. The throbbing in her head was getting bad again, the cramping in her belly worse. She wondered if she was bleeding. It was not her time, but how could she not be with pain this bad?

"Can you continue?" Skeleton Hamza's smoky voice asked, seeming so close, so comfortably close to her.

"I can, Skeleton Hamza," she replied softly, holding out her empty ramekin. Dane Wunds refilled it with another few drops of his mystical clear liquid and red tea. She gave him a wan smile, thankful for this small kindness yet wary of the fleetingness of its comfort, wary for her future.

"You men can't know what... it's like. You stick. You stab and stab and walk away. You don't think of what happens after: the pain, the hurt. It's everything horrible wrapped up into one thing. But we—we *women!*—have to sow what you plant. You take all the credit for everything, but you don't do anything but hurt and kill and hurt again." This was too difficult a subject to put into words. How could she explain the feeling of having her clothing ripped away, to bare her skin? And then the horror that comes after, with the realization that it was not enough, that they wanted *more*. So they cut away her skin and stabbed her so deeply she could feel it in her bones. How could she explain the feeling of being split apart like corned meat that had been stewing for days?

Of blood and tears as the only lubrication for the slicing of her soul? Even if she could explain, it was pointless to try. They would never understand. "I don't expect you to know what it felt like. You can't know how horrible it is to have *him* inside me, forcing me to be something I wasn't. To feel him still there!"

As she smacked the thin magical collar at her neck, she felt tears falling down her cheeks. She glared at Lord Haphenasis, so infuriated by the indifferent smirk on his face that she barely noticed her own crying.

"You are my prisoner," he said, shrugging.

A large, heavy hand fell on her shoulder. She jerked away from it and wiped her eyes, her cheeks. "Ignore him," Ishtower said. "I know how hard it is to separate emotion from situation, but please concentrate on what happened next."

Vie nodded. She was trembling, but whether from physical exhaustion, emotional exhaustion, or the sheer agony that was crushing her, she could not say. "I just want to go home. I *did* just want to go home. I didn't want to deal with him. I didn't want to take anything. I didn't think he'd be there. I had heard he had gone away, that the tower was empty. All I could think of was home... of my..."

No, Vie thought, gathering herself up again. *They don't deserve this. These are men. Just the immediate facts matter.*

"I got an arm free and grabbed one of those pedestals. There was a box on it, I'm not sure what of—glass, maybe? Crystal? I'd seen it flickering earlier. It was pretty. But the ropes—I couldn't see them—pulled me closer to the magus. It felt like I was being ripped apart. And then the pedestal fell down. The box on top of it.

"It shattered on the floor. Not like glass, where it breaks and tingles and leaves its pieces everywhere, but exploded, like fireworks. There was something there, I blinked because it was bright, but there it was, a little gleaming bolt of fire. I don't know what you magi do, or where all these things come from, but this was alive, like the dragon. It looked about, confused. When it saw me, it stared, buck teeth of energy nibbling on a fiery lip. It was like it was asking what I was doing, but that's...," Vie gave a snort of laughter, "that's just crazy.

"But maybe I was crazy. Maybe I am. Maybe I was just so damned desperate that I'd have made a deal with the Dark Mistress herself. I asked it for help." The absurdity of it brought out a full laugh from her. It was odd in the silence of the Keyhall. There had to be forty people here, and she was the only one she could hear. "The energy thing smiled at me. It was cute in its own strange way. With a high-pitched little laugh, it flared like when you blow on fire and tiny sparks leapt out. Everything a spark touched caught. It was great to see, but if it was going to save me, it wasn't working quickly enough. I was still being dragged backward to the magus.

"Still, I watched it. It was more satisfying than giving in to my fear. The one became two and then three and more. When I felt the Lord Haphenasis's hand on my leg, there were more than ten of these things giggling their silly language. But they were coming for me. That's all I cared about. I saw them and I knew that once they reached me, the magus would burn and I'd be free.

"I guess he thought so, too. He did some magic to the fire critters, but must have felt it wasn't enough because, with me in tow, he ran out the door and down the stairs. It didn't feel like he gave a... cared how I followed him, because I kept hitting myself on the walls. Then, I hit my head.

"The next thing I knew I was on the ground outside the tower while it burned."

Chapter 3

"OLD BUILDINGS ARE LIKE THAT. WOOD ROTS, UNLESS, LIKE the wharves down by the bay, they're painted each year in tar. Stone and brick are stronger, but even those aren't perfect. Look at the eastern wall of the Temple of the Mother up Crescent Street, and you'll know what I'm talking about. That was what? Fire? Place looks like it's melted. Stone's tougher, yes, but it's not perfect.

"I'm a thief. My job's to find ways to get in. When I was a kid, I said 'to the four hells with people' and went mouse. It lasted almost a year, until a really scary run-in with a pelican-hawk. I scared the shit out of that prick when I became myself again. Made a tasty roast, too. In my time as a mouse, I learned how mice work, what they look for, how they find it. In wood, it's the knots and poorly cut wood planks. In stone, it's the caulking and drill holes. When rope rots and crumbles, what's left?

Holes just big enough for us—for me. When the caulking crumbles and the rains wash them clear, it's the same thing.

"Places where there's lots of water get it bad. And when I got in the Apocryptein, there was lots of water. A big pool of it, water dripping down from a big metal spigot, the huge basins—I can only guess they were for bathing, but I've never seen none that big before. But it smelled of fire, wildflowers, and street filth. Never seen no toilet that fancy before.

"Didn't pay much thought to that room, really. All I cared about was that I was in. Off this room was the big room—the entering hall, or whatever it's called. *Fooyay* or something. Nice place. I liked the mural in the middle of the floor. It looks a lot like this thing here," Vie said, tapping the mural of the oak under her feet. "Pretty as the floor was, I liked the sculpture under the twin stairs more. You know the one, with the big fight, the wizards... pardon, *magi*, going up against the others. Fancy work there. There was a little light shining down on it from the glow balls above it, but I didn't spend much time looking at it, as there's no way I could pack that up in my little gift bag.

"I scaled the stone handrail going up to the bannister. Stone and my claws are good friends, you know. On the second floor, there were easy chairs and a sofa. Some nice vases were set out with flowers—by the way, the blue ones? Yeah. Those are stinging bluebells. Any idiot knows that not only do they sting to the touch but, after a couple days, they reek of a latrine. They're the worst flowers to have in a house. Anyway, though there was a silver tray with crystal glasses and those fancy bottles for liquor on them, it was no place for treasure.

"I should'a just grabbed these and run, but there's no way to pay for a life away from Sludge with just this."

Vie's mouth was horribly dry after this long stretch of speaking. She would have loved to have had a chair to sit in, wanted to ask about one, but asking for one here felt wrong. What were the protocols for talking with the magi? Could you ask for a chair to sit in? To steady her wobbling legs, she took a deep sip of the ramekin. *Yup, pomegranate.* It was nice and hot and it filled her throat and belly with a comfortable burn.

"So I went up. And up. And up. Seven more levels of this place and nothing but dust, mice—"

"There are no mice in the Apocryptein!" Lord Haphenasis snapped, interrupting Vie.

She arched an eyebrow at him. "Did you spend a year with mice? Do you know what to look for? I doubt it. I know from mice, and there were others there, you mark my words."

She took quiet satisfaction in seeing a couple of the assembly whispering to one another behind their hands. The chubby lord's affected smugness did not touch the seething cauldron of irritability in his eyes.

"The tenth floor. That's where I found lights again. These were bright. The place smelled clean, of use, of people. Here, *Lord Halfass-ness*, you are right that there were no mice. I did smell you, though. I smelt you on the stairs, on the big wooden door that was the only thing beside the lights. The whole thing was a big entryway to the door. Trust me: you make something like that, and you're telling thieves *Come here for treasure!*

"Most people would leave the place locked, though."

Vie paused to let this idea sink in with the other magi. Petty prodding though this was, it felt good for the misery she was feeling. The political battles that came with insults and doubt were easier to win than those based on merit alone.

"It was locked!" Lord Haphenasis snapped. *I'm getting to him,* Vie thought, quite happily. If she were to be killed for her trespass, she would at least make sure that she was not the only one going down. Sludge had taught her that any fight where both parties lost was still a victory for the loser.

"Oh, that's right, it was," Vie said, tapping her lip in remembrance. She reached up to the coil of black hair that sat high on her head and extracted one of the two silvery chopsticks holding it in place. The stick danced in her fingers as she pulled it down. With a practiced flick, it returned where it was, holding up her braid. "You know, I'd heard that the rich don't ever think that anyone'd be crazy enough to steal from them. That's why they don't lock their front doors. Anyone who's ever had to struggle knows better. Softness is no blessing. It's only an invite to lose everything—and, trust me, the more you have, the more people want from you.

"Behind the door...." She drifted away at the memory of that immense room. "Wow."

With the abuse the Innervein had been stacking on her and the quickness of the night's events, there had been no time to consider what she had seen, but now it all came back to her. Crystal figures, miniature chairs; ceramic drinking glasses, brightly colored vases, fancy coats of arms. Impressive jackets and robes filled one big part of this place. There were weapons on display on walls, and shelves of books and doodads and knick-knacks of precious metals and gems sat off along the far back wall. "It was amazing. I knew I've never seen nothing like that. I know a guy. He's a collector, but everything he has would only take up a small part of this room. I knew then that I'd found what I was looking for.

"I felt like a virgin in a pleasure house, where there's more than I could even stand. I wanted to stay there forever, to touch every pretty sculpture, to run my fingers through the fabrics and wrap myself in the coats and wear the jewelry, and maybe, for a little while, to feel as beautiful as those snobs from Hope Lane."

Bidden by her thought, those *ladies* from Hope Lane, in their wide dresses covered in ribbons, with lace collars that climbed up their perfect necks, nearly to their chins, shuffled forth. They always walked in pairs, a parasol in silken gloves, their faces done up in pale powder, their red cheeks wide with smiles. Pearls and gold at their throats or hanging from their ears. They were beautiful in a way Vie had never felt. She envied their easy lives, and while she had been chiding the magi for their carelessness, she would have killed for the chance to live that carelessly.

"I knew valuable when I saw it," she continued, after taking a deep sip from the still-hot ramekin of tea. *Yes, I know valuable. And knowledge is most valuable of all.* She looked at the men around her, their faces dark in the dull cold light of the Keyhall. There was only so much she could mention on this subject, so she buried the truth of her objective, and distracted them from it with the facts that she felt they needed. "It was a crystal dragon. Coiled in on itself like a cat, with its nose tucked under a wing. It was a beautiful mix of purples, blacks, and greens. I was drawn to it. No, I *wanted* it. But when I got close... I wasn't expecting *that*.

"It slid its head out from its wing and looked at me with its tiny, shiny eyes. Its little wings unfolded and flapped twice and it opened its mouth. I've known babies that could scream like the hordes of the four hells were hot on their heels, but this was something else."

It was only now, thinking about it, that the sound was not just a meaningless sound. It was almost as if there was a message in that roar. A greeting? Or was it a plea?

"A thief needs silence and speed. But, after that roar, I knew my time was done. I didn't want the damned dragon thing roaring again, so I made for a far wall, where most of the smaller things were. Having gone to the trouble of going in there, I had to get something. I couldn't let it all be a complete waste of time. The crystal dragon kept babbling to me the whole time I was there. Wagging its tail, flapping its wings—it was almost like a little puppy. But I didn't have time for it. And no way was I going to try jamming that thing in my sack."

She finished the last of the tea. To her everlasting joy Dane Wunds automatically topped it off with both the strange liquid and the tea. This new cup was just as hot as the last one had been. But this one she just sipped at, momentarily becoming distracted by how empty her bladder felt. With her arrival here, had she pissed herself? The tea was too strong to smell, but she hoped she hadn't. That was the last thing she needed—meet a whole lot of the magi, only to puke and piss all over them. She smirked into her cup.

"And then I was out of time altogether," she almost whispered to herself as the smile departed.

"'What is this now?'"

"*What is this now?*" Hamza repeated for clarification, but not, she knew, for her sake. It was for the sake of the others gathered in the Keyhall.

"Yes, that's exactly what he said. Those were exactly his first words to me. If you don't know who I'm talking about already, you'll know your blonde *brother* for the piggy-like face and barrel of a body. He was standing in the doorway of the..." she fiddled about for a good word that described the room. She went with her gut. "...*treasure* room with a glass in hand. Sure, I had disturbed whatever he had been doing, but so was he disturbing what I was doing.

"I didn't know what one of you wi—*magi* would do to me if you caught me, so I went mouse, thinking that he'd never find me, or that if he did, he'd think I was just another rodent that needed to be thrown out. All I wanted was to get out of there. My plan was to stay behind the pedestals and table legs and dash out through the door while he was looking for me.

"He said something arrogant and high and mighty about liking the fact I can change into a mouse but that I couldn't get out. Then there was a big boom, like thunder. I heard nothing after that for a while; my ears were ringing painfully. I thought I would puke it hurt so much. Then I was blinded by a big white light. While *Lord Halfass-ness* might not know how to keep someone *out* of the tower, he sure knows how to hurt people that come in. I could barely run, let alone think. Blind, deaf, I knew that was about it. I cowered where I was, sure I was going to die.

"Then something grabbed my legs and wrapped

them up. Whatever it was—ropes?—felt like needles going in my leg. Where the ropes touched me it stung like mad. I could feel it all throughout my body, and where it touched felt like it was swelling up. It burned and as I whimpered out in pain. I knew I was changing, being jerked back human again. I felt my body moving in itself. That…" Vie paused. A chill had ridden up his spine and she hugged her arms across her chest, took another sip of tea. The throbbing in her head was getting bad again, the cramping in her belly worse. She wondered if she was bleeding. It was not her time, but how could she not be with pain this bad?

"Can you continue?" Skeleton Hamza's smoky voice asked, seeming so close, so comfortably close to her.

"I can, Skeleton Hamza," she replied softly, holding out her empty ramekin. Dane Wunds refilled it with another few drops of his mystical clear liquid and red tea. She gave him a wan smile, thankful for this small kindness yet wary of the fleetingness of its comfort, wary for her future.

"You men can't know what… it's like. You stick. You stab and stab and walk away. You don't think of what happens after: the pain, the hurt. It's everything horrible wrapped up into one thing. But we—we *women!*—have to sow what you plant. You take all the credit for everything, but you don't do anything but hurt and kill and hurt again." This was too difficult a subject to put into words. How could she explain the feeling of having her clothing ripped away, to bare her skin? And then the horror that comes after, with the realization that it was not enough, that they wanted *more.* So they cut away her skin and stabbed her so deeply she could feel it in her bones. How could she explain the feeling of being split apart like corned meat that had been stewing for days? Of blood and tears as the only lubrication for the slicing of her soul? Even if she could explain, it was pointless to try. They would never understand. "I don't expect you to know what it felt like. You can't know how horrible it is to have *him* inside me, forcing me to be something I wasn't. To feel him still there!"

As she smacked the thin magical collar at her neck, she felt tears falling down her cheeks. She glared at Lord Haphenasis, so infuriated by the indifferent smirk on his face that she barely noticed her own crying.

"You are my prisoner," he said, shrugging.

A large, heavy hand fell on her shoulder. She shrugged away from it and wiped her eyes, her cheeks. "Ignore him," Ishtower said. "I know how hard it is to separate emotion from situation, but please concentrate on what happened next."

Vie nodded. She was trembling, but whether from physical exhaustion, emotional exhaustion, or the sheer agony that was crushing her, she could not say. "I just want to go home. I *did* just want to go home. I didn't want to deal with him. I didn't want to take anything. I didn't think he'd be there. I had heard he had gone away, that the tower was empty. All I could think of was home... of my..."

No, Vie thought, gathering herself up again. *They don't deserve this. These are men. Just the immediate facts matter.*

"I got an arm free and grabbed one of those pedestals. There was a box on it, I'm not sure what of—glass, maybe? Crystal? I'd seen it flickering earlier. It was pretty. But the ropes—I couldn't see them—pulled me closer to the magus. It felt like I was being ripped apart. And then the pedestal fell down. The box on top of it.

"It shattered on the floor. Not like glass, where it breaks and tingles and leaves its pieces everywhere, but exploded, like fireworks. There was something there, I blinked because it was bright, but there it was, a little gleaming bolt of fire. I don't know what you magi do, or where all these things come from, but this was alive, like the dragon. It looked about, confused. When it saw me, it stared, buck teeth of energy nibbling on a fiery lip. It was like it was asking what I was doing, but that's...," Vie gave a snort of laughter, "that's just crazy.

"But maybe I was crazy. Maybe I am. Maybe I was just so damned desperate that I'd have made a deal with the Dark Mistress herself. I asked it for help." The absurdity of it brought out a full laugh from her. It was odd in the silence of the Keyhall. There had to be forty people here, and she was the only one she could hear. "The energy thing smiled at me. It was cute in its own strange way. With a high-pitched little laugh, it flared like when you blow on fire and tiny sparks leapt out. Everything a spark touched caught. It was great to see, but if it was going to save me, it wasn't working quickly enough. I was still being dragged backward to the magus.

"Still, I watched it. It was more satisfying than giving in to my fear. The one became two and then three and more. When I felt the Lord Haphenasis's hand on my leg, there were more than ten of these things giggling their silly language. But they were coming for me. That's all I cared about. I saw them and I knew that once they reached me, the magus would burn and I'd be free.

"I guess he thought so, too. He did some magic to

the fire critters, but must have felt it wasn't enough because, with me in tow, he ran out the door and down the stairs. It didn't feel like he gave a... cared how I followed him, because I kept hitting myself on the walls. Then, I hit my head.

"The next thing I knew I was on the ground outside the tower while it burned."

Chapter 5

"MY JOURNEY TO THE LIBRARY OF DOMANI WENT QUICKER than I had expected it to," Lord Haphenasis began. "I found the original copy of Aler the Omega's *Splitting Worlds: An Exploration Outside Dimensions* within the first hour there. That such happened is a testament to the organizational skills of their librarians. Using the contents of a book to organize where they go and then subcategorizing them alphabetically by author's name? Brilliant! It is a system that all libraries in Traumanfang—and here in the Innervein—should adopt.

"But I doubt my opinions on the categorization of literature are necessary at this time. What matters is that Squite ventilated me back to the Apocryptein as the sun sank heavy into the western sky. By the time I had concluded a soothing bath, arranged dinner, and completed the various minutiae that comes after a trip, the sun had set long before.

"The moment of opening a new book is always so thrilling for the unknown mysteries contained within its pages. After sampling some of the salted Elbonian boar that I prepared, I sent myself into the physical being of the book to feel out its previous handlers. I could sense the elk whose hide went into the creation of the cover, I could feel Aler's pen dripping ink on me as he organized his thoughts to put on the paper. This truly was an original copy as I had been promised, and that... being able to connect to the greatest minds in creation, there is no substitute for that."

"While students in your annual seminar would find your skills at Tactile Recall to be fascinating," Skeleton Hamza said softly, "we would much appreciate it if you just focused on the details that we *need* to address in the present."

"You are, of course, right," Lord Haphenasis replied, glancing at the thief. She was standing in the spotlight created from the willpower of his collected brothers. As always, the Innervein adapted its own capabilities to match the needs of those around and within it. *They want to know about her. And the Veins.*

"I was settling in, a port and my dinner on the table next to me. All around me were the copious tomes of my own personal library. I was at peace and had just opened Aler's book to read his preface. That was when a horrible screech made me jerk, spilling my drink all over myself. Annoyed by this, but more concerned with the surprise that came from the noise, my senses tuned into the sound like quicksilver, and I recognized it almost immediately as coming from my old traveling companion, the Crystal Dragon of the Magi of Ulster. As you, my brothers, know, it is bestowed upon the most learned magus of our brotherhood. Not only is it a treasured part of my collection, I would count the semi-sentient creature among my friends. For it to scream like that meant only one thing —there was an intruder.

"I flicked a cloud at my feet, stepped on and raced off to my gallery. The door to the gallery was wide open when, not long ago, it had been closed and securely locked. And contrary to certain dubious claims," he said without acknowledging the thief with a glance, "the lock that I created for the gallery was no simple lock. It was protected with a telescoping shield, which wans and ebbs depending on what force it projected against it. None should have been able to get through without my leave.

"I was faced with two details. The first is that someone had penetrated one of the three places most important in the whole world to me. The second—and this was most disturbing—they had gained access to the Apocryptein. Not once since its creation 1,100 years ago has the building been visited by any who are not chosen to enter into its hallowed walls."

"Apparently, if Vic's testimony about the mice is to be believed, that is not completely true," Ishtower said.

"*If* being the key word, here," Lord Haphenasis said dismissively. *Just like Ishtower to pick a fight where a fight was not necessary.* "Mundane elements like air, even insects, are, in their own way, necessary. The blood spells protecting the building have almost entirely halted the building's decomposition. Moreover, these spells exist not just in the external framework, but also in the arcane fabric of the aether, upon which the Apocryptein was built! The blood of the sacrifices used in its creation have bled into

the Veins, binding it to the... to the site..." Lord Haphenasis trailed off, his mind racing.

"My lords, might I be able to interrupt myself for a
moment to satisfy a minor curiosity?"

"Is this directly related to the topics of this inquiry?"
Skeleton Hamza asked.

"I believe it is most directly related."

"Can it be done here?"

"If one of our esteemed hosts would be so kind as to
incite a transparency at the roof of this hall?"

With a murmur from the tattoo-faced warden of the
Hall who stood before Hamza, the wide dome twinkled
into nonexistence. Above their heads, stretching out into
infinity, was the enveloping rainbow of the Innervein.
Every color represented each and every Vein ~ not just
from Traumanfang, but from the other Eight Realms as
well. As they twisted and ascended, the colors seemed
to merge into one. At this moment in the rotation of
time, the colors combined into a singular void akin to
the deepest black. As the construct in which they stood
shifted over time, it was sometimes the black overhead
and sometimes a singularity of the purest white. As he
had felt near forty years past, when he first beheld the
Veins in their physical manifestation, Lord Haphenasis
was left breathless. There was such peace in them. Peace
and power and beauty. The Veins were the only lover he
had ever taken to, the only one he ever would.

For the past eighteen years, Lord Haphenasis had
been the warden of the Apocryptein. This meant he had
had eighteen long years in which to become intimately
familiar with the five Veins that intersected at the point
on which the tower was built. The five colors of Gho,

Re, Cha, Dei, and Wn were easy to find. He knew their neighbors in the color spectrum and because of the power that came with their intersection on Traumanfang, they were generally far brighter than their neighbors. With a glance, all five were accounted for. Usually, they beat and thrummed with a pulse of the most vibrant life, but not tonight.

"What is that?" one of his brothers asked, echoing his thoughts and confirming his concern. For some reason, the gathering of his brothers, the rippling that all had felt, everything he had seen—all of this had seemed unreal. Certainly, it was real, but it felt more like an automatic response to abstract events that just *could not* be true. That someone less intimate with these five Veins than he had noticed the problem above meant that the events unfolding around him were, in painful fact, real. Reality was crashing in on Lord Haphenasis in a way that he never imagined it could.

"It is tarnish," he said quietly.

Hamza twisted his head upward, as if his blind eye sockets had means to see the Veins above him. "Tarnish?" The awe in that one word lingered for but a moment before he adopted his more authoritarian one. "Curious. Is it localized or sinewy?"

"It's localized, but spotted."

"Now this is interesting. Is it in only one Vein from the Apocryptein's Riot or does this condition affect all five?"

"All five," Lord Haphenasis answered.

"Now there are six," Hamza mused softly.

Lord Haphenasis flicked his eyes on the sixth tarnished Vein. For centuries, the Ha Vein had burned less brightly than the others. Certainly the corruption of the Ha had been on the mend, and according to the elder generations of the Order, it would someday make a full recovery. After its many long centuries of solitude, it now had an even handful of its brothers for company.

"Lord Haphenasis," Hamza said softly. "What happened to them?"

"Perhaps I had better continue my tale to best illustrate that point," Lord Haphenasis mused aloud.

"Please do."

"There could be any number of reasons that the thief was able to gain access to the Apocryptein. Perhaps it was the mundane form she had chosen. Perhaps, as Dane Wunds hypothesizes, she is not at all from Traumanfang and, therefore, has some ability that had not been considered in the creation of the Apocryptein or in its defense. I know not. Apparently, all that matters is that she was there, in my gallery, walking through it as if it were her own home. She appeared as she does now, her dark trousers and simple homespun that marks one of her class.

"There in my collection, the burglar turned and met my eyes with her own, large, black. Then she was gone.

"Despite being unable to see her, she could not mask her presence from me. In her departure, I felt a surge of arcana, a vibrational hiss of air as it rushed in to fill a void. Had she ventilated to another place? No, that was impossible based on the resonance following the cast. The only other cast that resembled this kind of void-calm came with transfiguration—though, at the time, I considered it a highly unlikely ability considering the rarity of such a gift.

"A Thunderclap had struck fear into a tribe of

Yimenites when they had tried preventing my collection of the Relic of Eal. I figured this thief would cower in the same manner as they had. The whole room boomed with the vibration and I waited for her to reveal herself. It was to no avail. She refused to emerge. I theorized that if sound failed, then perhaps lights would be more effective in drawing her out. The Switch of Luna bathed the entire room in a blinding sphere of stark white light, yet still she remained hidden.

"This required some more drastic measures: a summoning, a binding, the drawing of her soul. A dozen different options flicked through my mind as one tune rose to the surface. Less a tune than a poem, a verse from a dusty tome so old that I cannot even recall its cover. It worked, however. An animal screech followed the spell's release. Coils of Imagination dragged a small grey mouse from under my display shelving. As it was drawn toward me, the mouse shed off its fur, to be replaced with the arm and leg of the thief you see before you now. I was satisfied that in moments, she would be in my hands to serve her punishment.

"Much to my chagrin, she was struggling against my mighty spell; and, worse, she actually *succeeded* in slipping an arm free long enough to grab a pedestal. She struggled to hold on to it as the coils reached up along her arm to re-secure her. She grunted as she twisted her torso for freedom.

"Time seemed to freeze as her motion reverberated through the pedestal, forcing the heavy stand to tumble after the thief. The glistening arcane plasmats box that had been set upon it tumbled toward the cold marble floor, where it struck with a loud shattering crash.

"I watched in awe as this happened. Never, in my many years of study, had I ever heard of an arcane plasmats creation shatter like this did. It could not have happened. It should not have happened. And yet, it did.

"As the box splintered into the remains of a dream gone sour, its lone energetic prisoner leapt out in a fit of gibbering laughter and a shower of sparks. Despite being in my collection for over a decade, I had never beheld a Kremsek before. They are rather curious creatures—not so blinding as the sun, yet if one stared at one too long, the after-images would be as uncomfortable to the eyes as the Switch of Luna must have been to her.

"Free at last after its long imprisonment, it was soon roasting red hot, tossing sparks arbitrarily. Each spark landed and sputtered into a perfect doppelganger of the original. Within what seemed a mere heartbeat, half a dozen Kremsek were running roughshod through the room. The Lap of Guillarm, the Chanina Vibraphone—everything I had accumulated over the course of my life erupted in such intense heat that the marble floors of that room had already begun to sear.

"I summoned a raincloud to smother the Alpha Kremsek and felt my hopes for saving my collection dissolve. The cloud generated just enough moisture to dissipate in a dull fog that was barely noticeable over the optical phenomena created by the monster's intense heat. I tried a hailstorm, a Gout, Dewballs; I depressed the room temperature, drew in a counterfire; but while I managed to slow the Kremsek's reproduction, nothing could actually stop or diminish it.

"In my head, I ran the numbers. By my estimate, no less than *sixty* Kremsek would spawn before I could smother even one. It broke my heart, but I did the only thing I could do: I threw up whatever containment I could and abandoned my collection and the upper stories of my home to the disaster that this intruder had wrought. I drew close to me the Coils of Imagination and the prisoner trapped within and bolted.

"Ten levels in two hundred harried heartbeats. Here, in the main foyer, I paused at the sculpture in the nook of the twin stairs. I looked on the faces of my charges, wondering what I could do to keep them secure. Ten levels above, the Kremsek were spreading. It was only a matter of time before they worked their way down here. Seconds, perhaps minutes. To buy myself and the tower more time, I grounded myself in the firmament of the floor level and tapped into the copious reserves of arcana of the Riot. With this energy swirling around me in a way it could not do so up in my trophy room, I blasted upward an explosion of force. I had hoped to strike with enough force to launch the Kremsek from the building. If I destroyed the upper levels of the Apocryptein in the process, then it would be a necessary sacrifice.

"Floor after floor crumbled to dust above me, but as my blast reached the Kremsek, it was deflected into the walls, blasting not just the flooring but the walls themselves into oblivion. Some Kremsek appeared to vaporize, but by this point those deaths were flickers compared to the roaring inferno that the others were. Offense became defense as I threw up shields to halt the fire monster's plummet toward me. Asbestos, stone breaks, Coils of Imagination, Cants, ice, firebreaks, curses... three hundred spells if one bled from my mind through my body. I used everything I had. For a long heartbeat, it seemed as if I had stopped them where they were. Still, I wanted no chances taken. I became a living rainbow as I assaulted the beasts.

"At last, panting, sweat tastelessly pouring from my brow, I knew I had done well. The beasts roared in their frustration at being trapped above me. I allowed myself a satisfied breath, content in my knowledge that my charges were protected from liberation. And yet..." he continued, the weight of his failure bearing down on him almost like a physical weight, "despite the copious protection I cast, a single small spawn had slipped through and dropped onto the flammable cushions of a nearby couch."

Lord Haphenasis shook his head. "I understand now how it took our brothers so long to round them up. They move like quicksilver and reproduce almost as masterfully. I...," he began. Why were these words so difficult for him to say? *Because failure is for lesser men. So do not consider them as being such. Instead look at it as it was....* "I made a tactical withdrawal.

"Outside, rubble and debris had been strewn from the explosion of the top floors. I hoped that someone or another of our Order, or—I will admit I would have accepted aid from them, too—even of the Sisterhood of the Heart, would have heard the explosion and ventilate to my side. Yet none came. The heat of my immolating tower licked my heels as a cloud carried me across the moat. Already its waters were beginning to steam in the muggy air that the Kremsek were generating. I threw Mullet's cloak over the moat to prevent the spread of the blaze and watched its containment snake around and upward.

"As the Kremsek consumed my wards one after another, I was left...," his voice catching at the last word of the sentence, "helpless." It took him a moment to find his voice again, during which time, he wished his brothers would say something to alleviate the responsibility of having to continue his story. He wished in vain.

"The Kremsek got hotter—I could feel it through Mullet's cloak. The stone walls of the Apocryptein—created by the great architect, Sidbisid Doma, in a time when architecture was the greatest art form—cried and bled into a slow molasses that dribbled down into the evaporating moat below. The spells that had required the sacrifice of a thousand lives petered out, enchantments that had been created by magi whose names had been lost to time diminished to nothingness, and with a mighty cracking of the ground and pedestal that was the Apocryptein, the last wall tumbled."

By the Veins, he thought as the image played out in his memory again. It struck him with surprising force. It was a moment of comprehension that came with the realization that everything had just changed. Hard, impossible, really, to believe, yet true nonetheless. *It is really gone.*

"Your tale appears to be lacking some details," one of his brothers said. In his distraction, Lord Haphenasis could not make out who it was that had spoken, but it served well to bring him back to the audience hall and out of his reality crash.

"That is because the story is unfinished. The Kremsek's laughter—amplified by the thousand fiery children it had spawned—morphed into a high-pitched roar, like it was infuriated at being unable to vacate the premises. Howls of rage echoed across the hill as the immense roar of fire swirled together, spinning round and round. There was another mighty *crack* and its scream was no longer that of rage; this was more akin to the whimpering screech of a dying animal. Indeed, I think it was dying for, as it burned, it coalesced into a single beam of flame that vanished in a twinkling of the eye.

"I will admit my sudden confusion at its disappearance. I stood there, ready for anything – or so I thought— yet oddly aware that the Kremsek was, in fact, no more. Indeed, even the tempestuous heat that had all but smothered Mullet's cloak was gone. Slowly, I started back toward the ruins of my tower.

"As the first one took to the air, I understood—with painful surety, for what followed supported my theory in full—what the cracking sound had been. We had kept them below, so deeply ensconced in the granite that they would never escape. Indeed, the very walls of the Apocryptein were sunk as deeply into the hillside as the structure stood tall. But the Kremsek had penetrated all the wards, all its defenses. Its purely arcane nature had some penetrating effect that could not, would not, be stopped."

This was the moment of truth. This was why his concern for himself was nothing and his relief at having his brothers present so profound. For once in his life, he was left without a theory, stratagem, or definitive means of attack. For once, he needed his brothers to figure out what to do next.

"Lord Haphenasis, what are you telling us?"

"I am verifying a fact that none of you dares to give voice to. I am telling you that the Kremsek destroyed the Apocryptein, gouged away the earth below, and shattered the crystals contained by stone, arcana, and blood and, in doing so, were consumed by the prisoners contained within.

"I am telling you that the Twelve Cataclysms are free."

Chapter 6

"ALL TWELVE?" A WORRIED VOICE ASKED.

Lord Haphenasis nodded. "I counted twelve beams of light taking to the night's sky. As they emerged from the remnants of the Apocryptein, I recognized their arcane vibrations. I am telling you, my brothers, that this woman freed the Twelve!"

As Lord Haphenasis had hoped, the assembly cast the entirety of its attention on the thief. Before there was mere inquiry at her presence, now, even he could feel the hate pressing into her. It had to be done. Despondent as he was feeling about the whole situation, he needed her punished for her hubris. Then, once she was out of the way, his brothers would be free to invest their attentions in the real problem—really the only problem that mattered now. *Put her to death, and let us be done with this.*

"I... I didn't," she said, hugging herself against the onslaught. Yes, there it was, the uncertainty, the acceptance that came in the lower classes when their betters speak to them with the word of truth. She turned to Dane Wunds and Squite, and the lord was happy to see both of his brothers turn away, doubt and pity wrinkling their faces. Even the bothersome Ishtower refused to meet her eyes.

A cough broke the silence. Out in the circle of magi, another orb floated down to cast its light upon one of the men. This one had a small face despite his large head and receding hairline. Neither handsome nor even ugly in the traditional sense, there was keen interest in the way Jetseb leaned forward to speak. "Accusations are all good, Lord Haphenasis. Certainly, the woman before us is guilty of breaking into the Apocryptein, but your accusation fails to consider a very important detail. You are laying blame at the feet of a convenient scapegoat."

No! Lord Haphenasis thought, annoyed at the scribe's refusal to move forward.

"Please elaborate, Runician Jetseb," Skeleton Hamza commanded.

"The Apocryptein was destroyed by the Kremsek, not this girl. What kind of people would we be if we blamed arbitrary events? No, I say we examine those events as they are. The Kremsek was in an arcane plasmats container and those do not break easily. Actually, they *don't* break at all. I'm much more concerned with how this could even happen. Who here would have the power to do something like that?"

"None of us could."

"That's not entirely true," Jetseb replied easily. "We know that the box could contain the Kremsek, right? And, before us, one of our brothers just admitted that he was able to all but stop the raging Kremsek in his tower. What's more, this is the same man who claimed to have brought the problem into our lives in the first place. No, my brothers, I think we all know that someone is quite capable of figuring out how to destroy one of these items."

It was in the *Buh Nor Bible* that Lord Haphenasis had first read the fatalistically true adage that "A mob is only as peaceful as its most violent member and, in a debate, a crowd will swing from one statement to the other, indifferent to neither and passionately in defense of both." He hated the truth of those latter words, but more specifically, he hated how judgmental the attitude of his brothers felt when cast upon him. He was thankful that all his brothers were so thoroughly trained in the practice of violence as the utmost final deed in any situation. Any less augustly pedantic crowd would be stoning him already.

"There are no spells capable of such a thing!" he retorted to the glowering oppression of the room. "Nothing in the history of our brotherhood has ever even come close to this! Not spells of construction, creation, mind, body, energy, placement, chronology, liquid, physical, nothing present, nothing past, nor even anything banned! In my research, both here and at the Apocryptein, I have endeavored to destroy some and any of you can read my reports from the library here. Quite simply, arcane plasmats cannot be destroyed unless brought into the Innervein and released to the aether! So do not even begin to lay the destruction of the Kremsek's prison upon me, when the culprit is standing right before you!"

Cannot.

Lord Haphenasis twitched, suddenly overcome by the word. Why did it stick in his throat? *Cannot. Can not.*

There was something about them that was not those two words. But it was. Lord Haphenasis touched them with his arcana in order to figure out why they were lingering like the cold brush of death's fingertips.

The problem was not that words, by themselves, necessarily carried power. Language could be classified as words spoken or used in specific ways to affect a particular purpose. But unless they were organized in the right order, for specific purposes that were socially acceptable, they meant nothing. Words had amazing potential, but were undermined by their definitions.

Names, on the other hand, were limited only by the evocation of what it represented. If one were to name a person, it was that person's being that was drawn on. No matter where or when a name was called, the named being theoretically could feel it. Get enough people together to call a name and it put stress on the being in myriad forms. In some it created arrogance born of self-knowledge; in others it created madness; and in still others it acted as a summons.

But what happened when a being responded to a summons? The most common response was simple—servitude to the words spoken by the summoner. Many of his brothers had a familiar – a being who came and went as their masters bid. Some of these familiars were animals, but several of his brothers had been able to bind a denizen of the other seven Realms. Such skills were greatly admired among the Order. Yet most summons were limited, as words alone seldom managed to fully describe desires, and therein lay the root of words' greatest limitations.

So were created *cants*.

Two pronunciations defined this linguistically derived variety of spell. The first was the ash, an older sound that had changed over time, but which had the traditional writing of æ, which allowed the phrases within the spells to be cast. The second was the longer ä that was, in essence, a barrier of the cast. Any who attempted to use the latter pronunciation of *cant* would realize that they could not.

Lord Haphenasis realized with a tremor of incredulity that it was the more colloquial use of the contracted form of "cannot" that was the name of a spell he had used earlier that night. Instead of thinking of it as a cænt as he should have, he had thought of it as a *cänt*, which allowed its casting.

If Osaizi's Cant had ever been cast previously, the individual who had would long ago have gone the way of the ages. The spell, itself, had almost been forgotten. It would have probably remained lost to time had it not been for his tremendous skill with Tactile Recall. Even then, his abilities had merely succeeded in bringing the concept of the spell into *allusion*. It required another decade of research to find enough historical mention to divulge the entirety of this unspeakable cant. When at last he had found it, there was only an obscure reference, one that was almost completely indecipherable, but Lord Haphenasis had not become Traumanfang's leading magus to be stopped by some clever obfuscation. When the vocal maze had given way, he had learned the name and story of Osaizi's Cant.

More importantly, he had learned how to cast it.

Until tonight, he had been merely content to just know the spell. After all, how could it have hurt anyone of import? In the long uncountable centuries since the creation of Osaizi's Cant, it had never been used. What could possibly have happened at the time of its creation to have caused its condemnation into oblivion?

Certainly nothing as serious as the release of the Twelve Cataclysms.

"Lord Haphenasis."

He looked up, slowly coming to the idea that some-one was speaking to him. "Yes."

"Did you hear what Runician Jetseb said?"

"Osaizi's Cant."

The assembly looked from one to another in the vain hopes that someone would know what he was talking about. It was a pointless endeavor. There was no way they could possibly know. There was such distaste in Lord Haphenasis' mouth that he could scarcely contain it. He wanted to brush his teeth or suck on licorice root or even to chew on a heady clove of garlic. Anything was better than the guilt he suddenly felt. He glanced upward at all of his brothers. Perhaps, because none of them knew the spell, none would have the intelligence to condemn him.

"Sorry?" Jetseb asked.

Lord Haphenasis smiled brusquely. "Forgive me. I drifted for a moment. Now, as I was saying-"

"No," Skeleton Hamza's quiet force boomed with what felt like a Thunderclap. "Sesellebach, repeat what you just said."

"It was nothing that I can recall now."

"As skilled as you are with Tactile Recall? No. I think not. Repeat those words."

A chamber pot appeared in Lord Haphenasis' mind: a convenient escape from this. If only he thought the leader of the Order would allow him to get away with such flight. Very quietly, he gave in. "It was Osaizi's Cant."

"I... is that a spell?" Jetseb asked. "Skeleton Hamza? Do you... have you heard of this before?"

Skeleton Hamza took his time in responding. When he did, his voice was quiet, yet none could quibble about to whom he spoke. "Indomitable curiosity is no blessing. What has been forgotten has been done so for a reason. We do not awaken demons on account of the damage they will do. Nor do we summon Otherrealmers unjustly. To do so is the very height of carelessness. We are magi of the Order of the Vein. We are above such trivialities."

"Hamza, you must understand that there is no harm in its learning."

"Isn't there? That spell was bound by oblivion, to be forgotten forever."

"And yet you know of it?" Haphenasis asked.

"No. I am ignorant of it. Or I was before you spoke its name. And now the Veins weep in my ear, damning us for allowing you in our Order."

Hamza's words were a bludgeon in Lord Haphenasis' gut. Whatever limitations his brothers suffered, they were nonetheless his brothers and students. Being the best of them all, it was his duty to rise above their limitations and, in the event they could not be taught, deal with the challenges himself. This was where he belonged. Since he was a mere toddler, wrapped up in swaddling cloths, the Veins had called to him. There was no other consideration for his future. How could the Veins claim otherwise?

"You may mean no harm, but look at what your carelessness has wrought."

The blind magus rose and, guided by its hum, stepped toward the floating image of Reservwyresport that had been unchanged throughout the night's proceedings. Lord Haphenasis would gladly have manipulated the image to illustrate his description of the night's events but he lacked the authority to do so. As learned an arcanist as he was, he had no interest in the quibbling political drivel in which the council thrived. As Warden of the Apocryptein, he got more than his fill of their regulations. To suffer it daily would be a punishment far too profound for the simple pleasure of an occasional hologram manipulation.

Hamza slipped the tip on his finger into the relief and stirred the air. Miniature people appeared in the streets of this holographic city. At first they went about the daily tasks of their common lives, but soon they were gathering in squares and streets and their interactions became violent. The violence became brawl and individual turned to mob; bodies fell left and right. When the people could not kill, they burned. Where they could not burn, they smashed. The globe spun. A different place. Here, there was a castle long dead and fallen to ruin. Yet as Hamza twisted his hand, the castle came to life again, in a dark way that invited naught but gloom. The forests surrounding it cracked and bled, and from its rotting heart, an army of the dead emerged like bees. These were harvesters of the pollen called life.

The globe spun again. A valley, long since locked away by the only route into it. The immense stone wall cutting it off from the rest of the world cracked. The crack grew until, with an explosive blast, it shattered into dust. In the resulting cloud, another army emerged, this one

colorful and beautiful and jerking in a way much unlike
the dead army. These were gearwork constructs forged
from metal, ceramic, stone—works of art with destruction
on the mind.

Across the face of Traumanfang, armies gathered to
battle the threats but, at each point, there appeared a single man who stood in their way. Like the funneling of an
army at a bridge, this single man cleaved his way through
all who came his way. Army after army fell before his terrible black sword.

"Stop," Lord Haphenasis said, unable to look away,
disgusted by what a single spell could do. With each
display of the Cataclysms' might, he knew a fresh surge
of guilt. This demonstration was sufficient. He got the
point.

"No." Hamza hissed with the power of arcana. "This
is only the beginning."

The holographic image turned toward the South Sea,
outside the city of Pavlodar. Even from as high an aerial
view as Hamza had taken, the lord could see the potency
of the destruction. Elemental storms wracked the waters
and the islands dotting the seas were swallowed whole
under the storms' might. Waves the height of mountains
slapped the ancient towers of the greatest city in the
world, leaving destruction and desecration in their wake.

Then, from as far out as Hamza could show, the image zoomed in on a woman's face. Even Lord Haphenasis
could feel the pull that she stirred. He knew her inside
and out and found himself wanting to protect her, to
keep her safe, and with such sense came the realization
that every single person in this room felt variations of the
same. In a flash, she was gone, replaced by armies of reli-

gious zealots and traders of the flesh. She was the single gem that the whole world would destroy to possess.

With a cracking of his heart, the image turned again, and he found himself wanting to scratch his nose as the people of the generic town he beheld now did. This was the illness called the Kassernian Flu, a horrible thing that distracted with a runny nose and never-ending cough, and murdered the future.

Another turn. Zombies wandered the streets, their eyes bruised and dark. Sleep had become a terror in the form of dreams that devoured these people when it fell. The sandman had been replaced by a nightmare that allowed no peace. Across the world, flu sufferers yearned for a clear breath, soldiers fighting for the girl fell, and those relieved at having no more sleepless nights in Pavlodar found cool relief in the cleansing destruction of their home. Pain and crime and hallucination come during the daytime exhaustion, but all were welcome releases from the horror that came at night.

Then, from the vents that the Order of the Vein help protect, they began. From the Blue Realms, legions of Fey, angered by the severing of an ancient treaty, poured out on their fantastic beasts, flying by the wondrous means that they had. Here, they claimed the tally deserved by the failure of the Order to fulfill their part of the bargain. The destruction they wreaked was palpable and, over the course of it, gasps as Lord Haphenasis' brothers beheld their destruction.

As one fell so, too, did the other. Where there were men, there were also women, and the Hearts imploded in the schism that came with the return of their founder. The Blessed—those wonderful people who were kissed by the aether and warped into the beautiful perfection that came with the strange coloring and physical alterations of their birthright—are annihilated. And in this holocaust, a civil war consumed what few arcanists remained after both the Order of the Vein and Sisterhood of the Heart were destroyed.

Then, the last image Hamza called forth was a disembodied smile, grinning at all the destruction that ravaged the world.

This was the apocalypse, a swath of destruction and terror that would leave the entire world in ashes. The Twelve fulfilled their legacy.

Twelve? Lord Haphenasis did a quick count. "Where is the last one?"

The image changed. Where before there was the mundane topographic aspect of Traumanfang, here was the Innervein. Despite the monochromatic colors that came from the relief, he could still identify each of his most beloved Veins. There was Wn. And Gho. And Cha... and all were tarnished as they were now. No... not as they were, as they would become. The brightness that suffused each paled, faded. And one by one the unique flavors dwindled into a generic dull grey. The Innervein began to crack, stiffen and dry out. The pleasant ululations were no more. The entire Realm had become nothing more than a dead husk and the aethir dwindled into nothingness.

"You do understand this, do you not?" Hamza asked the silent room.

"How is this even possible?" someone asked. "It's not possible, is it? The aether is eternal. It cannot be destroyed. It just can't! Can it?"

Hamza lifted his eyeless face toward the round walls of the room. Stretching high into the rafters of the room were portraits of all the Skeleton Keys preceding Hamza. Traditionally, for their portrait, each must wear the same robe, leaving each one looking oddly similar to the next, where the only differences between portrait were their faces and the backgrounds, depicting where each had come from. Seven hundred and thirteen portraits were hung in this room, and even without eyes, the Skeleton Key's gaze fell upon a single one. It showed a bright-eyed man with a smile as wide as the evening sky. The plaque beneath his portrait read *Feliz Durawk.*

"According to ancient record, Feliz Durawk postulated that the aether could be dissipated into the Nine Realms and, in doing so, strengthen the values of arcana within each one. A brilliant theoretician and cosmologist, he tested his theories on the Ha Vein. It was these tests that tarnished the Vein, a scarring that it has yet to recover from. Before today, he was the only one who had ever allowed a Vein to be tarnished."

Lord Haphenasis felt the eyes of the assembly upon him.

"With his escape today, is it any wonder that Gho, Re, Cha, Dei, and Wn have joined the Ha in imperfection?"

"I am wholly to blame for everything?" Lord Haphenasis asked quietly. "The tarnishing was a result of the Kremsek's destruction of the Apocryptein. It was not due to Durawk's escape. And we are conspicuously avoiding the fact that none of this would have happened had the girl not broken in."

"Was it not your duty as warden to erect the minor

wards to prevent such an intrusion?" Hamza asked.

"It was, and I did! Would you be satisfied with a list of all the spells that were surrounding the tower?"

"That will be unnecessary," Hamza said. "Yet what good is protection if the *protected* is corrupted?"

"It was locked up."

"And was freed by a spell you cast."

"It was an accident."

"Accident or design, your actions have released the Cataclysms upon Traumanfang." Skeleton Hamza's voice dropped into an authoritarian roar. "Sesellebach tel Haphenasis, Lord of the Khary, Warden of the Apocryptein, Possessor—former—of the Dragon of the Magi of Ulster, you stand before your peers accused of the worst crime we have ever witnessed in the course of our existence. Have you any more to say before judgment is passed?"

Judgment? Me? Not the thief? Lord Haphenasis could not wrap his mind around the words that were being said to him. *No, this was wrong; it was not supposed to be like this!* He needed his brothers to plan a means toward saving the world, not to condemn the wrong person.

"You are hereby sentenced to an eternity of imprisonment within a crystal and hereafter labelled by the most damned of titles: *Cataclysm*."

Chapter 7

THE SURPRISE LORD HAPHENASIS FELT AT THE VERDICT APpeared in his puffy lips; their opening and closing imitated those of a fish gasping for breath. It was as if understanding the words Skeleton Hamza said were just beyond the edge of comment.

"No," he said at last, quietly leaking out the words from his disbelief. "No. I am no Cataclysm."

"You have been judged," Skeleton Hamza replied, seemingly indifferent to the man's confusion.

"No! This... this is a farce! You are upset, I understand that, but it is no reason to condemn me for what is clearly an accident!" Even as he spoke, tiny ribbons of light began to appear in the air. Reacting to the presence of arcana, Ishtower stepped before Vie, shielding her from the quickly angering magus.

"Haphenasis," Ishtower said, reaching out to his

brother. "Settle down. You're channeling."

"Leave me be, miscreant!" the lord shouted, pulling away from him. "What is this, brothers? You scorn me but praise the girl? Is that it? Are you so addled by your hormones that you would sit there and allow this thief to ply your minds with her... her wiles? Where is your decision about her actions? Where is your mighty wisdom when it comes to someone who matters none?" Each question increased the threat in his body until, at last, he reached a boiling point of danger. Around her, the assembled magi were getting to their feet, pulling power of their own, ready for the standoff that all seemed to know was coming. Ishtower grabbed her by the waist and hastened her toward the relative safety of a wall, where simple waves of his hands drew up shimmering barriers between them and the irate lord.

"Lord Haphenasis, power down!" the Warden of the Hall was shouting.

"How dare you!" Lord Haphenasis roared. Back at the Apocryptein, Vie had seen his power and thought that impressive. He had destroyed her senses with just two spells, then bound her in another. It had taken only three spells to humble her to his potential. Yet potential was exactly what he had displayed at the silver tower. Now, he was all but invisible from the arcana spinning from and seething into him. Above her, she could feel the mighty dome groaning against his buildup. The great doors crackled as he drew arcana into himself. His face was growling into a rictus of hatred and disbelief and Vie found herself horribly, terrifyingly frightened.

"How dare you all!" the lord repeated. "If this is what it all comes to, then so be it! I served faithfully! Every day of my life has been geared toward the betterment of our Order, and here you stand, ready to scorch my body away from me so you can cast my spirit into banishment. Well, come along, then! You shall find me no pushover!"

He stood there a long moment, waiting for his brothers to execute the attack. Arms splayed to the sides, he seemed ready for anything. Around him, his brothers glanced from the accused to one another, almost as if silently asking, "Are you going to take the first shot?" Vie felt her heart pounding in her chest, wondering if the wall Ishtower had built for them would be enough once the sparks really started flying. The only thing preventing her from shrinking down and escaping through a crack was the knowledge that doing so would hasten her death.

When at last the first attack came, it did so from a place Vie had least expected. Skeleton Hamza slowly raised his hands out before himself, palms out toward Lord Haphenasis. It was a disarmingly peaceful movement, entirely neutral. "Brothers. Stand down. Has Lord Haphenasis not just complimented us on our ability to use our minds before we resort to histrionics of the flesh?"

While Vie did not fully understand what the eyeless master said, she understood a backhanded compliment when she heard one. Apparently, so did Lord Haphenasis. The energy he had drawn to him continued to snap and seethe, but his eyebrows furrowed in doubt.

"Lord Haphenasis, you heard our judgment, and your reaction is understandable. Yet in giving free rein to your emotions, you failed to consider a small point. How can we execute this sentence if there is no Apocryptein in which to store your crystalline prison?"

The lord frowned.

"It is true that you need to be punished for your crimes against this Order and against Traumanfang, but what good is a sentence like this?" The Skeleton Key paused for a moment to let this question sink in. "We already have twelve Cataclysms loose upon our world, do we not? Where is the wisdom in removing our—arguably —most powerful magus from this war when there is no guarantee that he will even survive it? No. That is why this is a suspended sentence to be appealed at the end of the catastrophe spread out before us."

"I need your word that none will attack me," the lord said, stubbornly rooting in. Amazed as Vie was by his distrust, she was more amazed by the way the other members of the assembly whispered behind hands to one another. From what she could see, the Skeleton Key's sentence came as a complete surprise to all.

"It has already been given. You know as well as any that statements given by the Skeleton Key in the Keyhall are official decree."

"So what was that business all about?" he asked petulantly.

"To ascertain just where your allegiance lies and how much offense you would take to such a title."

"This was a test?"

A thin smirk spread across Hamza's face. "I have always prided myself on my abilities to teach. The title of damnation stands, but I will allow a proviso. Aid us in whatever manner necessary—and I know your expertise on the Cataclysms is considerable, so such manners will be tested—in the recapture of the Twelve, and it will aid your appeal tremendously. How do you respond?"

"As if I have been shamed. Most embarrassingly so."

His shoulders drooped and with them so, too, did the pulsing energy that had been snapping around him. In the darkness that followed, he looked far smaller a man than he had been just a moment ago.

"Good. Use it. Now, brothers, we must stop the Cataclysms. I open the floor to any ideas, speculation, and conjecture you have to offer. The facts remain as such: the Twelve Cataclysms are loose. We have no containment for them, and we cannot allow them to be killed. Give us options, brothers."

"We have the blueprints of the original Apocryptein," Jetseb said. "We could rebuild it."

"That then raises the question of containment," another brother said. "The Apocryptein was built at that particular veinal intersection because the lines reinforced one another to create a uniquely amplified pool of power. What would happen if, due to the Kremsek's fire, we could not rebuild in the same place."

"We would have to find an alternative."

"The crystals housed both their bodies and souls, did they not?"

"Their souls, yes, but their bodies were discorporated. They currently exist in spirit forms without any corporality."

"Will they be able to reconstitute their shells?"

"It is only a matter of time before they do."

"How long?"

"Six months," Ishtower said from beside Vie. The light wall that he had created had already disappeared. Vie was having difficulty accepting the fact that only moments ago, she was fearing for her very life. Now the men of the room were carrying on a regular conversation as if nothing had happened at all. If her headache and cramps were not already one for the records, this would have given her one, if not the other. "As a Martialist who has focused on weaknesses and strengths in all manner of beings, I can give you that number solidly."

"How would you know this?" Lord Haphenasis asked the large, dark-haired magus.

"Who do you think was called in to look after the Apocryptein these past three years when you're here, giving your classes?"

"You? Please tell me you refrained from dirtying my library with your drunkard's filth!"

Ishtower smirked at him. "I even read your theories about their corporality and state of mind upon reintegration. That said, brothers, Lord Haphenasis has made some good points concerning their status."

"Perhaps it would be better if I elucidated this topic." Vie had no idea what that meant, but Ishtower gave the lord the floor to babble. She was not sure if it was gentlemanly or insultingly done. "They will likely start out as disembodied spirits. But they will be hungry and will seek out a feeding source: a Vein, a population, animals, a forest, what have you. Once they have reconstituted, they will be the Cataclysms they were in their lives. Our best bet is to strike them now, while they are weak and disoriented."

"And how can we track them?"

"Each one has been tagged with a vibrational beacon that can be tracked through the aether. I will need some tools to cobble one together, but I already know their arcane 'scent' and could set it into the tracker."

"Then it is settled," Hamza told the assembly. "We

have a six-month window, gentlemen. Lord Haphenasis and Ishtower, you have your task: seek out the Twelve, while they are weak, and contain them."

"Only we two?" Lord Haphenasis stammered.

"How many trackers can you make?"

"Several. Enough for everyone else who knows their scents."

"And does anyone else know their scents?" Hamza asked the assembly.

Not a single hand was raised.

"Is it something that can be taught?" asked one of the younger council members.

Lord Haphenasis considered this. It all came back to words. A man could learn phrases, but the vibrations were like individual words. When one listened to someone talk, it was sometimes exhausting to listen for exactly one word from a sea of information. If one was told to listen for the word "too," and only "too," meaning "also," it would prove a challenge for one who was well versed in the language. Ask a novice to listen for "too" and they may jump when they hear the word "two," as in the number, or "to," used as a preposition, or even "to-morrow." If they jumped at every misheard vibration, they would exhaust themselves and never be right.

"The scents could be taught but not rationalized."

"How long will you need?"

"With the crystals in our possession, it would require at least a week of intense proximal meditation to pinpoint the specifics of it."

"In their absence, we need something. Could you re-create the resonant scents?"

"I believe so, yes."

"Preliminary training will begin in half an hour. You will have six hours to teach us. Brothers, all pribers and magi of the Obsidian should meet in Whirl's lecture hall for training. Additionally, I ask for volunteers. Any who desire should join the others. You will be our hunters while these two concentrate on the direct threats. If there is no other matter, that will conclude this assembly."

Vie could not believe what she was hearing. Had they forgotten her in the madness of the threats that the Cataclysms brought? If so, it was a stroke of luck that she could hardly have expected. For the second time this night, she found herself not exactly giving thanks to the Veins or gods, but at least acknowledging their existence.

"Only we two?"

"Ah! How remiss of me. Vie of Sludge!" Of course they had not completely forgotten about her. That would be too easy. No. Her punishment would be something horrible, no doubt. Death, public stoning, life as a hedge-hog, something like that. "In dealing with the myriad of problems that have presented themselves this evening, I had little time to pay you heed. But now prepare for your own sentence. You are guilty of trespassing on Order property, of wanton destruction of Order historia, of playing the role of accessory to an attack on one of the Order, of the gross attack and irreparable damage to Order estate, and of aiding and abetting the release of the Twelve Cataclysms. Such crimes should deserve death."

Vie's heart raced. The single word, should, kept her from screaming obscenities at the men surrounding her.

"However, we have far more pressing matters to deal with and, to that end, your punishment shall be a contin-uation of one that was already in effect. You are bound by a Choker of Sorrow to Lord Haphenasis. You are his subject, body and soul, until such a time as either he chooses to release you from the obligation or you have completed your mission of recapturing the Twelve Cataclysms. In the unlikely event that the Choker of Sorrow is removed, you are nonetheless bound to continue your service of Lord Haphenasis and his team as if it were still part of your being. In essence, by your trespass tonight, you have given your life over to servitude of the Order of the Vein. A re-evaluation and appeal of this will be held only upon the successful completion of this assignment. Do you understand this punishment as it has been stated to you?"

There was a time in her life when she would have fought these men tooth and nail. She would have ground her heels into the floor and shouted at them until she was hoarse. They would have backed away from her wrath, surprised at how violent and dangerous she was. And then, as one, they would have fallen on her and killed her. But that was before. Before she had found a little peace and love, and the responsibilities that came with such things. Now, she looked around herself and thought. There would be a time for riotous anger, for wrath and tantrums, but right now she needed to consider something greater than herself.

"Squite," she said softly to the wizened old man beside her. "Remember your promise."

He averted his eyes.

"Remember it!" she hissed.

"Vie of Sludge! Do you understand your penalty?" the Warden of the Keyhall boomed.

Squite did not move for a long time. He merely stared at the floor, at the scorched marks where Lord

Haphenasis had been standing while he had been futilely fuming against his own judgment. Then, finally, he nodded ever so slightly at her.

"I understand the punishment you have given me."

"Then may the Veins have mercy on us all."

Chapter 8

"THAT WAS A SPECTACULARLY BALLSY THING YOU JUST DID," Ishtower said. Vie was not certain if he had been officially designated a guard or if he was still just the conduit that was leeching the majority of the wards' pressure from her. Either way, she did not care. She was exhausted. Tonight had been far more emotional than she cared to contend with. She ached all over, she was nearly blind from the headache pounding against her, and the tea she had sipped all throughout the trial had gathered in her belly like a massive cock possessed by the dark men of the islands of Kostany. At that moment she wanted only three things—a piss-bucket, sleep, and home—and talking while she walked was nowhere on that list.

She mumbled an inquisitive response to the handsome magus. Although everything in this immense maze looked alike, she thought she knew where they were going. Upon her arrival, after she had spread a massive puddle of vomit across the floor where they had—what was it that they had called it?—*ventilated* in, Squite guided her up to Dane Wunds's quarters. It was there that he had first attempted to purge her of the wards that were beating her up. Of course, at the time, she was giggling and incoherent, a distracting drawback from the spell that Squite had cast on her in order to get her to the healer. It had seemed like a dream, one in which she was being assaulted, but around her everything had been pretty. Pretty and funny. There was that strange feeling inside herself, too, like she could feel her heart beating and the blood pumping through her body. It had made a funny song for her to hear. She could not recall anything she had said, but every word that had come out of her mouth had sent her into peals of laughter. Sadly, nothing had even a trace of such sentiment now. She sighed with the sadness of her reality.

"Can I get another of those laughing spells?" she asked Squite.

"Sorry, dear," he said, shaking his head. He exhaled a small cloud of smoke from his nose. Vie was so out of it she had not even noticed him lighting a pipe. The smell was sweet and delicate yet it made her stomach clench. A wave of coughing struck her. Doubling over, she hacked and coughed and felt sweat gathering clammily at her brow.

"Put that out!" Dane Wunds snapped at the old man. "Smoke is hardly healthy for the infirm."

"Since when?" Squite asked.

"Since always."

"Dat ain't true. When I was a li'l boy, healers like yerself encouraged it. Dey said it 'got de heart beatin' an' de lungs breavin'.' So you can take yer prescripshun an' shove it."

Dane Wunds responded by hexing the bowl into explosion. With black soot, dark ash, and tobacco settling into each and every one of his many age lines, the ancient man looked like a demon. It was quite hilarious. Or it would have been had Vie not been too distracted by her body's protests of the wards to care.

"She is my patient, so whatever treatment I say goes."

"Damn kids an' yer newfangled ideas of healin'," Squite grumbled, pulling a rag from a pocket in his feathery cloak.

"Laughing spell," Vie repeated to any of the three magi with her or to the two trailing behind. Ishtower she was not sure about, but these two, she knew were guards. They were much younger than the three she was walking with—even Ishtower, despite his raven black long hair, had creases of age set in his eyes—and moved with the self-important annoyance of all guards. One thing she appreciated about them was that they were holding their tongues. There was nothing worse than kids who thought they knew better, casting their opinions and insults where they were not needed.

"Can't," Dane Wunds said, pressing a cool palm to her head. The simple contact quieted her heaving, and she felt the clamminess of her forehead disappear almost at once. "Emotional manipulation is extremely taxing to the body. After your near-death upon your transformation into the mouse, there is no way I want to try anything risky."

"Yeah, better I die when the Cataclysms kill me."

"This is no laughing matter, girl," Ishtower said,

wrapping a strong arm over her shoulder to keep her walking.

"Who's laughing? Not me, that's for sure." She limply pointed at Dane Wunds. "His fault."

"Death, I mean." There was such sadness in his voice that Vie had to look up at him. Some of her hair had come loose and was getting in her eyes. It was hard to see him through it. "When it comes, it will be horrible and you will not want to be anywhere near it."

"I'm no girl," Vie said, changing the subject. Death was a subject to joke about, not look in the face. Ishtower's moodiness did not lend itself to joking, so that led her to avoid the subject. "I'm twenty-eight or so."

"A right old lady," Ishtower replied.

"Here we are," Dane Wunds said as they turned a corner. He hurried down the corridor to the first door and opened it. "Come, get her inside and set her on a bed."

"This isn't where we were before, is it?" Vie asked. In the room Squite took her to earlier, she remembered a couch and table and desk covered in various bottles and potions and pots and glass filling up a single cramped chamber, now she was looking into a well-lit chamber twice as long as it was wide. At the far end, past two opposing rows of beds that stretched a ways down, there stood a large window that looked out onto the rainbow of the Innervein's Veins.

"No," Squite said, helping Ishtower lay her on a bed. "Dis is de recovery room."

"Wait," Vie said, pushing against their efforts. "Privacy first. I need a bucket."

Squite and the two younger magi looked embarrassed at the thought of her pissing in their company, but Dane Wunds and Ishtower were indifferent to it. Despite this, only the ancient magus averted his eyes. As she squatted over the bucket, Vie made a point to stare at the two young magi in the eyes, as if accusing them of perversion. One actually looked away under her gaze. The other looked to be enjoying himself, the little pervert. While Vie's experiences with men had never forced her to engage in bodily release fetishes, she knew well that they existed. She wondered at this young magus, enjoying her simple act of making water, and once more asked what it was that made men the strange things they were. Were none good? Or was drawing this kind of freak, or freaks like Lord Haphenasis, or even of *him*—abandoning her just when she needed him most—just a curse she had contracted in being born to Sludge?

"Shit," Vie said, looking into the bucket. "I am bleeding. Two weeks early, too. Thanks lots, magi. Want a look?" she added for the benefit of the eager-eyed pervert.

"Enough," Dane Wunds cut in, nudging the bucket under a neighboring bed and handing Vie a cloth. "Thank you for your escort, gentlemen, but you can wait outside."

"We were told to look after her while she was here," the pervert said. Vie could feel his eyes on her naked flank as she mopped up her blood.

"And you are in the way here. If you do not leave, I will take this up both with your superior and with Skeleton Key Hamza. If you leave this room right now, I will even put in a good word on your behalf so that when the time comes to hunt down the Cataclysms, you just might be counted among the number."

The modest one, a stout young man with short dark hair and a baby face, turned right around and made for the door. The pervert lingered a moment, weighing desire with desire. At last he, too, turned and left the room.

"Kids," Squite said with a shake of his head.

"Full of piss and vinegar," Dane Wunds replied as he helped Vie into bed. "Thank the Veins we were never like that."

"Speak fer yerself!" Squite cackled. "You could stew leeks wif my blood! But business is business, an' dis is damn peculiar stuff."

"How so?" Vie asked, closing her eyes. The room was tilting slightly and she felt like puking again, but for the moment, there was a gentle comfort to the queasiness of her body's sensations.

"Everyfing," Squite replied. "A *firteenf* Cataclysm."

"One in my lifetime is bad enough," Ishtower agreed. "Now, all are loose."

"You blame me?" Vie asked. Something pricked into her arm. She did not even bother looking down. All she cared about was the comfortable warmth spreading from that point. With a hand at each of her elbows, Dane Wunds began a soft chanting. "Oh, that's nice."

"This should knock you out in such a way as to lessen your sensitivity to the wards," Dane Wunds explained. "I'll be here to draw what additional pressure there is. If worse comes to worst, the kids outside can replace Ishtower as conduit."

"Where's he going?" Vie asked.

"To attend Lord Haphenasis' lecture about tracking the twelve."

"To answer your question, Vie," Ishtower said, "to be

honest, I don't know if I blame you. This is so far above me that I don't even know what's what. But I do know that going to that lecture will probably be a waste of time. I doubt I'll learn anything new, but in case *Thirteen* forgets something, I should be there to correct him."

Squite snorted—not quite a laugh, but neither was it a cough. "I knew dere was a reason I liked you, kid. But don't you forget yerself. You let dat man hear you talk such, you might be askin' for trouble. I been around long enuff to know Lord Haphenasis ain't no one to be underestimated. He's de best because it's who he is. He may've been born into nobility, but since den, he's sure as de Four Hells earned it. Contempt and grudges won't be of use. You treat him wif respect, keep your disapproval to yerself, an' you just might live frough dis all."

"I'll take your caution to point," Ishtower said, the frown plain in his voice. Hatred ran deep and Vie found herself curious as to what it was that caused these two to hate each other so mightily. "Anyway, girl, as I said before, that was brave."

"Thought you said 'ballsy.'"

"I did."

"What was?" The heat from Dane Wunds's treatment was massaging all the aches and pains from her body. Even her head was beginning to feel a little better. Sleep was pressing hard at her temples.

"Ignoring Hamza to get some response from Squite. Before I go, might I ask what was going on between you two?"

"Since you're comin' wiv us, why not? Before we went into de Keyhall, she made me promise to bring her back ta Sludge before any judgment be carried out."

"Didn't you say you were in the Apocryptein to find a way out of that place? What possible reason could you have to return there?"

Sleep was closing in on her. When she woke up, it would be time to leave and begin the grand experience of tracking down the Twelve Cataclysms. Before that could happen, it was her time. It was a tiny victory, but she had secured the freedom to collect them. Darkness was pulling her in. Before it did, she saw the three of them, each one as large-eyed and beautiful as they had been every day since their birth. "My children."

Chapter 9

"THE FIRST THING TO KNOW IS THAT NONE OF YOU WILL BE able to find the Cataclysms by yourselves."

A low grumbling answered Lord Haphenasis' statement. Whirl's lecture hall was the largest amphitheater in the Innervein, a room designed in the ancient tradition of a central stage at the base of a wide pit of benches spread out in a semicircle. The room could hold more than a complete class of magi, which consisted of six Summons of 50, bringing the total to nearly four hundred. The room was now completely packed. Lord Haphenasis looked out at them all with satisfaction and a certain amount of disapproval. Not for his part, mind you; but this was a futile lesson that, at best, would provide them with motion that mimicked progress.

"This is no insult to your skill. It is a mere fact of precision. Allow me to give you an example." He snapped his fingers. "Who can tell me which musical note was created with that action?"

The criticism that had greeted his opening statement gave way to uncertainty. Perfect. A teacher's first duty was to create doubt and discomfort. Only through the acceptance of ignorance could one actually begin the slow process of learning.

"That was what musicians would call a C *sharp*." He brought his other hand close and snapped again. "And that? Please raise your hand if you think it was the same."

A large number of hands shot up.

"Different?"

A more scattered assortment of hands went up, this time more hesitantly than the first group.

"How many of you feel that you do not know?"

The number of hands that went up dwarfed the amounts of both the first combined. Ignorance was often a silent torture, one best suffered in silence. The learned knew enough to ask questions, for from interrogation came challenge and growth. The ignorant never knew enough to ask questions, but what they could do was suffer discomfort. With this simple series of questions, Lord Haphenasis had weeded out those who had raised their hands in surety from those who did so because of their peers' reactions. In the third option, he found truth. The discomfort that came from uncertainty always gave way to a neutrally nonjudgmental option, and in finding this, opened the mind toward the lesson rather than the distraction of discomfort.

"Good. The truth is that they were different. A musician who has spent his life learning the differences between sounds would have a better time identifying the subtleties of the two sounds, but as none of you are experts in that profession, I doubted any would be able to do so. I hope you understand my earlier statement now.

"For the past eighteen years, I have served our Order as Warden to the Apocryptein. Every single day, I have descended into the bowels of the construct to inspect my prisoners. When I first came on, there were only eleven. The twelfth came nearly a decade into my time there. But I am getting ahead of myself."

Twelve crystals of varying shades and colors appeared around him. They were almost uniformly the same in shape and dimension, with flat tops and bottoms but with precise cuts in its sides to create a fancy pattern of fractaled light that reflected a singular pit back in upon itself. Each one—for the sake of the presentation—was double life-sized, roughly three times the size of a closed fist.

"Here they are, such as they were last night. Each prisoner has been given a name pertaining to the nature of his or her offense. We have the Whim, the Lich, the Mother, the Theorist, the Bard, the Devourer, the Plague, the Possession, the Tempest, the Butcher, the Tinker, and finally, the Possessor.

"Just as each note has a precise sound, each of these also has a specific thaumatic vibration that we can use to identify one from the other. Right now, I ask you to close your eyes and feel the vibrations as I did each time I descended into their holding room. It will be a jumble, but that is quite acceptable. Do not let this intimidate you. In a moment, we will listen to them individually. As you listen to them all, try to differentiate one from the rest. If you are unable to do so, there is no shame, for you have not yet been taught the differences."

He did not warn them he would reproduce the vibrations. He merely did it. Those who had skill at identifying or tracking arcane *scents* would be able to hear it. Those who did not would not. It was as simple as that. Despite this, Lord Haphenasis amplified the vibrations to a point where any who were sensitive would pick up on it. He was pleased to see that the majority of those assembled in this hall could actually pick up on the vibrations. Their concentration formed a rictus of struggle in their faces. He quieted the vibration.

"I can see that many of you could sense the vibrations. Now, as the general din continues in the background, I will pull one vibration at a time into the forefront so that you can feel each one as the individual that it is. If you are able to identify one from the orchestra, congratulations, you have taken a step toward comprehension of this lecture. But whatever you feel, keep your exultations to yourself. Truly, we need as profound a concentration as you can muster."

The Whim was first. It was a playful vibration, such as one could be. It dipped and swirled about, passively aware of the way it bounced and cajoled positivity from its complex rag. While each one had their own strengths and weaknesses, each vibration was an echo of who the individual was in life. Lord Haphenasis had long imagined the Whim as a curious individual who picked at the world like a cellist plucking at his strings.

Next came the Bard, whose song was alluring and seductive. He had never liked this one. Even from within, he could feel the potential that his song carried in it. This was a voice that could alter reality as it chose. He knew the story of the Bard, how he had become so obsessed with the other realms that he actually sang himself into the Blue Realm, where the Fey lived. It had caused a war between the two dimensions, and it was only through a treaty between the Order of the Vein and the Fey King that the war was halted. Such power over reality was dangerous, and every time he visited this prisoner, he was filled with unease and distrust.

One by one, he played the other ten vibrations for his brothers. He did it first in order of capture, then backward from most recent to oldest, then he played only female, then male, then neither. Again and again he played the vibrations for his audience. Each time, he tested them, asking questions about what they sensed, how it felt, what distinguished one from the next, where they could feel the resonation, their emotional response to the vibrations. Time and time again he repeated it. Time and time again, their answers were suffused with uncertainty. Half the time that one of his students seemed sure of which vibration they were sensing, the answer proved wrong. These drills continued without pause until the time-keeper declared it was time to move on to the next part of Lord Haphenasis's lesson plan.

"Already?" he asked, surprised and most dissatisfied. How could two hours have passed so quickly and with such meager progress? Frowning, he nonetheless moved on to the next stage of the training. During the short time he had been given to prepare this lesson, Skeleton Key Hamza had been very clear about the timeline.

"You have until dawn."

"Why dawn?"

"You mentioned that the Cataclysms were released as disembodied spirits. As I'm sure you know, the secrets of ventilation were unlocked after the study of spiritual form. At first it was the fragile barriers between dimensions that we were first able to explore, but then we learned that such travel can occur entirely within Traumanfang. We will have to assume that our escapees can move quickly. At dawn, they will have had an entire night to move. There is no telling where across the world they might be. We need to find them and recapture them now, while they are still weak and disembodied. Once they reform their bodies... well, I don't need to tell you this."

Indeed he did not. As spirits, they were disembodied potential whose only real capability was feeding. With bodies, they would be in a position to exert that potential upon the world around them. That was when the Cataclysms would begin to rail against the world for their imprisonment. While some, like the Whim, had given themselves freely, others had rained death upon not just the Order but the entire regions in which they were captured. Each one who was allowed to reform would make their job all that harder. Hamza's deadline made altogether too much sense.

"While I am not pleased with this progress, we nonetheless must press onward. This next round will be a running test. My assistant will pass out parchment and quills to all. Your job is to identify exactly which of the Cataclysms you sense in the cacophony. Once each round is complete, I will display each one so that you can feel how each scent stacks upon the others."

The results were unsurprisingly bad.

"No! Do you feel the tittering here? The despondency? That is the Lich. This is the emotion of utter loss and failure! Again!"

By the fourth round, when the timekeeper had given him the signal to stop, Haphenasis had his face buried in his hands. He was hungry, exhausted, and beyond irritable. Had the Lich been manipulating his emotional output? He could not tell. Remaining in his seat before the assembly, he considered telling them all just to leave. They could not get it. Some, certainly, were not useless. They could pick out the different vibrations, but it was a painstaking process. In the time it took them to find the correct vibration, the Cataclysm would have vacated the locale.

"Lord Haphenasis?" the timekeeper prompted.

Rubbing his eyes, he groaned his way to his feet and stared out at the scores of magi seated before him. How in the name of the Veins could they be so oblivious? If only it were the right time to be truly offensive. If it were, he could damn them all for their limitations. Sadly, there was no time for that. There was no longer time for anything save to solve the problem of epic proportions that was the Twelve Cataclysms. Taking a deep breath, Lord Haphenasis set his mind to the task at hand.

At the end of the lecture, he packed his things into his travel ruck with a lesser sense of foreboding, but with nowhere near the sense of satisfaction that his lectures normally brought him. It was acceptable if one or two of his students failed to grasp his message, another thing entirely when all *but* one or two failed. He left out the demonstration for any students who wanted further experience with the vibrations. Much to his dismay, none of the group were descending the stairs for immediate further practice; instead, they were all slowly working their way out the two doors at the back of the room. He hoped there would be enough time for them to take advantage of the practice tools later.

"Were you able to teach them?" Skeleton Hamza asked from the back of the immense hall as the last of the students exited.

"Teach? Oh, indeed. But teaching has never been a problem for me. As the old expression said, *you can lead a horse to water, but you cannot make it drink.* So the question, then, is not whether I have *taught* them, but more a question as to whether or not they were able to *learn* anything."

"I trust your ability in this," Hamza said.

"You trust in the abilities of a *Cataclysm*," the lord scoffed. "Is this what you are telling me? If so, why go through with the whole trial? Why have you labeled me so?"

"Teachers only provide their students with the tools necessary to solve their own problems."

"If crypticism were an art, your frescos would decorate landmarks from here to the Manitou Plateau."

"Lord Haphenasis, do you trust me?"

"This is not about trust."

"Yes, actually, it is. This is all about trust. I trust you to do what is right. Just as I need you to trust me to lead you and your brothers the way the Veins choose."

"And my brothers?" Lord Haphenasis scoffed. "There are maybe three in the whole group who might have a shot in the Vein to be able to actually track one of these Cataclysms. The way I see it, I will personally have to find every single one and cajole them back into their cages."

Skeleton Hamza said nothing. He merely stood in the back of the room with a curious smile on his face.

"What?" Lord Haphenasis asked irritably.

"As I said. This is all about trust." And with that, he left.

Chapter 10

METALLIC COPPERY BLOOD WAS GOOD FOR MANY THINGS. Congeal it and cook it with a meaty base and it made some tasty black pudding. Ancient Knokni used it to measure their devotion to their dead god: the more they spilled, the more their devotion. It could be mixed with spells and potions to channel their potency, as had been done with the Apocryptein. But one thing Lord Haphenasis was quickly learning was that it was insufficient to block out the characteristic stink of Sludge.

"Remind me again why we are in this den of rejection and want?"

Lord Haphenasis frowned at a sailor who had collapsed with his bottle on the side of the muddy lane they walked down. Constantly sailors carried by the tides of the Singing Bay came here to deposit their wares. As the wharves and piers were adjacent to this corner of the city, the sailors needed a place to stay. Sailors being what sailors were, they brought desperate hunger for all forms of recreation and privation. It was for this that Sludge sprung up from the sloppy runoff of Reservwyresport.

"It is simple, really," Ishtower said, pausing to let an early morning deliveryman trot his horse through the muddy lane. "Our companion said that we had to collect her children from her friend. You told her that she was crazy to think we would—and I quote—'waste our time with children.' Vie's response was that she would abandon them over her dead body. You said that could be arranged. It was then that I convinced you that seeing the world from her perspective might be in everyone's best interests."

Lord Haphenasis tenderly prodded the bridge of his nose just to see that it was still attached to his face. It was. The pain that throbbed from it into his eyes was all he really needed to listen to, but a reminder was not out of line. The coppery stink was still there, but at least the bleeding had stopped.

"I believe your exact words—after a whole slew of cussing, of course—was, 'You're right. How much trouble could a couple whiny brats actually be?'"

"They're not very whiny," Vie said, leading the way through an alley littered with sleeping bums. However, in the grey obfuscation of the early dawn, Lord Haphenasis was not certain that they really were people.

"Why must they always sleep out in the streets around here?" he asked, stepping lightly to avoid one broad tramp who had spread out crosswise in the alley. "Is this really a shortcut? Would the main thoroughfares be more conducive to travel to our destination?"

"There are no 'thoroughfares' in Sludge," Vie explained as she moved. "There are only lanes, back alleys, and ways. The thoroughfares you speak of only go to the docks. Everything on the river side of the docks has no real roads. No point, really, what with how it gets washed out every time a flood comes."

"The fact that we are even struggling through such a mud land raises some serious questions about Squite's loyalties."

"Come on," Ishtower groaned. "You know that he can't. Sludge is too inconstant to allow for Venting in here."

"You speak as if you know this place," Vie said.

The big man shrugged and avoided the accusation by ducking around the remains of a wooden kiosk that looked to have been ripped down into the middle of the street. Much of it had already been stripped, but the broken wood had been largely abandoned. Nothing lasted long in Sludge, not even trash.

"Would it not have been better to attain our destination from the wharves?"

"No, the mud is too thick on the water side."

"I could call a cloud to carry us to our destination."

"Would you give it a rest? You've been groaning and complaining ever since we got back. This is happening. Accept it."

Accept it, Ishtower said. Why not? What was one more bit of insanity to throw into the embers of the night? It did not matter that the Twelve were loose, nor that it would be an easy enough matter to flex Vie's choker and force her to join him at a quiet eatery where he could set his hound to work in pinpointing the first of the Cataclysms. With Ishtower's punch to his face, however, he had given in. Even now; after decades of authority, of title, and of fulfillment of power; physical confrontation made him cower. It was a sad truth, but also one of frustrating reality. How was it that over the course of a single night, he could stare down the entirety of his Order, and be swayed by a single act of bullying from an old pain in the neck?

"I will accept this, but this is the last time this happens."

Ishtower's response was drowned out by the horrifying sound of a retching peon from somewhere in the ediface beside them. The buildings here were little more than shanties of driftwood, half of which were haphazardly leaning into their neighbor, the other performing tricks of balance and engineering that made Lord Haphenasis think there were some arcana manipulators in these slums. He realized, as they wove from one lane to alley, that he had not even seen the sky in several minutes.

"Are you certain you know where we are going?" he asked. The discomfort he was feeling now had nothing to do with simple aesthetics; this came from a deeper sense of distrust. Hamza had left her in their hands, a wildcard, a rogue element that none knew or *could* trust. Ishtower had been so easily taken in by her charms that he wondered if there was not more at work here than he could outright see. What if she was leading them to a trap?

"What? Don't you trust me?" the thief snarked.

"Enough." With a twitch of arcana, he triggered the Choker of Sorrow. The thief's progress stopped and she turned toward him.

"Haphenasis? What are you doing?" Ishtower asked.

The lord flicked a wall between himself and his

brother. He was alone with Vie.

"Haphenasis! What is this?"

"I need some answers," he replied, staring at the woman as he spread his consciousness toward her. In her head there had to be the truth of this. It was only a matter of prying. Through her eyes he pierced, passing through walls of bone and flesh and, surprisingly, a series of those carved from arcana. He wondered where she had learned to build such things. *Of course*, she was a morpher. There would have to be a certain degree of innate compartmentalization to control the odds and ends of the different sensory inputs. It was a natural thing, perfectly understandable. Most peeled away easily enough, but as he pried, he found certain parts of her mental geography to be odd, strangely shaped, as if the continents of her mind refused to conform to the standards of normal people. Because of this oddity, it took longer to find her memories than expected.

When he did, he was in a room unmarred by the destitution that defined Sludge. This was a place of relative comfort, even—if that clockwork owl were truly silver and functional—of wealth, far dissimilar to the world that Vie was now leading them through. But here, there was pain, excruciating pain. He stepped ahead a ways to avoid the pain and found her exhausted, with three babies at her breast.

So she is a mother after all, he thought. Comparing her age at the time and her age now, he was not sold on the idea that this was not a trap. Much could happen between the birth of children and the present. He flipped his way through the pages of her life since then and found her more at the present, and poked his way through her most recent thoughts.

Coming to himself again, he found himself sweating, an unfamiliar pressure in his loins. *Of course, it was the childbirth.* Phantom sensations often came with heavily traumatic memories of the pried. Vie was on her hands and knees in the muddy street, panting.

"There is no trap," he absently told Ishtower. "She truly is taking us to her children."

"You seriously doubted her?"

"Why are you so surprised?"

"To be honest, I don't know if I am," Ishtower said, tapping on the wall. Lord Haphenasis dropped it as the Martialist hooked a hand under Vie's armpit.

"Leave me alone!" she snapped, slapping his hand away. The rage in her eyes was almost a living thing as she glared at Lord Haphenasis. If looks could kill, this would have disemboweled him. "Don't you *ever* do that again."

"What are you so angry about? I was the one who might have been at risk had this been a trap."

"My memories are my own," she said, rising shakily to her feet. "You have no right to them."

"By the decree of my brothers, you are mine. I have the right of acquisition. I can do with you as I will."

"Then I *will* fight your will with everything I have."

He did not even shrug to acknowledge her petty rebelliousness. He merely commanded her through her choker to "Lead on."

Without another word, she did, moving ahead of them. Feeling satisfied with this momentary security, Lord Haphenasis followed her from a couple of strides behind. Ishtower took up beside him.

"Watch yourself," he warned.

"Hmm?"

"Even the gentlest of women have tigers inside them. This one, I fear to think of what might be inside her. You know I have no love for you, but with her, you're putting yourself on a dangerous road."

"She is bound to me. What have I to fear from her?"

"Asks the man whose house was incinerated thanks to her."

It was salt in a fresh wound, but Ishtower's reminder did not spark the contempt that his remarks usually deserved.

"What do you suggest, then?"

"Befriend her, or, as that is so highly unlikely from you, at least seek not to aggravate her any more than necessary."

"I did not trust her not to jeopardize us."

"Really. Her jeopardize us?"

"I had not realized you had become impervious to knives or crossbow bolts."

"We've been set on the tracks of the *Twelve Cataclysms*—who, may I remind you, are *the* most dangerous people that have *ever* existed on Traumanfang —and *you're* worried about a crossbow bolt or a knife to your back?"

"When you put it like that, it does seem a rather trite concern."

"As cruel as that tongue of yours can be, next time just use it. You sound dumber when you assume then when you actually speak."

Lord Haphenasis's rejoinder drowned in his throat thanks to a screech from Vie. She had just turned a corner in the maze that was Sludge. Hastening to the corner, Lord Haphenasis was met with a bona fide commotion or people jostling, shoving and pointing. Vie was pushing her way through the crowd, and toward the three-story building licking the sky with its flames.

"Yue!" Vie screamed.

"Come on," Ishtower said to Lord Haphenasis and hurled himself onto the roof of a nearby grocer's kiosk. "There will be no fire brigade down here. Not enough room for the fire wagons to get through. I can cool the flames if you can contain them. Fire needs air. Choke that off and it will die."

Lord Haphenasis nodded and lumbered up on the roof with far less grace than his athletic brother. Lord Haphenasis pulled out Mullet's cloak and wove it though the building's open windows. Once there, he focused his consciousness into the foggy firmament of the spell and spread through it over the burning areas. The heat seared his consciousness but he was not to be deterred by something as trivial as a vicarious pain. Besides, even as he burned, he could feel the chill of Ishtower's spells and took mild comfort in this partnership of elemental counterbalance. His first target was a tapestry that was roaring up a wall. He spread himself out over the tapestry, separating it from the air it needed to consume. Then he moved further along, reaching from one flame to another, moving quicker with each area, until he has split himself so thoroughly as to hit dozens at once.

Time never seemed to function as it should when he worked like this. The biggest problem with fire is that while a combatant concentrated on one thing, obscure or hidden flames could smolder and deal lots of quiet damage. The trick was to smother as much as possible all at one time. It was a task made difficult by how widespread the blaze was. It felt like he had been at it for days, or at least hours when, finally, he felt no more heat and all open flames were gone.

Lord Haphenasis pulled his mind back into his body and clutched Ishtower's arm so as to keep from tumbling over. Channeling through a spell like this always left him a bit disoriented while simultaneously utterly exhilarated.

In this courtyard, dawn had finally decided to touch down, but they had succeeded in saving the building. It was a larger building, one of surprisingly permanent materials and care. It had been built to endure, with an elevated entrance and flood-resistant stucco tar. The dark tiles of the roof were stained and black scars covered the building's exterior near its windows, but with the combined skill of the two magi and the water tossed on from nearby citizens, the building was still standing. A cheer for the heroes burst from the crowd. Ishtower flashed them a smile and gave a wave. Lord Haphenasis was uncomfortable with the whole thing and simply nodded at the peons.

"Do you see Vie anywhere?"

"I can call her to us."

The magi climbed down off the kiosk and crossed the street to where a pair of flatfeet were questioning what might have been the proprietor of the building.

"Better not. Just make ourselves conspicuous. Let her come to us."

This tactic irked him, but he held his tongue. He made the command as unobtrusively as he could.

Vie appeared through the still-smoking doorway a moment later, dragging three creatures behind her. She was furious. "Again! You son of a bitch! How dare you pull me away from my children when I am in the middle of shouting at them!"

Ishtower cleared his throat in distaste.

A giggle came from one of the imps lingering behind her. All three were nearly black with soot, virtually indistinguishable from one another in their simple shifts and short pants. One had longer hair and one was much bigger, but all three had streaks under their eyes. They had clearly been crying.

"Don't you start!" she snapped at the children. "This is hardly a laughing matter. Burning down the Released Stout? Where is Yue anyway?"

The longest-haired child spoke. "Auntie Yue was busy so she told us to sit in the big room, but then the Goatman told us that we were in the way and that nobody wanted to see a bunch of kids in the big room. So we had to leave the big room and go somewhere else. I asked him where can we go and he said in the basement."

"What happened there?" Vie demanded.

"There was a big box!" a different child said.

Vie groaned. "Which of course you opened."

The second child nodded with a big smile on his sooty face. "It was full of balls so we played some balls."

"What kind of balls?"

"They were black! And who're these guys?"

"Don't change the subject. Was it coal?"

"Yup!" said the largest child.

"And you set it on fire?"

"I didn't!" the long-haired one said.

"I did!" the large one said. "Not only that, I juggled three of them!"

"Were they flaming?"

"Oh yeah! *Fwoosh! Fwoosh!*"

"And you dropped them."

"Well, they were pretty hot."

Vie grabbed her child's hands to inspect them. "Do they hurt?"

"Not really. A little. But I juggled fireballs!"

"And threw them into the coal bin."

"It wasn't at the coal bin—"

 "It was more away from him—"

"But once it dropped in—"

"It was so quick—"

"We tried putting it out—"

"But that only made it burn more—"

"You threw whiskey on fire?"

"*Fwoosh!*" the large child giggled.

"All right, all right, I get the picture," Vie said, rubbing her eyes.

"I don't think we should get into trouble because Bon juggled fireballs. Not many people can do that. It was really impressive and you'd be really proud of him for doing so. And who are these guys, and how come they're staring at us? What, you've never seen kids before?"

Ishtower did not even try to hide his smirk.

"Kids, these are two gentlemen I had the *pleasure* of meeting tonight while I was at work, the magus Ishtower and Lord Haphenasis."

"Which work? The work that Auntie Yue does or the work that you don't talk about?"

"You're magus?!"

"A lord! Mom! Can I show him how I learned to greet a lord?"

"Gentlemen, these little firebud shits are my three *charming* children: Bel, the firstborn, is the talkative girl.

Braden is the small quiet one. And Bon... Bon! Pull your shorts up this second or I'll tan that hide! What do you think you're doing showing your ass like that?"

Ishtower snorted back a chuckle though Lord Haphenasis saw no humor is having a bold child flashing his backside.

"Bel told me it's the best way to greet a lord."

"I did not, you liar! Mother, I have no idea where he got such a silly notion. Lords are to be honored and curtsied to." With this, the girl bent her knees, fanned out her shift, and made a horribly awkward curtsey. Lord Haphenasis was too affronted by the boy's decision to flash his butt to bother correcting the girl on her poor attempt.

"Never mind," Vie sighed. "Have you seen your Auntie Yue?"

The shortest of the three, Braden, pointed up at the scarred building. Vie's face paled in the early dawn light. "No. She was still inside?"

"Nope," Braden replied, giving his mussy head a shake. "Up there. The roof next doors." Several people had gathered up there and were in various stages of undress. One of them glittered like gold as the morning sun struck her. "She's sparking in the sun."

"Thank Re," Vie sighed.

Chapter 11

To Vie's surprise, when Yue had caught up to them, Lord Haphenasis suggested they retire to a bathhouse where they could clean themselves up and find some breakfast. That notion suited her just fine. There were long nights and there were *long* nights. Tonight had been the latter. In fact, the last time she had endured such an ordeal-wrought night was nearly eleven years ago when she gave birth to her little litter. She had no illusions that the magi would bring her incalculable difficulties in the days to come, but the promise of food and cleanliness brought her such relief that she was able to ignore the threat these men brought.

Knowing the area better than everyone else, Yue and Vie led the way to the closest bathhouse. They walked arm in arm at a leisurely pace that neither magus chose to protest against. Vie's roommate, best friend, and occasional business partner looked horrible. Her normally

perfect golden fur had been smoked with ash, but fortunately there appeared no scorch marks. She was dressed
only in a short robe that barely touched the top of her
thighs. As they walked, Yue told her how she had been
with a client when the bells rang, alerting all to the fire
in the building. The little robe was all that she could secure in time. Behind them, the kids were showing signs
of sleepiness, the boys falling in without complaint, while
Bel, clearly thinking that this was 'girl time,' grabbed her
mother's free hand.

"What are they doing here?" Yue whispered of the
magi as they walked.

"You remember the last thing you said to me before
I left tonight?"

"I told you to not get caught."

"Well."

"You got caught!" Bel squealed.

"Shush, child."

"You got caught?" Bel repeated at a whisper.

"Oh, sweetie," Yue said, pressing Vie's hand.

"How? Didn't you go mouse?"

"I did, but they're magi."

"Honey, tell me everything," the sympathy was plain
in Yue's voice. It felt wonderful to have a trusted friend—a
woman, at that—at her side again. The challenges of the
night were so much the smaller for her company.

Vie told her everything. Too tired and still suffering
the lingering aches from the Innervein, she stuck to the
details with a distance borne in companionship. The kids
were awed by her recollection of the arcane world, but
their questions about it were cut short with promises of
"Later." Despite her reluctance to go into super-descrip-

tive language, her story continued until long after they had entered the warm waters of the bath. Yue listened quietly as she helped scrub soot off the kids. When at last Vie finished, Yue was bringing her a small slice of absolute contentment in the form of a hair massage.

"What now?" Yue asked softly as she slipped Vie's long hair into a braid.

That was the question, wasn't it?

Across the wide social pool, her three children were splashing around, clearly reawakened by the comfort the hot waters brought. Always at the lead of trouble was the talkative Bel, her mischievous smile able to so quickly turn venomous despite its playfulness. Bon always gave life to Bel's suggestions, which for now consisted of discovering just what a bar of soap tasted like. Vie rolled her eyes as he spat the bar out of his mouth with a volley of suds. Little Braden, the smallest of the trio, was also the shyest. He watched his twin sister and brother with a wide-eyed hunger that yearned to learn, but was always reluctant to join in their mischief. When he did, it was with the surety of comfort that came from being part of a group. They were beautiful, so beautiful. Vie sucked in a breath to keep herself from tearing up in worry.

What was going to happen to them? To all of them? Was she making the right decision in collecting them? There was no telling just what kinds of dangers were in store for them. Hamza's demonstration in the Keyhall had been quite clear that whatever hells were unleashed upon Traumanfang would strike everyone. There was no escape. Scant comfort that it was, by being in the front of the battle it might save them all some torture.

Vie scowled. "It's horrible. Wherever that jackass

Lord Haphenasis goes, I have to go, too. All because of this." She flicked the choker around her neck.

"I had wondered where that came from. The turquoise is really quite flattering on you."

"It also makes me his slave. Fire and brimstone, Yue! Isn't Sludge bad enough? Why do I have to deal with this now, too? Maybe if you told them that the kids were little imps, the wizards would let us go."

"They are little imps."

"You're only saying that because they burned down the Stout."

"Isn't that enough?" Yue asked, her dark eyes flashing their honesty with a proverbial slap to Vie's face. But as always, the harshness was tempered. "At least you're not in prison."

Vie felt tears brimming. This whole event was too much. Her exhaustion was too much. She turned away from her friend just in time to see Bon dive under the water.

Her children. They were the greatest medicine for self-pity, fear, doubt, and just about all other negative emotions. They never let up with their demands and madness, which meant that she could never let up either. But at least the momentary twinge of tears had been washed aside.

"Stop trying to see if your brother can breathe underwater!" she snapped at Braden.

Her youngest glanced mischievously at Bel for confirmation. The look was enough an admission of guilt for Vie. "Pull him up this minute, or so help me, I'll kick your little butts through all four hells!"

Unrestricted free time was too much for the kids to

handle. With a sigh, Vie rounded up the imps and got them dressed for breakfast. It had been a long time since Vie had been able to come to such a fancy bathhouse. Her regular place was by far the cheapest one around, run by a shrew from Hess, who reeked of sulfur and swamp. The old shrew refused to set up a common room, claiming that one encouraged lingering and socializing, which meant a reduced turnout of bathers. Under no circumstances would Vie subject herself or the magi to such a disreputable venue. More importantly than the squalor of that house was that the magi were clearly rich. That meant opportunity. That meant high class. At least for what Sludge had to offer. Still, merchants and other wealthy folk made their way to Sludge from time to time. That meant the Ivory Shower.

Like all good houses, the Ivory Shower was always open. One of the biggest draws of this bathhouse was that each bathing area—men's and women's alike—had a waterfall that mimicked the Singing Falls which cascaded a ways up the River Sing Wing, near the old city, Reservwyre. The cultural designs and murals on the walls were lovely and often drew crowds who spent whole days here. One could even rent a bed in one of three social rooms to pass the night. The second room was geared more to that of a massage lounge and the third was an expansive cafeteria that looked out on a small enclosed garden. The kids were so excited to be able to be part of a sit-down meal that their behavior was surprisingly good.

Until they saw the broad table off to the side of the room.

Bon rushed up to it and gave a detailed account of everything set out upon it.

"Mom! Mom! Buttered figs! And black pudding! Roasted tomatoes! Boiled eggs! Scrambled eggs! A big pot of green liquidy stuff that smells amazing! Duck and chicken and fried fish! Squiiiiiid! Whooaa yeahhhh! And salmon...," he said, sniffing "smoked salmon! With a side of bacon. Bananas and strawberries and pineapples and hooselberries! Eww... turnips and cabbage... Bread! Buns! Bread! And... why does this bread have a hole in it? And jam! And butter! And cheese! And more cheese! And... Blargh! Do. Not. Smell. That. Cheese... What's this? Porridge! And coffee! With an entire jar of sugar!"

"Save the sugar for others!"

"Awww..." Bon said, a large spoonful just inches from his mouth.

"Mom?" Braden asked, tugging at Vie's sleeve. "What's with all the food over there?"

"It's called a buffet," Yue told him. "You can go up and eat as much as you can put onto a plate."

"But what if I don't have room on the plate for everything?" Bel asked, eyes popping nearly out of her head.

"Go back for more," Ishtower told her while handing her a plate. She grinned at him and got in line.

For a time, silence reigned while everyone enjoyed heaping portion after heaping portion of the delicious food. Much to Vie's private satisfaction, because this was still very much Sludge, and few of the patrons had the high-born opinion that came with the rich, Lord Haphenasis seemed on edge throughout the whole meal. Twice, when a late-night reveler shouted out that they were out of coffee, Lord Haphenasis visibly jumped. What did he expect, that the fires would creep back and kick him again?

"This has been extremely generous of you two gentlemen," Yue said, settling back into her seat for one more round of hot herbal tea. It always amazed Vie how she could so easily slip from the simple language of Sludge to the primmer words of the higher classes. As a child, she had been bought by a pleasure madam and been trained relentlessly in the finer qualities of pleasure, including those of the mind. While Yue had taught her much over the years, it was nothing to the wealth of learning that her golden friend had received. "Not only did you save many lives by killing the fire in the Released Stout, but here we are, enjoying a fine meal after a thorough cleansing."

"That was nothing," Ishtower replied, smiling handsomely at Yue. His attraction to her was as plain as day. Vie took some of the credit for herself, having arranged her friend's hair and done her eye shadow using the cosmetics set out for public use in the ladies' bathing area. "I'm glad we could do so."

"It was interesting to use that particular variation of that spell. I had used it on other spells before, where I channeled my consciousness through—" Lord Haphenasis began babbling before Yue smoothly cut him off.

"We were so fortunate to have you in the neighborhood at such an odd time. Just what were two elite gagi doing down in Sludge at that hour anyway?"

Vie hid her smirk behind her own teacup. Such a plea of ignorance coupled with compliments had earned them a bonus on more than one occasion.

"Something about her children," Lord Haphenasis said dismissively of Vie.

"Now that you've collected them, what will you do?"

"Preventative medicine."

"What my far less charming brother is trying to say," Ishtower amended, clearing his throat, "is that we have been tasked with a tremendous responsibility."

"Oh yes! Vie mentioned something about the eleven dangers...?"

"Twelve Cataclysms," Lord Haphenasis said, taking the bait. "The Apocryptein's greatest purpose was that of prison. If the twelve prisoners manage to reform their bodies, they will unleash untold destruction across the face of Traumanfang.

"Wait," he said, interrupting his own flow of thoughts. "Did you say 'collected'?"

"Well, yes," Yue responded. "That is why you came back here, is it not? You captured Vie, and with her comes all her responsibilities. As they have no father, who else can look after them?"

"No," Lord Haphenasis replied, stirring one of his chopsticks through a large bowl of porridge flavored with large slabs of bacon. Everyone else had already finished, but he was still working on his third helping. Even Bon, who never lacked an appetite, had been defeated by the buffet. "I believe you misunderstood our reasons for coming back here. This had nothing to do with collecting them and everything to do with saying good-bye to them. You are their nanny, are you not?"

Yue smiled politely and said quite simply, "You must be fucking joking."

Ishtower laughed. Lord Haphenasis blushed. Vie groaned when she caught sight of Bon's eyes lighting up at the foulness of her language.

"Don't even think of it," Vie cut him off before he could even begin asking.

"If they were left in your care before, why can they not remain there?" Lord Haphenasis asked, looking to Ishtower for support. "Where we are going is no place for children."

Yue took a slow, measured sip of tea and spelled it out for the dense wizard. "Sweetie, the Released Stout just burned down, and I'm positively blue with worry about where I will sleep in the upcoming weeks. While I have been able to do quite well for myself over the years, much of my life was caught up in the Stout. In fact, I am quite distressed by it—oh, I know, I look so calm and serene on the outside, but a lady must keep up her appearance—and just how I might look after myself. I fear I will have to resort to begging favors of unsavory creatures like *Rosalind*."

"I have no interest in this Rosalind," Lord Haphenasis snapped. "We have urgent business that will only be hindered by these urchins."

"The point is that if I am asking for favors, it will be difficult enough for just myself. Now tell me, who in their right mind would take in a pleasuress who has three children in tow? More to the point, how can I make a living looking out for these angels? Look at what happened the one time I attempted such a task."

"You lived at that hovel that we just put out?"

"What is a hovel to one, Lord Haphenasis, is a palace to another," Yue said politely as she smartly kept her eyes down. Vie knew the look; Yue used it to hide her anger in situations when doing so would be less than ideal. "My popularity has afforded me a certain class of clientele that has provided me with certain comforts. That I have my own room is a huge benefit. Yes, the Stout has been the

home for many young women like me and I am content
with that. But the fact remains that without my own lodg-
ing, I will have no way to care for Vie's children. Nor
could I do so with the kind of love and affection and
attention as only their mother can give. Is not, after all, a
mother the best guardian of her own children?"

Well said! Vie thought. It was her firm belief that it
was Yue's wit that kept her best clientele coming back to
her. While a skilled, attentive lover drove men insane, it
was the freedom to flex their minds with a caring soul
that they could not resist. Her tongue had brought more
than one man low.

"That goes without saying," Ishtower agreed.

"Then would it not be better to leave Vie's children
in her own care?"

"Of course, but you are suggesting an unrealistic option. She has committed a crime against me—against all
our brothers—and she has to serve out her punishment."

"So you will leave her here?"

"To paraphrase you from a few minutes ago, that
would be inconceivable. Wherever I go, she must go, too.
But the simple matter is that it is no place for them."

"Who died and made you our father?" Bel demanded. To her credit, Vie was surprised she had held her
tongue for this long.

"Is that child talking to me?" Lord Haphenasis asked
Vie, pointing a chopstick at Bel.

"Darn tooting I'm speaking to you, big guts!"

"How rude!" Lord Haphenasis said, too shocked to
let the enormity of the insult get to him.

"Wait'll you let her get going!" Bon added.

"Enough from you," Vie said to her children.

"Enough from all of you! We three are going after the Twelve Cataclysms! Children are simply not allowed. It is too dangerous."

"And Sludge isn't?" Bel asked.

Lord Haphenasis' jaw dropped. A wrinkle appeared over his pale brow.

"Tell us more about the Twelve *Catasisisis-ums*," Braden added, breaking the silence with the wide-eyed wonder of curiosity.

"Ca-ta-clys-ms," Ishtower corrected him.

"It sounds better than Sludge," Bel added. "Sludge just makes you think of poop."

"Poop is awesome!" Bon said. "Squishy, squeltchy, *ppppppttt!*"

"Well, I hate poop. And he poops a lot."

"Like a grown man!" Bon said proudly.

"Which might just be why we tried burning it down tonight."

"Bel!" Vie snapped, aghast to hear this from her daughter. "You didn't!"

"No, but why not? You called it a dung heap, yourself, didn't you? You said, 'What a rotten stinking pile of driftwood and shit sandwiched—" the complete exactness of Vie's quote was cut off by Bon, who, at a nod from his mother, had slapped his hand over Bel's mouth. Despite this, she struggled to get out a few more words. Bon simply laughed, happy that his superior strength gave him the upper hand over his sister.

Letting her children wrestle out their problems, Vie turned to Lord Haphenasis. "As you can see, my children will be fine with us. They come with me and that is that."

"No, they shall not," Lord Haphenasis said. "As they

say, the apple does not fall far from the tree. The same night you burn down my home, your children try to burn down Sludge. What kind of a life are you teaching these children? Five years old and they are already fit only for prison! You are enough of a liability in my care. There is no way we can bring them with us as well. But, if you insist on pursuing this inane course, then I will have only one alternative: to give them to the local constabulary."

"Imprison them?"

Lord Haphenasis nodded.

"Just like you put away your twelve little problems?"

Lord Haphenasis nodded again.

"Who have all escaped now?"

Lord Haphenasis did not nod this time.

Yue took up the argument. "So you think the local constabulary will arrest them? Even on your advice?"

Lord Haphenasis' face darkened. "I am a lord. And for nearly two decades, I have been of service to this city. I see no reason why not."

"Because of their age, most likely. Since they can't go in a prison, they'd be sent to an orphanage."

"Yes, that is an alternative."

"Which they'll burn to the ground within a day or two."

Lord Haphenasis looked at the three children.

Three toothy grins supported Yue's accusation.

"That would leave you to pay for the destruction of the place, as you were the referring agent. Credibility is a horrible thing to lose, isn't it?"

"Are you... are you using her children to blackmail me?"

"Should I?"

"No! Besides, from there, they would end up in a foster home."

"Which they would escape from in an hour. And knowing them, they would come right after us, wherever we were to go."

Lord Haphenasis's shoulders slumped. He looked at Ishtower, who had been quietly sipping his coffee this whole time. "Are you going to add anything?"

"Nope."

"Of course not. I suppose I could give them all the Choker of Sorrow."

"You will do no such thing," Vie interjected.

"I do not trust you or your mangy street urchins. If we have to bring them with us, then it might be for the best that they be bound like their mother."

"No. They come and I take responsibility for them."

"Torture for disobedience?"

"Fine."

"Fine."

"Lovely!" Ishtower said, leaning forward. He gave Bon's dark hair a ruffle. "Now that that's taken care of, let's hunt some monsters!"

Chapter 12

LORD HAPHENASIS LOOKED FROM ONE MISCREANT TO THE next. Each one was strikingly similar to its mother. They all had the same coal black hair that shined in the right light, a round face and long, skinny limbs that showed just enough meat to separate them from the malnutrition of poverty that classified so much of Sludge. The one area where they differed were the eyes. Certainly all four—mother and three children—shared the darkness of eye that was common in people from Featherwind, but where the mother's eyes were large and al-mond-shaped, these childrens' eyes were huge. He did not like them nor did he trust them. There was just a little too much of the madness of the Fey in them. Children, he had been taught, were to be seen and not heard, especially not by nobility.

If it were up to him, he would cast the little wretches back into the street from whence they came, where they belonged. And good riddance! Were it not for the brute that his brother magi had saddled him with, it would be him alone dealing with the great forces of evil, pitting his own wisdom against theirs. It was a challenge he would gladly have taken.

"The sooner we are done the sooner we can be rid of you," he grumbled, reaching into his travel ruck. The drawstring bag with its shoulder strap was the only thing he had managed to extricate from the Apocryptein during his retreat. Fortunately, it was blessed with a ventilation gap, one that was linked to his apartments in the Innervein. From it, he had access to a large assortment of items and personal needs. With but a thought, whatever he had in mind came to hand, as his hound now did. Setting it upon the table drew everyone's attention and brought the table to silence. Even the brats suddenly clammed up, curious about the silent orb with variance widgets jutting out from it.

"What's that?" the smallest of the three asked.

"If you must know," Lord Haphenasis sighed, wishing he could just get his work started without having to answer even one question. "This is a hound. Ishtower, could you make yourself useful and distract these peons while I concentrate on tracking down the escapees?"

"Let's do as Lord Haphenasis asks, little one," Ishtower said.

"But what is it?"

"Do you know bloodhounds?"

"Bloodhounds?"

"Big brown dogs with big folds all over their faces and big ears?"

"Nattie Bee over in Market Square has a big dog that sounds like that, only her dog has small ears and they're all pointy and sticky-up-like and it's got a little tail that goes *whoosh* when it wags it. She calls it Dorey Dell and puts it in her basket." The speed and volume of language that Bel spoke with interrupted Lord Haphenasis's concentration. He cleared his throat, hoping that it would encourage the girl to quiet down.

"Does it have a high-pitched yip when it barks?" Ishtower asked.

"Yuh-huh!"

"That sounds like a techichi."

"Maybe, but alls I know is that it is cute, but you gotta be careful with it 'cause it doesn't like strangers."

"Quiet!" Braden hissed at his sister. "He can't tell us about that doodad if you're blathering."

"Have you seen a bloodhound before?" Ishtower asked, looking from one kid to the next. None nodded, even Vie and her golden-furred companion seemed to have no clue what Ishtower was talking about.

"Really? You've never seen a bloodhound? Single greatest hunters in the world. They can even track scents that are a couple days old and even through thick snowy drifts. You give one something with your quarry's scent and the dog will wander around sniffing for it. Whenever it catches a trace, it goes to where the scent is strongest. Before long, you've got your prey. Lord Haphenasis's hound works under the same principle. It will track the 'scents' of the twelve prisoners for us."

Lord Haphenasis could feel the energies of his prisoners already. One of his jobs as warden of the Apocryptein was to look after the prisoners' well-being. In their cases, it was to ensure that they were still "alive" within their crystals. This meant constantly delving deep into the underground vaults of the prison. There, as an under-warden, he often sat for days, listening to and studying the thaumatic hums the crystals produced. As only psychoplasmic residue trapped within a containment field at the center of each quartz crystal, the hums were the only thing able to exist outside of the crystals.

It was for the event of an escape that all wardens were trained in the reproduction of their vibrations. For the hound to work, he needed a scent. As the newest of these creatures had been interred for about a decade and the oldest had been there for over a thousand years, finding an actual scent would prove to be impossible. The hound was designed to work on thaumatic vibration. Warden Curtai, his predecessor, was quite impressed with Lord Haphenasis's ability to master their vibrations within three weeks where it had taken him several months.

Even now, each vibration ran through his head, as familiar as his own name. Placing the hound on the palm of his hand, he pushed the vibration he had recreated into it. The hound responded to being fed its target by dropping a small spindle from its base. As it became more and more familiar with the scent, the central orb began glowing a dull green that soon took on a topographical representation of the whole world. Around it, the variance widgets began spinning until, in moments, they settled in, showing the relative location of the first convict in relation to themselves.

"North by northeast," he said, "about a thousand kilometers from here."

Ishtower grunted. "He travelled fast."

"You heard Hamza during the assembly, did you not? Each of the convicts is essentially an isolated energy source whose primary function now is to gather enough sustenance to recreate their bodily shells. As disembodied entities, their speed of travel is potentially as virtually instantaneous as our Veinways. However, as circumstance has started us here, in Reservwyresport, let's say we find something closer? I would so hate it if we had to backtrack."

Lord Haphenasis repeated the procedure with each of the other eleven vibrations and recorded their locations in a small ledger withdrawn from a pocket on the interior of his coat. By the time he had finished, he looked up and found the rest of his party had abandoned him to his work. No wonder it had grown so quiet. He wondered where they had gone off to, but quickly squashed such concern. If they were not here now, it might prove to be a prime opportunity to abandon them.

He rose from the table, sneaked one last mouthful of smoked haddock into his mouth, and made for the doorway.

"Not trying to desert us, are you?"

Ah. Of course, they would be seated on the benches outside the cafeteria. The three children were sprawled out on one, asleep, their limbs and bodies intertwined like a Gordian knot. Vie had been dozing and came to with Ishtower's words.

"You were not in the cafeteria. I had thought I might find you."

"Of course," Ishtower replied dryly.

"Where is the other one?"

"Yue left a short time ago," Vie said, yawning. "Ishtower has been politely entertaining me."

"Why would you humor a thief?"

"Whatever else she is, she is our partner in this adventure. I thought it good to get to know her a bit. Quite an interesting story. You should give her a moment of your time. You just might learn something."

"And are we satisfied with what we learned? Perhaps she gave you a good price for her services?"

"So, where is our first target?" Ishtower asked, ignoring the snark in the lord's tone.

"Call me surprised that you chose to ignore the dangling bait," Lord Haphenasis replied with a cocked eyebrow.

"Trust me, I would gladly argue with you all day, but I think we all have better things to do."

"Yes, like go home, as luck would have it."

"The Innervein? Your hound can track them through the dimensions?"

"No, not our collective home. I mean my home. It turns out that the first of the twelve has returned to the scene of the crime. We are off to the Apocryptein."

Chapter 13

"WHICH ONE ARE WE AFTER?" ISHTOWER ASKED AS THEY stepped into the black sociable carriage that Lord Haphenasis had called to carry them up the hill to the Apocryptein. As the bathing house was on the edge of the labyrinthine ghetto of Sludge, it was only a short walk to a thoroughfare. The base of the hill was only three districts away from there. Despite this, the lord was annoyed with the fact that Squite had not come running when he had called. Vie thought he might have fallen asleep. Although she got some shut-eye while Haphenasis was working, it was nowhere near enough.

"The Butcher of Fitch," the lord said, settling his ample backside into the far back of the carriage where he wedged himself beside his brother wizard. "Please spare me some room there."

"Who's that?" Bel asked, clambering up to sit opposite Ishtower. She glanced around toward the front of the cab and then down again, eager to inspect every-thing that made the wagon special. "He sounds interest-ing. Is he very handsome? Does he have big muscles and wear fancy clothes?"

"Didn't you hear, Bel?" Vie asked, getting in to sit in the middle of the rear-facing bench beside her daughter. "He's a butcher. That means he cuts up animals and sells them to people who go to his shop. Does this great and mighty butcher make sausages, too?"

"Yeah! Sausages are the best!" Bon added quickly so as not to miss an opportunity to share his thoughts on the matter.

"Don't be stupid," Bel nagged. "How bad would be one of the twelve *catacams* if he was just a simple butcher? You know he isn't, right, Mommy?"

"Of course. I'm only teasing you."

With all her children secured in the vehicle, the driv-er closed the door and they were off, moving down the road at a slow walk due to the traffic that always came on at Shema. The gentle swaying of the carriage as they moved would probably put her children to sleep before long. For that matter, she wondered how long it would be before she gave in to it, too.

"Maybe he killed people for fun and sold those bod-ies to his customers," Bon added after thinking about the issue for a moment.

"So what did he do?" Braden asked the large lord sitting opposite from him.

"So now you want to listen?" Ishtower laughed. The three kids nodded. "Naturally, once their imaginations have run rampant, they finally settle on the mundaneness of reality. You remind me of my own children when they were your ages."

"That one is not far from the truth," Lord Haphenasis said, nodding at Bon, his hands folded across his large belly. Despite the clear wear of exhaustion playing about his small teal eyes, he was remarkably alert and comfortable. It seemed to Vie that this sitting and chatting could well have defined his life. And he played the role of social host quite well in spite of his proclivity towards insults.

"How so?" Bel asked, twisting around on the padded bench to get cozier.

"He killed for fun," the lord replied, looking down his nose at the kids either for a nonchalant effect or to see how they reacted. He need not have bothered for their total captivation was well in hand. Scandals and horrors were always of utmost enjoyment to them.

"What's he like, Ish?" Bon asked Ishtower, throwing half the poor wizard's name to the winds.

"You ask me and I'll say *trouble*, but if you ask Lord Haphenasis, you'll get a story. Since we've got some time to kill before we reach the Apocryptein—especially in this damned traffic—we'll let him entertain us, yeah?"

"So what's he like, Lord Hat?" Bon asked the fat man.

"A great deal more patient with ignorant children, I'd warrant," he snapped. Then, after the kids settled down a bit and Vie encouraged Bon to apologize and call the man by his full title—as required of a man in his position—the lord grudgingly took up the tale of the Butcher of Fitch.

"Nobody knows where he came from nor what his story is. Some believe he was a barbarian who got lost and found himself in a land far from home. Others think he was born from a blacksmith and was sent out to seek vengeance for the death of his father. One or two think he was the bastard child from a realm of darkness, set loose upon our world as a precursor to an invasion. Whatever he was, it cannot be denied that he was a big man with muscles growing upon his muscles.

"More remarkable than just an intimidating visage that awed all who came close was his sword. This weapon was a thing of beauty, a deeply black blade over a perfectly balanced hilt whose functionality gave it a beauty of purpose that any who looked upon it could readily understand. This was a black sword of death. And it was sharp enough to slice the wings from a fly.

"In his vagrant wanderings, he always seemed to stir up trouble, picking fights with strangers, stealing food when he was hungry, savaging whatever lands he came across. But it was not until 500 years ago when he trekked through the Sargewaters that his rowdiness caught the attention of the local lord. Not willing to put up with a murderous problem in his realm, the king sent a platoon of his soldiers to destroy him. It was a wonderful thought, but he underestimated this butcher, for the Cataclysm cleaved the entire platoon in twain, leaving all but one dead in his wake. The lone survivor, saved by his own cowardice, fled the slaughter of his peers and reported the disaster to his master. Infuriated by this, the king sent another patrol, this time armed with heavy armor, long spears, and bows. Alas, this group fared no better than the first.

"With this second victory, word of the butcher spread like wildfire. People from all over the king's lands began a great exodus, fearing for their lives, knowing too well that if the butcher came calling on them, it would mean the end of everything. Already having suffered a severe blow to his able-bodied soldiers and seeing so many of his remaining charges departing, the lord petitioned to his neighboring kingdoms to aid in the removal of the menace.

"These neighbors were no petty fools, looking to squash any opposition to their desires. They heard the plea and weighed their options. In the butcher, they beheld a great threat to lands, people, and livelihood. It was decided that they would enter the battle. Not wanting to underestimate the butcher as the first king had to suffer, the neighbors agreed to send an army. Before this mighty force of soldiers, the ground quaked and rumbled and, as one, they tracked the butcher to a small farm on in the Duchy of Fitch. There they gave the butcher the choice: surrender and let his crimes be judged, or die there where he stood. The man laughed and said he quite enjoyed life and that neither option worked for him.

"The order was given and one million arrows were loosed at him. The sky turned as black as night as the arrows soared. Then, when the first had finished, a second volley was ordered. Again the day became night. It was then that a scout rode forward to inspect the dead body of the butcher. Much to this rider's horror, the butcher remained standing, arrows protruding from his every body part. Yet despite this, he merely stood there, laughing. The scout reined in his horse and fled back to his general.

"'Impossible!' the general roared. Nonplussed by his archers' failure, he sent in the infantry with their long pikes and swords. One hundred thousand blades were sent, and 100,000 blades were hacked into this butcher;

yet, despite all this, 100,000 men were left dead in that field, and not one among the corpses belonged to the Butcher.

"With the defeat of their army, the kings begged the Order of the Vein to intervene. If brawn could not stop him, then what about arcanum? A group of thirty of my ancient brothers arrived in the fields of Fitch and beheld the terrible warrior deep in the throes of his bloodlust. Watching him in battle they quickly divined that so long as he possessed his sword, he was unstoppable. Using an entire repertoire of spells, our brothers stripped him of his blade and captured his body within a prison of arcana.

"It was then that a curious thing happened. The king who had brought forth the initial complaint had come along to bear witness to the Butcher's great comeuppance. Thinking that the threat was over and hoping to obtain a trophy to reimburse his great loss, King Sargewater reached down and picked up the blade. As he stared into the depths of its black iron, his features bled until all traces of him were gone. Alerted by his horrid cries of utmost agony, the magi looked over at the lord and were startled to see not a trace remaining. Instead, there stood none other than the warrior who they had just imprisoned."

"No!" Bon exclaimed.

Lord Haphenasis almost smiled at how masterfully he had captured his audience. "Indeed. And what of King Sargewater, you ask? Why, he was nowhere else but in the confines of the arcane prison that my ancient brothers had made."

"How did he take that?" Vie asked.

"He did nothing of the sort. He was a desiccated

husk, broken and stripped of all life. Our ancient brothers realized that the connection between the Butcher and his ebony sword went deeper than previously expected. He and the weapon were linked as if one."

"Where can I find a special sword like that?"

"Only in your dreams, Bon," Vie said.

"If the Butcher escaped from his prison every time someone grabbed his sword, then how come the wizards captured him?" Bel asked.

"Magi, child," Lord Haphenasis corrected. "We are called magi, not wizards. It is a common mistake that the peons of the world make."

"Magi," Bel hastened to say so that the lord would get back to his story.

"They were quick to react to the returned threat and, as they had done before, they separated him from the weapon. Once the two were split once again, my forebears wrapped the weapon in a bubble of arcana, cutting it off from anyone who would touch it. With the Butcher and his sword in tow, they then transported both to the Apocryptein. Once here, they cast the blade into the Riot deep in the heart of this hill."

"Riot?" Braden asked.

"Where the veins of arcana intersect, they whirl in a mix of stabilized energy that we call Riots. Riots create boils of tremendous energy that we can sometimes harness to amplify our abilities. Where two or more Veins intersect, that available energy is boosted even more so."

"How many Veins intra-spect here?" Braden asked.

To this, the lord actually smiled. "Five."

"That's a lot."

"It is. It is one of only two locations across the face of

Traumanfang where five intersect. Any spell we cast here draws upon this power and it multiplies. Our powers wax in the presence of the Veins, but even more impressive are those of our Order who are able to store this potential in our own veins."

"Enough with the secrets of our brotherhood, Lord Haphenasis," Ishtower interrupted. "What happened to the Butcher of Fitch?" The question got a flurry of enthusiasm from Vie's kids.

"You are right to draw us back to this. After all, we must still plan out our strategy in dealing with him.

"The five-pronged Riot here at the Apocryptein was the only place where my brothers felt secure that their spells could smother the incantations embedded in the butcher's blade. They secured the weapon in the deepest cavern and melted the rock around it to trap it there forever more. It has remained secure here ever since."

"And the Butcher?" Bel asked.

"Has been imprisoned in a crystal prison for the past 500 years."

"Is he still alive? Because, if he isn't, he's probably not going to be very happy about being locked up like that. If it was me, I'd be all like, 'Murder! Kill! Piss on! Drool!'"

"Bon!" Bel snapped. "What a horrible thing to say."

"Sadly, your bother is probably correct. We have no idea how or if he has been aware of the passage of time. If he has been..." Ishtower paused to consider this. "We have no idea. We could be in for a tremendous fight."

"That is utter nonsense," Lord Haphenasis said. "Your ignorance of this is embarrassing to me and our Order. These are dissembled spirits humbled and trapped.

There is no way that he would be able to gauge just how much time has passed. Even if the Butcher were capable of understanding that a long time has passed, he would still be unable to recognize just how much has, in fact, passed him by.

"What's that dumb look for? Have you never woken up, looked around, and been confused by your surroundings? Has a drunkard like yourself never seen the light coming in from a window and not known what time of day it was? I see no reason why it would be any different for our charges. No, the only real cause for concern is the Butcher's goal."

"His sword," Braden said.

The lord nodded. "His sword."

Chapter 14

DEEP IN THE BEDROCK UNDERNEATH THE APOCRYPTEIN, THE magi had buried the sword well. It had begun with a winding spiral staircase that cut far below the moat surrounding the tower. It had delved into cavernous recesses that time had all but forgotten, where ancient civilizations had carved their symbols into the stone. There, amid the silence, they had etched out a nook in a massive slab of ultra-condensed limestone and split it in two. The black blade was enshrouded with dozens of spells that both prevented seekers from thinking of it and of terrifying illusionary wards that would have forced even the most ardent explorer back. Once done, the weapon was laid to rest between the stone fragments and sealed. As a final protective measure, they had collapsed the tunnel and all traces of passageways down into the sword's lair.

None, not even Lord Haphenasis, had been able to venture into the ebony sword's stony prison since.

"Could it be possible to find a way down there?" Ishtower asked.

"None. If even air were able to reach that condemned blade, it would be a small miracle."

"Disaster, more like it," Vie added.

"So upon the Butcher's release, he would naturally be drawn to his weapon."

"Naturally."

"Could we assume that its power could restore him?"

"It is my theory that with the energies of the sword in hand, it would sustain his disembodied form with silent energies, rejuvenating him almost instantaneously into vibrant corporality."

"Where would such energy come from?"

"It would have been stored up with the weapon when it was imprisoned. The passage of time does not mean the dissipation of arcana. With its prison along the riot, the energies of the Veins would have maintained its latent potential."

"Sadly," Ishtower frowned, staring at the narrow vault of wood set between the two carriage seats. "All this points to the simple fact that we absolutely cannot allow the Butcher to reclaim his sword. What can we expect from his personality?"

"I would have thought you well-enough versed in his lore," Lord Haphenasis suggested.

"Doing battle is best done with as dynamic a picture of your enemy as can be created. Humor me."

"The man was a roaring brute of incredible stature, a violent killer with unparalleled skill. Beyond his abilities, we know nothing of who he is and where he came from."

"Did anyone ask him?" Braden asked.

The boy squirmed under the critical stare both magi leveled him.

"Sorry," he whimpered, burrowing into his mother's side.

"If he is so terrifying, shouldn't we call in our brothers?"

"What? A single warrior is more than the great Ishtower can handle?"

"Nice try, but there is a reason why he was considered a Cataclysm. Any one person with the skill and evil temperament enough to wade through the countless soldiers of several duchies isn't going to be asking polite questions about tea. He's going to be out for blood."

"Could his spirit access the sword's prison?"

"Not likely."

"Now is a great time to toss aside the cryptic answers, *Botch*."

Lord Haphenasis rolled his eyes. It was an old nickname, one that Ishtower had taken to calling him back when they were raw recruits, away from home for the first time. Ishtower claimed that it had come from the then-lordling's "unwieldy" and "haughty" given name: Sesellebach. Trying to pronounce it was too much of a chore for the ill-tempered youth that Ishtower was. To simplify, he had adopted *Botch*. To this day, Lord Haphenasis hated the name with a passion.

"Fine. It is highly unlikely that the spirit would be able to burrow its way through the astral pitfalls surrounding the weapon. They begin at the fourth sub-basement, a ways yet before the tunnels were collapsed. Any spirit that seeks out the weapon would find itself transported to a faraway locale if not outright dispersed."

"How would he be able to access the sword if it were still locked up?"

"It would be impossible. The spells and containment are so absolute they would easily have survived even the destruction of the Apocryptein."

"There is no way to break the spells?"

"There is the possibility that extreme heat or intensely focused arcane power trained on a single spot could eventually dissolve the barriers and melt the stone on which our ancient brothers had enveloped the weapon, but I can think of nothing that could generate that kind of heat, nor anything that would have the patience to do that."

"How much time are we talking about?"

"Several centuries. Our brothers were quite thorough. Just as the weapon will be in a state of hibernation because of the Riot, so too will it bolster the spells trapping the blade. It was an amazing feat of precision skill."

"High praise coming from you," Ishtower mocked.

"I praise anyone and anything that earns my admiration."

"So should we get backup? Hamza offered the entirety of the Order to come to our aid."

"Are you afraid, Ishtower?"

"I have no fear of your butcher. I merely ask for the precaution of having a squad of our brothers on hand in the event of unforeseen complications. You may be unfazed by the protective sheath made for his sword, but something doesn't feel right about this."

"The fact that you neglected a drink for breakfast?"

"Leave it!" Ishtower growled. "The point, Lord—what was it you called him earlier, Vie? Because it seems so fitting to use right now."

"What? During the trial?"

"Yes. It was something witty: a play on his name."

"Lord Half-ass-ness."

Ishtower smiled coldly. As if he needed another nickname with which to slander the lord. "Ah yes... The point, Lord *Half-ass-ness*, is that while we may be able to contain the soul, that weapon is deadly. Who knows what kind of a world would be created if that man were to get hold of his weapon? Think of what he'd do to this city."

"I can and do. Traumanfang is far more populated now than it was all those years ago. But the point is that there is no way the Butcher would be able to access his weapon! It is for that simple reason that it would be utterly pointless to call in our brothers. They are *busy* enough without us demanding protection from a disembodied spirit whose only means of immediate physical reconstitution lies well out of reach!"

"Fine. Since you seem to have all the answers, let's play it your way. How, then, oh great leader, should we approach this situation?"

With Ishtower's grudging acceptance of Lord Haphenasis' logic, Lord Haphenasis mapped out his plan of attack. Ishtower, being the more physical of the pair, would take point and ferret out the butcher's spirit while Lord Haphenasis would come in behind, drawing upon a full quota of arcana to recapture the spirit. The lord figured that here at the Riot, he might still be able to create a permanent enough containment field that would allow the Cataclysm to be delivered to their brothers.

Upon stopping the sociable carriage a lip down from the crest of the hill, the children started making a ruckus of excitement, demanding that they be allowed to go up the hill to watch the two magi at work. Naturally, Lord Haphenasis refused, citing the potential danger for the children. Arcana, while easily controlled in the hands of a skilled magus, could sometimes strike errantly. No, they were much better serves staying there with the carriage. When the imps proceeded to bemoan the unfairness of it, he got fed up and ordered Vie to do her motherly duty and force them to stay put.

Apparently, she was still bothered by the thought of him commanding her, for she made a most sour face. Nonetheless, she did as he ordered. The whole deal was explained easily and quickly. Despite this, she counted the children once. Then did it again.

"Where's Braden?"

"There he goes!" the large one said, pointing up the hill to where the smallest of the children was running with all the boundless speed of childhood.

"Ishtower! Get him back here!" Lord Haphenasis snapped. If that damned child reached the top of the hill, he might call the disembodied spirit down to him. Did the urchin not realize that the magi's plan was designed to protect him and his family? Lord Haphenasis was beginning to think that ill-thought action was all that he could expect from these peons. And to think that while recounting the story of the Butcher, Lord Haphenasis had almost been swayed in thinking that this particular imp had enough sense to possibly enjoy a future in arcana.

But now his well-laid plan had gone the way of bad writing. Ishtower hurtled after the foolish boy. The lord watched him move with distaste—he had always found running and leaping through trees to be a horribly overrated activity. As such, one of the first spells that he had learned was the name of clouds, which he could summon with a gesture, and command to do a number of feats. For the moment, that constituted a solid shield of elevation. Floating a half meter off the road, the cloud carried him after the fleeing pair.

Much to his satisfaction, the ditzy child had come up short at the top of the hill. Oddly, Ishtower had the boy's arm in hand but was not retreating with the boy in tow.

"Why is he still here?" Lord Haphenasis snapped, settling down onto the ground beside them. "Return him to his mother at once!"

"Look," Ishtower said, pointing at the Apocryptein.

Lord Haphenasis did as his brother bid and was struck with a gale of force such as he had never before felt. Under a bright blue sky, the place looked vastly different. The lovely green orchard was scorched black and silver, stained by the fires of the Kremsek. For so many years, the tower had stood insoluble, fifteen stories of precision given physical form. He could still feel its wooden floorboards creak beneath his slippered feet, the howl of this wind breezing past the windows, the view of the city below. His fingers recalled the cool comfort its stone brought him on a sweltering day. His nose, the tasty tang of his winery mixed with the gentle musk of the building's arcana. The after-image of his expectation had demanded an upward glance. To see nothing but warm blue skies where his regard lifted jarred him. He forced his gaze downward, where the tower's remains lay crumbled amid the fallen and ashen trees. And somewhere in all that were the remains of his wonderful books—now nothing more than the charcoal dust of fine and ancient paper—and the bottles and bottles of his personal winery. The '32 Ghortsneck that he had almost popped open when he first bought it; he had been saving that for a special occasion, but now its sweet nectar would never kiss his tongue. The lovely down mattress that he had made from the golden feathers of a Vulphon goose would never be his to relax in again. And his collection... all of it was gone in a puff of smoke. Lord Haphenasis thought that coming up here would be business as usual. It had not even occurred to him that seeing the Apocryptein like this would touch him. But this was no simple caress to be brushed off; it was a visceral chill, brutal in its heavy-handedness.

Lord Haphenasis dropped to his knees, shuddering as if he were stricken with a high fever. It was too much to take.

"Botch?" Ishtower asked, his voice seeming to come from a great distance.

"All gone," the lord of nothing said as both images of his home—the past in its fullness, and the empty whole he now saw—blurred from tears.

"Botch, get a grip on yourself," Ishtower said, grabbing his shoulder.

Lord Haphenasis pressed his palms into his eyes, hoping that enough pressure could convince them to see what he desired: that his home would be back where it was.

"Lord Haphenasis."

Hearing his title pulled his ears back to the world but he was not ready to return. Not yet.

"Lord Haphenasis," Ishtower repeated. "Please. We have a job to do. You can mourn it later."

A *job*. *Later*. They were mighty words but, in the wrong context, they were not enough to pull him away from his agony of loss.

"Please, Lord Haphenasis. I need you."

I need you. Three words that could never be taken in another context. Three words he had never heard at home as a boy while growing up. Three words he would have given his life to hear his parents say. Three words whose simple recitation had compelled him to study in a way none before him had. They were an idea that he had long believed in, that with his power, with all his decades of intense study, he would be the answer that no other could provide.

He never thought that Ishtower, the brute who never had a kind word for him, who always sought to ridicule him, who always had a joke or an insult, whose mighty abilities relied entirely on the physical, who had spent so much time in a drunken state of bullihood that he could barely rationalize the world around him, was speaking those mighty three words.

If Ishtower could not solve this problem, that meant it was a question of the mind. A problem of the metaphysical, a dilemma of the soul and the immaterial. That meant a question needing the finest mystical mind in all the Nine Realms. The question was what could possibly have made Ishtower admit this terrible fact?

Lord Haphenasis forced his body to stop its shuddering. He wiped his cheeks and grabbed the arm that Ishtower had extended for him. Rising to his feet, he hiccoughed and asked, "What is the matter?"

"That," Ishtower said, pointing across the bridge stretched across the moat.

A man stood before them, his back toward the two magi, a long black sword in his hand. A string of curses came to Lord Haphenasis's mind but settled into the much more eloquent "Oh no."

"Mommy, why is the big man with the sword naked?" came a young voice down by his waist.

"And why is he flexing his butt cheeks like that?" asked another voice. The children and the woman had decided to join the magi while Lord Haphenasis was struggling to cope with the loss of his entire life's work.

"I can flex my butt cheeks, too! Look!" This came from the middle one, the big one without a brain. He stepped away and dropped his slum drawers and proceeded to mimic the warrior before them.

Lord Haphenasis did not even bother to look at the child flexing his scrawny little butt. He was having too difficult a time trying to process the simple presence of the man.

"How can this be?"

"I couldn't keep them back by the wagon," the woman said.

"What? No, not them," Lord Haphenasis said of the children. "Him! However, in the Nine Realms was he able to access that blade?"

In response, his mind jumped back to the previous night, after Vie had broken into the Apocryptein, after she had released the Kremsek, after he had fled the tower with her in tow. Here, almost exactly on this spot, as a matter of fact, with the scoring heat of the Kremsek's fire singed his eyebrows, he had heard a sound that at the time he had attributed to the shattering of the Apocryptein's wards. The tower had imploded in upon itself, but now, trapped in his mind's eye, he could see the events as they really happened. The cracking had come first and with it came a seismic undercurrent; in response to that, the Kremsek had shrieked and the tower had fallen. Only then did the Twelve Cataclysms escape, riding the edges of a dissipating series of fire-monsters.

"By all the arcana in the Veins..."

"What happened?" Ishtower asked.

"It was the Kremsek."

"What?! How?"

Lord Haphenasis could not answer his brother magus; he turned toward the woman. She stood there like a dumb cow, oblivious to reality. Whatever intelligence she had was wasted on the horrid luck she carried with her. He had heard of totems of ill reputation that could drive a man insane by their mere possession, yet he had never seen one. Until last night, when he beheld this raven-haired woman breaking into his collection room. Could he ever have considered that she would carry with her the secrets to the destruction of everything he held dear? It was such a laughable notion that even now he could feel hysteria bubbling up in his chest. How absurd that she would bring about his ruin and in doing so would lead to the deaths of everyone across the face of Traumanfang. Once the Butcher noticed them, he would kill them all. But such knowledge just simplified matters for him. If they all were to die anyway, then he would at least get his revenge on her. So with vengeance in a heart that pumped murder as if it were blood, he turned toward Vie and his lips uttered the most lucid truth he could imagine.

"This is all your fault!"

Chapter 15

THE SENSATION CAME IMMEDIATELY AND WITHOUT MERCY. IT was a tightening, quick, complete, excruciating. Lord Haphenasis had reached out a hand and Vie's air was cut off at her throat. The magus' eyes had drained out all of the green from the teal. They were two glowing gimlets of the palest blue. They were the color of death.

So complete was the choking that she could not even gag. Her mind shut off and she dropped into instinct, clawing at the collar at her throat. Because of the arcane nature of the Choker, her nails cut not into the magical object but into her own skin. Serving to bring herself more pain did nothing for her breathing. Death approached with each passing moment.

Far away from her, Bel and Bon shouted. Screamed at the magus. She watched them as they were shoved aside at a wave of his free hand. They tumbled, crying, into the grass. Crying for her. Ishtower was there, striking his brother with colorful blasts of arcana, but it had no effect. The lord waved his spells away as easily as he had her kids. The kids were crying, terrified. Terrified like her.

Escape. It was all she had now. Escape, like a mouse through a hole. Shrinking down. Shrinking. Done! Free! But, alas, she had only freed herself to choke faster. The grip was clutching harder now. Eyes swelling. Body twitching, clawing. Writhing on the ground, with the magus a tower standing high above her, gloating in his destruction of her life. On her back now, still unable to gasp. Clawed forelegs cut. Pain. Agony. Was he laughing? Was he crazy? Stop him! But how? Smaller was no good. Become harder? Smaller was death. But bigger? Was that an option? Feelings changing, an image cracking, revealing something she had never seen. It was escape! Or only possibly. Reach for it, grab it, whatever! Stretch, stretch before blackness. Reach out. Reach... too far....

She could feel it in her chest: the closing blackness, the throbbing pain of her body yearning for air. She was dying. Her children... what of them? What about them after this was all done? It wasn't fair. One last stretch... one more....

A curious feeling. Empty space all around, empty, yearning for something to fill it up. It was a shape—*the shape* she had noticed—surrounding her. But what was it? Nothing she had ever known. Was this death? Was this the glory of Capo? The fires of Fracture? No, her bulging eyes told her, this was no death, and she was out of time.

She had seen this shape in her dreams, maybe nightmares, this void surrounding her, but she had been too afraid to explore it, afraid of what it might mean. But now, now, she only wanted to live. She let go. Her limbs bled out like batter in a pan, filling the gaps, expanding into the mold. It hurt! But pain meant life, she pushed herself quicker, could feel the walls of the mold against her. It felt right, it felt... the magus... was he backing away? Was he scared? Quicker now, quicker, there! It was done! It felt so wonderful. Every part of her was screaming with glory and triumph. Was she still suffering? No.

She was breathing. One large gulp came after another, such sweet nectar down her throat, tickling with its arcane purity. This air was so thick with the headiness of arcana here. She could taste the Riots in the air. It was amazing. It was orgasmic and her skin tingled with its touch.

The children were yelling something at her, screaming, terrified. Was he going after them now? No! She could not let that happen.

"No!" she roared. Was that her? It could not be. *I will stop you, I will. I will crush you, rip you, bite you, hit you, strike you, stomp you and you... and all of you! I will burn you, cook you, roast you, freeze you, smother you, just as long as you leave my children alone! Leave them alone! Stop it!*

"Stop."

Stop it!

"Monster, you *will* stop."

Who is speaking? Calm. Air. Breathe. Again. Breathe. Calm. Use your eyes.

After what felt like an eternity, Vie managed to open her eyes (Did she? Or were they already open?) and focused through them. It was a man, naked as the day he was born. His body was rippled with muscles, and he was bearded with a dark, unkempt mane of hair. He held a sword in hand. Vie had never seen one so massive. There were specks of light dancing at the edge of her vision and the man drifted in and out of focus. It was the man from the tower, the one Braden had run up to see, but he seemed so much smaller than he had before. Why was that?

"You will leave these people alone," he said. Was he talking to her?

"Or you will die."

Chapter 16

Lord Haphenasis rolled over. His head was pounding such as it had only done once before, during the week of hell that was his Validation, the weeklong test that came before his indoctrination into the Order as a magus. He could not see clearly. Dabbing his forehead, his fingers explored into the stinging recess of a painful gash at his scalp. His face was half-soaked in blood. Channeling his arcana into his own body for a moment, he took stock of his injuries: three cracked ribs, abrasions on his right arm, a number of bruises and bumps, but mostly scratches.

All things considered, he had gotten off lightly. He was thinking straight for one thing.

It should never have happened in the first place. The Choker of Sorrow was a potent spell alone, but Lord Haphenasis had spent nearly *two decades* soaking up the energies of this Riot. Before he was a potent arcanist but, after all this time, there should be none as capable as he was. What had possibly gone wrong?

The fault could not have been inherent in his own abilities. It must have been an aberration coming from the woman. Metamorphism was a rare talent on Traumanfang to begin with. An average metamorph would turn into a large dog or a beast of relatively similar size to their natural form. The reason for this came thanks to one's arcane potential; most suffered a lack of connection which prevented greater transmutation. But Vie could shrink down into a mouse, which was a beast of tremendous fragility and weightlessness. It required precision, skill, and quite a sizeable potential, and that alone should have set off a host of alarms in his head when he had first met her the previous night.

Maybe it had. He did, after all, bind her with the Choker of Sorrow in the first place. And, of course, there was the obvious sign at the Innervein. She had become violently sick from the wards protecting their arcane refuge. The sickness practically defined her as being an Other-realmer.

But a *dragon?*

Dragons were mystical creatures that seldom came through the fluctuations of Veins between the nine Realms. For the most part, they were too big to fit through the gaps. For the second part, they held humans in contempt and as such had no business with the peoples of Traumanfang. "We laugh/ At the little people/ And their little might/ Making little meals/ That leave our bellies/ Only partially filled," Mozer's epic, *A Sending of Dragons*, quoted. If Dragons fit into the pyramid of aristocracy, they hovered higher on that plane than

even he did. In the same epic, Mozer defined them as "...
aloof from the world of man/ Whose breath could sear
the sky / Haughty to hear / Laughing at the arcana we
whelp." Of the hundred or so magi that stepped through
the fluctuations into the dragons' realm of Lamytal, only
one had ever returned. He was a man named Trey Faire
and his reports showed them as undisputed masters not
just of the various animals and plants in the realm, but of
the very air they breathed.

This simple burglaring mother could not be from
such a wonderful legacy. She was simply too dirty, too
downtrodden—too much a simple peon—to master the
poise and potential of a dragon.

A guttural growl brought him back to the moment.
It told him that the woman's mystery could wait for another day. Right now, he was cracked-ribs deep in a fight
for his life.

Sure enough, there was the mighty dragon, hovering
a few steps away in sapphiric majesty. She had wings like
a bat, a long mane of hair that stretched from a flaring
crest of spikes at the corner of her jaw. Four massive legs
hammered into the ground, leaving large imprints in
their wake as a tail the thickness of an oak lashed the air,
threatening with its dorsal needles. Her dark head sported a thick beard and powerfully dangerous eyeballs that
spun in their incensed sockets under a crown of horns.
His burglar had become a massive monster, mighty and
dangerous, mystical and hideous.

Lord Haphenasis had never seen anything more
beautiful.

She seemed to sway awkwardly, a seven-limbed beast
thinking it only had the hands and feet of a normal per-

son. Twice, she tried rocking back on her hind end, and twice she tumbled to the ground, falling into the well-pruned raspberry bushes of this part of the hill. Hissing and spitting, she flailed about with as little control over herself as he now had. The difficulty of her new form was little bother compared to what her transformation's entitlement implied; theoretically, dragons—originating from a dimension known for its arcane purity—would be able to shrug aside the most potent spells that he and his brothers could muster. Already, this concept had been proven in the destruction of his choker. The throbbing in his head was evidence of that. It had blasted him just about at the moment of her transformation to the majestic monstrosity before him.

But, like all theories, it had to be put to the test. One circumstantial sample was insufficient to prove a theory. In practice, arcana was no different from science, and the same observational rules applied. Establish the theory, test and experiment, and then, when all possible variables had been explored, the only things left were either failure of the premise, a validation of the original premise or a new concept that would then lead to new tests. The query: would a magus who had soaked up the power of a five-Vein Riot be able to penetrate the inborn defenses of a dragon? He dipped his fingers in the mystical currents surrounding him. There they were: the lovely purple and green, the cyan, periwinkle, and saffron, all five familiar colors of the Riot. They swirled into him like old friends, charging him with a colorless fire of determined might. From this, he layered the potential before him like a shield. His defense and offense at his command, he was ready for the dragon.

He needn't have worried.

"I will not repeat myself, beast!" someone with quite a peculiar accent bellowed from behind the dragon.

Vie's attention spun away from Lord Haphenasis and toward the speaker.

It appeared to be the day of surprises, for there, standing proudly in his heroic nudity, his mighty obsidian sword held out before him, stood the Butcher of Fitch.

"These people are under my protection!"

These people are what? Lord Haphenasis wondered if the dragon had not bashed his brain in harder than he had previously thought. There had never been any record of the dark man's heroism, only his penchant for destroying armies. *What in the Four Hells is going on?*

Of course. It is opposite day. That has to explain it. A day where the conflux shuddered, disrupting all normal laws of the world and allowing contrary concepts to take charge. That would be the only thing that would actually enable the burglar from Sludge to really be a dragon. It would also be the only thing that would allow the Butcher of Fitch to stand tall and stare down the same dragon seemingly for the sake of protect him and the children.

"What? Next, I'll look over and the Apocryptein will still be there?" he mumbled, half on the verge of hysteria. Still he looked. "Piss on it...."

"No! You've got it wrong!" the youngest child said, poking the butcher's leg. "She's my mother."

"Your mother?" the Butcher asked the boy.

"Yes! That man was hurting her."

"The fat man?"

"I am not fat!" Lord Haphenasis heard himself saying. "My belly is my body's representation of satisfaction at the amazing meals I have enjoyed."

"No, that is definitely fat," the Butcher replied before addressing the boy again. "How was he hurting your mother? Where is she?"

"That is our mother," Braden said, pointing to the dragon.

"Are you sure about that, Braden?" Bel asked nervously.

"Yeah, if that's mom, then she got big! And sharp and pointy and wingy."

"This is really your mother?" the Butcher asked of the dragon.

"She looks different than normal, but her glowy thing—what Senecale calls an 'oo-rah'—is still mom's."

The Butcher looked from the dragon to the boy and back again. "Is it normal for big spiky things with wings to have little boys?"

"I don't know."

"Me neither."

"This is all wrong," Lord Haphenasis said, against his better judgment. He wanted to blast the Butcher, but there was no way he could while the dragon stood in his way. The energies he had called whipped and hissed about him, so powerful that they were beginning to sear and warp the grasses he was standing in. "Why have you not yet killed the boy?"

"Are you talking to me or to that?" the Butcher responded.

"You!"

"Why would I do that?" The Butcher asked, his face stretching long into an expression of profound confusion.

"Because you're the Butcher of Fitch!"

"I am?"

"Obviously."

"It is?"

The dragon snaked her head down to be on level with the Butcher. When she spoke, it rumbled out as a boom that oddly maintained her natural undertones and inflections. "DO YOU KNOW WHO YOU ARE?"

"Sure I do!" the butcher said cheerfully.

"WHAT'S YOUR NAME?"

"What is yours?"

"I AM VIE. THE BOY AT YOUR HIP IS MY SON, BRADEN."

"Hi!"

Braden giggled. "We've met already, silly!"

"Are you sure of that?"

"It just happened a few minutes ago," Braden replied.

"I mean, my name."

"What is your name?" Lord Haphenasis asked, wondering how it was possible that there had never been record of his true name.

"What's yours?"

"I am Lord Haphenasis, but you were saying about yourself. You are...?"

"I am."

"THE JACKASS WANTS TO KNOW YOUR NAME."

"Ask him," the Butcher said, pointing at Braden. "He knows it."

"Enough with the riddles!" Lord Haphenasis shouted. "Just tell us your name, for the love of the Veins!"

The Butcher's face grew very cold. The sword tip that had fallen to the ground now stood at attention, ready to impale opponents both great and small.

The threat was as clear as the day. The arcana that

Lord Haphenasis had called to him hissed at the man and snapped with a thousand tiny heads of fireworks. A cold sweat broke out on his neck, and he knew the sudden terror of certainty that if this man wanted someone dead, nothing could stop him.

"Hey," Braden said, pressing his hand against the butcher's leg again, "he wasn't telling you what to do. He was just confused."

"Why?" the Butcher asked, his attention so thoroughly withdrawn that his sword drooped again.

"Because we don't know your name."

"Oh. Well, that's okay."

"Oh-kay?"

"Okay."

"HE IS ASKING WHAT IT MEANS."

"Oh!" the butcher said, scratching at his conspicuously exposed crotch. When he had finished, he simply looked about him, from the skies to the trees to the boy to the dragon, at the road that led down the hill, and back at the ruins of the Apocryptein. It was as if he were simply checking everything out to see where he was and what was going on.

"Well?" Lord Haphenasis prompted.

"Yes, I'm quite well, thanks."

The dragon chuckled with the sound of boulders tumbling down a hill.

"What does 'oh-kay' mean?"

"I don't know. What does 'oh-kay' mean?"

The dragon chuckled again. Slowly, its features melted, layer upon layer folded inward and upon itself until the dragon was no more—there was only the burglar Vie, standing there in the same black leggings and dark tunic she had been wearing when Lord Haphenasis had first met her. Her eyes were tired and her neck bruised and scratched to the point of bleeding. Her cheek was pink and her arm sported several small cuts. Lord Haphenasis took some satisfaction in the fact that he had been able to dish out some pain to her. She stepped toward the Butcher and squeezed one of his mighty wrists.

"It means that everything is all right."

Chapter 17

"WHAT?" ISHTOWER SNAPPED, STARING FROM VIE TO LORD Haphenasis to the Butcher and to each of Vie's children in turn. He had limped his way back to them after the awkward time in which she was different. There were twigs in his hair and leaves poking out of his robe.

"You are not to do anything toward him."

"And my reason for this would be?" the magus snapped, glaring at Vie.

"Because Braden doesn't want you to," Bel said. "He says that he's a big friendly forget-a-lot and that he's really not out to hurt anyone, but that he won't let anyone tell him what to do, and that's why he was mean to the other people long ago."

"And how would your boy know this? And what in the Four Hells happened to you? I tell you, woman, a toss like that won't soon be forgotten."

It took Vie a long time to reply. "Braden has always known things that others don't. I can't explain it, but he can see someone inside and out, and if he trusts the Butcher, that's good enough for me. As for myself... I don't know."

Bel took her hand. "I need a moment with my mother. Excuse us."

The pair stepped away from the others. They drifted to a small grassy spot that looked down onto the rubble and refuse of the Apocryptein. The previous night, after being knocked senseless, Vie had come to not far from here, with Lord Haphenasis standing over her, his attention on the collapsing building. As she looked at it now, she could almost hear it still cracking and popping with the broiling rage of the Kremsek. She pressed her hand to her temple and rubbed the bump there. A moment later, she found her fingertips delicately tracing the scratches and cuts she had clawed into her neck. It felt normal, and in her head, there was no lingering pollution of Lord Haphenasis' thoughts. The choker was gone. But how?

"What happened to me?" she asked her daughter.

Bel did not respond.

"Bel, what happened?"

After a pregnant silence, Bel snorted.

"Baby? What's wrong?" She looked down. Tears rolled heavily from the girl's downturned eyes. "Baby, what is it? It's fine, you can talk to me."

"It's not fine!" she sobbed. "I wanted to talk to you, but I can't! I don't know how to say it. I don't know what to say! How do I know I can talk to you after that... that.... What was that? Was that you?"

Vie knelt and wrapped her arms about her nearly hysterical child. The girl tried pulling away, to show her fear by pushing against what she thought was wrong but, after a few moments, she gave in to her mother's embrace. "Bel. Bel... Bel, sweetie... it's fine. I'm fine. It's all right. Be brave. It's fine. But I don't know what happened. That's why I need you to be strong now. I need to know what happened. Can you tell me that? Bel? My brave little leader? Can you?"

Bel hiccoughed. "Was that you?"

"Baby, I don't even know."

Glimpses. Flashes. Total uncertainty of... instinct? Was that really what had struck her? Was it some magic that hit her? She had fallen into her familiar mouse form, that much she knew. But after that she had lost it. There was nothing to compare it to. She reached for something on the edges of her imagination and, as she grabbed it, there was a total loss of sensation. Survival was all that mattered. Whatever it was that she had touched made the whole world different. It sparkled and smelled and everything about it was wrong but also so strangely right, like the small, distant place was something she had never experienced nor belonged to before.

"What happened to me? Lord Haphenasis tried strangling me, and I went mouse. But after that, Bel, I felt like I changed again."

"You were a dragon!" Braden whispered. Vie had been so lost in her memory that she had not even noticed his joining them. She glanced around to see if Bon had come too, but he was with the big naked man with the sword, poking at a large stone that looked as if it had been flung from the exploding tower. The two looked oddly at ease with one another, almost like two pieces carved from the same chunk of stone. It was a worrying sight, but was that just a mother's fear of rejection from her own children? She had been told that her children would one day grow up and develop interests that set them apart from one another, from her, but that time could not be nearing so soon, could it?

"Bray... don't be silly. How could I be a *dragon*? I'm no different than anyone else."

"You were! Wasn't she, Bel?"

"Why are you so excited about this?" Bel asked. "Stop being *stupit*."

"Because she's a dragon! It's just... it explains so much... I mean, I could always feel it. I knew there was something special about us."

"Braden, I just told you to stop being so stupit. Everyone's special."

The bickering brought Bel's fire back to her. The fear was forgotten for now, but Vie knew it would come back. It meant that between now and then, she would have to prove her love for her daughter, however she had to. Plus, there was the mystery of herself. She needed an adult's perspective on this, a magus', ideally, for if anyone knew about what had happened to her, it would be one of them. Whatever the case, she needed something rational to counteract the horrifying possibility that her son had stated. Was she really a *dragon*? Did dragons even really exist? No, that was a silly thought. They were creatures from stories and could not really make it to Traumanfang. But what if such a thing were possible? What if Braden were truly right? Not far away, the two magi were talking animatedly. About her, no doubt. Or about the Butcher. Suddenly she longed for the simplicity of life from two days ago, where she knew how bad life was and what she could do for herself and her children. Life was not good, but she knew it well.

A dragon!

Vie could not get the idea out of her head. The notion was both fascinating and completely terrifying. At the Innervein, a number of magi had asked her about her family. They were so certain that she was more than a regular woman, but she could never have expected this. What did that mean for her? What would that mean for her *children?* If she was one, would they not be dragons, also? Having seen their mother change shape like this, would they try it as well? How would it change their lives?

A small hand gripped her fingers and she returned the squeeze with all her heart.

"It's... okay."

She smiled and pulled her youngest son close and held his head to her chest. She gestured Bel to join them. The girl hesitated. For a long moment, Vie wondered if this situation had pounded a wedge between them. Then she came. Vie held all the more tightly for this and pressed kisses into her jasmine-smelling hair. To have this destroy her girl's trust in her would have ruined her. "Thank you, baby. I swear we'll get to the bottom of this. I promise you." Within moments, Bon was there, too, undaunted by her transformation, and just eager to be a part of the hugging. For a long moment, all three of her children were where they belonged, safe in her arms, and the madness of the past night disappeared. For a time, everything was as it should be.

Then all four were wrapped up in two mighty arms.

"The hells?" Vie snapped, jumping nearly out of her skin.

"Embraces are fun!" the butcher said, his warm breath pleasantly full of morning sunshine and cool breezes.

The moment ruined by this odd man, Vie released her children, pulled herself away from the big man and, in doing so, realized just how naked he truly was.

"We need to do something about this."

"By all means," Lord Haphenasis said as both magi came up to join them. Vie doubted he was talking about the Cataclysm' nudity, however. Both magi moved with the unshakable rigidity of a wall. Flickers of arcana snapped in the air around them. Despite this lull, both were prepared for war. "Why, Ishtower and I could throw him in a Peacott Eggplant and summon our brothers to help bury that wicked sword of his deeper than it was before. Or, better yet, how about you just go back where you came from. I believe you have caused enough trouble here for one lifetime. In any case, step aside while we handle this."

Vie stared into the bitter teal of the magus' eyes. She felt her fingertips moving, unsummoned, to the tender flesh of her throat. The choker was gone and something told her that even if the lord had wanted to wrap another about her neck, it would not stick. She had never had a moment of such freedom. To have him in her head, just outside of consciousness, was horrible. As a person, he was not horrible—he had no wretched thoughts of lechery or of filth—but he was unwavering, a mountainous presence that panted at her with intense eyes that she could not resist. But now, she was free of his commands and his judgmental thoughts. Emboldened by her sudden liberation, she strode up to him and glared at his blood-caked, pudgy face.

"You have no more say in this, little man. You lost all right to that the moment you tried killing me."

"Is that not an exaggeration?"

"I think we both know what you wanted."

"Look behind you, and you will see what I want. Oh, but you cannot see it. Why? Because it all went up in the smoke that you cursed it to!"

"I am no longer your slave, and the destruction of the Apocryptein is as much your fault as mine."

"How typical of an underclass to dream of a world of equality instead of the reality of irresponsibility that it is. This whole mess is very clearly your fault. You broke into my home. You set the Kremsek loose. You let that damned monster free the Cataclysms! You burned my whole life down!" The energy that peaked during the height of the magus' rage dwindled into a quiet shell of self-pity. "You burned it down."

As he had gone for her throat earlier, she went for his during this moment of vulnerability. Life in Sludge had trained her well to go for such moments as this, for opportunity never came again. "Everything I do, I do for the sake of my children. What's your excuse? What do you care about other than yourself?"

"Now?" Lord Haphenasis looked past her at the wreckage of the Apocryptein. "Well, since I have no more tower nor wine nor books to read nor collection of artifacts, the only thing I give a damn about is undoing the damage *you* wrought by freeing that Kremsek! Included in that mandate—which came down on me from a group of my peers in the arcane world, I might add—is the endeavor of clearing my *own* name through the apprehension of the Twelve Cataclysms—beings, I will also add, that will rain destruction upon our entire world —and, unless I am greatly mistaken (in this instance, I know that absolutely not to be the case), that man right there is *one of the Twelve!*"

"Huzza!" the Butcher said, smiling. "Is there a prize for such a thing?"

Vie looked at the man with his dark beard, his immense muscles, at the breadth of his shoulders, the curiosity in his simple face. In his eyes, she saw the same restless curiosity she knew so well in her own children. There was trouble there, and uncertainty, but also a lost kindness. "With my children he's harmless."

"Are you insane? Can you not see that black weapon of immensity? That single blade has laid waste to countless innocent people!"

"Of course I can see it! But my boys understand him." An image came to mind. "And, you know, a moment ago, I think I remember you two going off to talk and leaving Bon, here, alone with the Butcher. If you really wanted to tackle him, wouldn't you have done so then?"

"What?" Lord Haphenasis asked, completely broadsided. Vie's long hours and conversations with Yue had given her the ability to confuse men. It felt good to strike this annoying man in a way she was familiar with. One day, perhaps, she would sick her... *dragon*... on him, but for now, Sludge was erupting comfortably from her mouth.

"I should be the angry one here! Why? Because you let Bon wander off with him. If you really thought this man was so dangerous, would you have let that happen? You know what I think? I think you either know my sons are right, or you don't give three damns about my children. If I'm with people who don't care about our needs, then by all Four Hells, maybe we're better off without you. Come on, kids."

She began walking down the grassy knoll toward the lip where she hoped the carriage was still waiting for them. Bel and Braden fell right in beside her, but Bon lingered a moment.

"Mom? What about him?"

"Since the magi know what to do with him, we're leaving him with them."

"What?!" Lord Haphenasis stuttered.

"But I don't wanna." There was an insistent pleading in his voice, a certain fear but, whether it was for himself or his new friend, Vie could not tell. Nor did she care.

"What do you mean you are leaving? You cannot leave!"

"Vie, wait!" Ishtower was finally getting himself involved. She had wondered how long it would take before he would join the conversation. She turned to acknowledge him with a level stare and her arms across her chest. "How certain are you about this?"

Vie looked over at the naked man. The whole ordeal had proven too interesting for him, and so he was entertaining himself by picking at the raspberry bushes for any leftover berries. The prickers on the bushes seemed not to bother him in the least. He must have found a sour one, for his face was puckered up.

"I trust my children. Besides, you can't keep me with you if I don't want it."

"You hear that?" Ishtower asked Lord Haphenasis. "I don't like this, either, but until we find another way to deal with him, I think she's got the meat of this. Who knows, having him with us could make our job easier. Come on. If we have any shot at dealing with all twelve, we have to put some faith in something."

The magus glared at her for a long moment, his jowls clenching and unclenching, then he glanced at her children, whom she knew were staring back at him with their large black eyes. At last, he looked away, toward the remains of the silver tower.

"We had better not be making the last mistake of our lives."

"Speaking of mistakes," Vie said, moving close to him. This close, she could smell the faint hint of the cheap perfume that they had at the bathhouse. The cut on the fat man's forehead had left his right eye dark from blood, but the teal inside was as fiercely cool as ever. He looked miserable and beaten. She wanted to just leave this as it was and move on, but she could not. She had one last message. "I'm going to say this once, and what you do with it is all on you.

"Look at my kids. Just look at them. Now look at me. Do you see us? Do you see who we are? Good. Because if you do anything against us—if you try to hurt us or if any of us are hurt from your neglect—I won't just leave you to clean up your mess, I'll kill you."

Chapter 18

From deep in the catacombs of Lord Haphenasis's travel ruck, he pulled out an adjustable pair of trousers and a bathing robe that he thought would fit the Butcher. He had several, but the man was an absolute mountain, standing a solid half foot taller than the already imposing Ishtower. Add to this a chest and arms that would make some trees envious, and finding a suitable fit made for a challenge. At least, it did in theory. As the Butcher pulled the white robe over his arms and tied it closed at the front, Lord Haphenasis frowned at how well it actually fit him. His hands found their way to his sizeable belly and he considered the notion that maybe he had been enjoying his food a tad too much in recent years. The trousers, on the other hand rode high, to just under his knees, leaving his large bare feet and hairy ankles to poke out. It was hardly a dignified look, but Lord Haphenasis cared little for this. That the Butcher was even with them when he should be locked up irritated him to no end. Not having the foresight to link his travel ruck to his trophy room came a close second to his immediate annoyance.

Ishtower sidled over to Lord Haphenasis. "Aren't you the rankled one?"

"Ishtower, please," he replied. "The last thing I need now is your sarcasm jibing me. I have enough of a headache stressing about the myriad terrors this monstrosity will unleash on us all."

"She's something to worry about, too," Ishtower said, lingering a moment with his brother as the other five had begun the short walk to the carriage.

"I *was* talking about Vie. A *dragon*?! What will Hamza say to that?"

"Probably something prophetic like, 'There must be a reason why it was her that broke into your home and started events down the path that has been set before us.'"

Lord Haphenasis frowned at his brother. "Levity aside, this just keeps getting worse."

"Much as I hate to say it, I completely agree. I can't think of anything good to some from this." Ishtower leaned against a tree, pulling weight off his injured leg.

"I assume you are mentioning this because you have devised a solution."

"Not a solution so much as a cry for help. I've sent a Whispering Wail to your Ventagist here in town."

"Saying?"

"Saying that we've got an experiment before us." The smile on his face was the same that tended to precede his more mischievous antics back in their informative years. It filled Lord Haphenasis with dread, for it seemed he was always getting this smile before something horrible happened to him.

"No."

"I haven't even said what my plan is."

"I do not need to know. That smile is giveaway enough."

"I thought you would be happy to retire in a comfortable hotel for some sleep or to meditate on all this."

"And risk the entire city's population with her presence? Or his presence? Who is to say that she can even control her transformations? Maybe you do not recall the legend of the Glimmer, but I certainly do."

"Spare us your stories," Ishtower said, pushing away from the chestnut tree against which he had been leaning. "Once you get going, there's no stopping you."

"Just like the Glimmer. She started as a regular morph, one who could change into a rava. But over time, she began experimenting with different shapes, and soon was able to shift from rava to woman to dog to ostrose and even to mythical beasts like a sphinx. Somewhere along the way, she had forgotten her true form, so if asked to return to normal, she could not. There is a theory that because of the constant changing, she had become addicted to the rush and could not stop."

"Your point?"

"The point is that the nature of a morph like the Glimmer was one of motion, and eventually, that motion led to a situation of predictability: danger. I ask you what do you think the nature a dragon is? What about the Butcher? And you want to throw both into the midst of a large population? Stick with your physical world and leave the thinking to those who are better suited to it."

"Pompous ass!" Ishtower hissed. A popping of latent

arcana exploded around him and just as suddenly vanished. He took several deep breaths and lifted his face to the warm morning sun before saying, "This has been an emotional time for you; violence such as you aren't used to has been forced upon your body. Maketh-El, you tried killing the thief! I've seen people snap before, and you've recovered from that better than I'd think possible. And, because of that, I'll forgive this slur. But clearly you need to rest."

Lord Haphenasis opened his mouth to hit Ishtower with several vibrations of snark, but saw little point in it. The Martialist was right—even if his choice of words were far below acceptable for such elevated company. Misery loved company, after all, and, at this moment in time, there was no one as miserable as Lord Haphenasis.

"Besides, do you really want to stay here any longer than is absolutely necessary?"

With his ribs aching from a heart problem that no medicine could touch, Lord Haphenasis sighed. "Which hotel were you thinking?"

"Three years ago, the Order had the symposium here. That fancy place with the pond in its back garden. Off the road toward the State House. Golden lion statues out front. Fancy. Nice chamber maids."

"The Gilded Lion?"

"That was it! We take the carriage there and then we'd have some privacy. Hopefully it would give the big man less opportunity to gut people."

The Gilded Lion was an historical treasure built 300 years ago for King Triphsaela the Fourth, as a summer retreat from the main halls of the traditional castle. While the monarchy was dissolved a few short generations after his death, subsequent mayors and governors did not shy from renovating it into a hotel that catered to visiting dignitaries. Ishtower was right. They could not stay here, and the Golden Lion was as good a place to venture as any and its private chambers and vast gardens would limit the butcher's socialization.

Lord Haphenasis nodded his agreement.

"Best send out another Whispering Wail to have a healer meet us there. My spells have staunched the bulk of my injuries, but I would rather have a professional see to the damage than take care of it all by myself."

"Then let's round up our motley bunch."

That evening's sunset roasted the clear sky in pale lavender when Lord Haphenasis glanced out at it from the large suite of apartments they secured for themselves. As he had brought them up, the bellboy filled their heads with the stories of the ancient kings and dignitaries who had once stayed in the same suite: Rubbold II, Duchess Zisi, Sheik Associ el Thefa, four different Emaks of the Sisterhood of the Heart and no less than five different Skeleton Keys. The rooms were adequate. Comfortable and filled with furniture both classic and tasteful, and empty wardrobes that made Lord Haphenasis sigh. It was comfortable, indeed, but it was not home. His room opened into a short corridor off of which were the chambers for the others. Vie, Ishtower, and the Butcher all had individual accommodations, while the children all shared the one which had a door connecting to the Butcher's. Oddly enough, Vie was the one to suggest this convenience, as it was only they who had any control over the massive man.

Over the next day, Lord Haphenasis got some

much-needed sleep and took care of the smaller details of everyday life—getting fitted for a new wardrobe, filling his belly, and contacting his brothers in the Innervein. Toward the end of the second day, a group of his brothers had arrived to take up a number of other rooms in the manor. They updated him on the situation of the other Cataclysms, about which Lord Haphenasis was anxiously curious. Two summons had been sent out into the various corners of Traumanfang to hunt down the vibrations. As of that point, none had uncovered any sign of the other eleven. This news was disheartening but unsurprising. The only positive detail that came from their apprehension of the Butcher was that the demonstration the lord had left in Whirl's lecture hall had started to be put to use. When he asked if it had been Hamza's order, the messenger reported that it was largely of individuals' own accords. It seemed that over the past day, some of the more corruptible of his brothers had begun a gambling pool to see who would tag the next Cataclysm.

Lord Haphenasis strongly disproved of this. It inspired haste, which often begat negligence. He could not help but feel concern for his brothers. Adequate in arcana that many might be, he worried that they would jump the gong and either attack the wrong person, or else would botch the capture and, in doing so, be obliterated. Yet, gambling aside, if it got more of his brothers involved, so be it.

With the arrival of his brothers, there were two who sat with him as he set his hound in action. Of all his brothers, only these two were intelligent enough to sit with a master at work. They had gotten a team of brothers together to investigate specific points that Lord Haphenasis pinpointed. This was a tactic that he vehemently supported, as it evoked precision. While he, himself, would be better served here in Reservwyresport, where another of the Cataclysms had been found, it was decided that these teams—such as they were—would track the other ten. He made a point to convince these two to have the others stalk but not to strike, yet the gambling purse had already reached several hundred gold coins. The pair insisted that their team had kept out of the pool for fear of distraction.

All in all, that first several days in the Gilded Lion had been immensely productive. The role of commander suited Lord Haphenasis immensely, and the distraction of leadership gave him a wonderful chance to ignore the more absurd and complicated details that came with Ishtower, Vie, and the Butcher.

Chapter 19

BEL SHRIEKED AS THE COLD WATER SPLASHED HER. BON had taught the Butcher how to curl up into a ball and jump in the water. Despite being unable to make much sense of the world around him, the big man learned physical tasks with amazing speed.

"Bon, you jerk! How come you had to teach him to ball-fall? You're getting me wet!"

"Guess that means you should come in and swim instead of play with flowers," Bon said, swimming over to the shore of the man-made lake to get out. "You, too, Braden. What're you watching us for? Come on in; the water's nice!"

"It isn't cold?" Braden asked. He was sitting on the edge of Vie's bench, watching his siblings and new friend eagerly.

"A little," the Butcher replied, holding his thumb

and index finger just a little ways apart. "But it's only like this much. Now it's like being in warm water."

Braden giggled. Vie nudged her son with her toe.

"Go on there, kid. Get some fun while you can. Don't know how long we'll be here, so you enjoy every bit of it that you can."

The boy smiled shyly and stood awkwardly. Back in Sludge, kids swam nude in the murky waters of the river. Here, though, all were required to wear bathing gear: shorts and shirts tied with a woven rope that covered up their nudity. It seemed such a foolish rule to her, but Vie had always known that the customs of the wealthy and poor were vastly different. Braden strolled over to the edge of the pool and dipped a toe.

From out of nowhere, the Butcher grabbed him under the armpits and hauled him into the air. Vie's stomach got caught in her throat. Was he planning on hurting her boy? Had the his kindness and sincerity all been a ruse? She felt a scream for help welling up.

With a giant smile on his face, the Butcher roared and tossed Braden into the water.

Vie stared with held breath, waiting to see if she needed to act. There was his head. He coughed and spat out water. As he wiped his unruly hair from his eyes, he giggled. "That was fun!"

"Roar!" the Butcher laughed, flexing his imposing muscles.

"Me next?" Bon screamed as he swam over to the giant.

"Only if you get over here before I count to three! One! Ten! Schwenty! Five!" Bon was there, in the big man's immense arms, next to be turned into a child missile.

Trembling slightly, Vie realized she had risen from

her seat. Slowly, she sat down again, wary of the constant vigil she had been keeping these past four days. It had been difficult to reconcile the magi's story of this man with the man-child before her. Despite her insistence that the Butcher was harmless, she knew in the deepest corner of her heart that such was a lie. The first reason for this certainty was the sword that lay under her bench. It was disguised in a bolt of cloth to resemble a fishing rod, but she could feel its power, nonetheless. Being close to it gave her a constant sense of misplacement, like a big gap between the floorboards. You knew that if you let go, whatever you were holding onto would disappear forever. Last night, Ishtower had put his finger right on that feeling: "It's like we're being watched." Yes, that was exactly it. The thing drew attention to it, almost as if it were a jewel to be coveted. In the closeness of the weapon, she could understand why the Butcher had been forced to fight whomever came his way.

That did not explain the man's darkness, however. That first day, at the Apocryptein, when Lord Haphenasis had tried commanding him, he looked ready to kill. There was no mistaking the truth to that look. He truly was the Butcher when it came to others telling him what to do. When the threat of command was not heavy on him, he was quite the opposite: a big kid, as eager to do new things as Bon, as observant as Braden, and as inquisitively talkative as Bel.

"Who are you?" she had asked him the previous night as he gobbled down a loaf of rich brown bread topped with a ladle full of noodles and sweet custard. The strange concoction was the latest of such that he and Bon were sampling for the sake of—as Bon said—"a cook-ery revolution."

"Who do you think?"

"Why do you always do that?"

"Do what?"

"Answer direct questions with a question?"

"Do I really do that?"

"Yes, you do."

"Huh. That's strange. I wonder why I do that."

"Because straight answers are for ninnies!" Bon said, sticking out a tongue heaped with tea leaves and half-chewed sausage. "Don't wanna be a ninny, do you?"

"No way! Ninnies are for nonuns!" the Butcher bellowed. "That any good?"

"No worse than that spicy red powder on steak."

For their four days in the Gilded Lion, all other attempts from her or from Lord Haphenasis or Ishtower to find out just who he was and where he came from had gone as smoothly. The magi had contacted their Order to tell them about the oddity of the situation. Curious to see just what this Cataclysm was like, a number of their brethren had been by to get a feel for just how much of a threat the Butcher was. Vie had spoken to a couple of them after they had interviewed the man-mountain. All of whom were left as perplexed and confused as the one before. About all they could gather from him was what they could see with their own two eyes. He was big, strong, and carried his sword with him wherever he went. The first two days, they had insisted he be kept to his own room. That had not worked very well. The first night, he managed to destroy half the furnishings of the place. The noise had woken up her kids just beyond the thin adjoining door, and so all four spent a long night of playing,

talking, and giggling. Since then, they had learned that
he needed little sleep, but so long as he were kept entertained, he would likely remain so for extended periods
of time. Lord Haphenasis had suggested that he be given
books to read, but the man became listless with those
that were full of words.

It was Braden who came up with the idea of picture
books. The single book in the Gilded Lion that boast-
ed pictures was a boring old book called the Buh Nor
Bible, yet despite this, the Butcher had quickly become
lost in the images. A magus was sent to the markets of
Reservwyresport to get more. Since that first night, there
had been no more sleep-killing noise from his room.

In addition to the picture books, the magi had found
whirligigs, a kendama, and an odd untangling puzzle that
never was fully untangled and always seemed to re-tan-
gle itself afterward. After the picture books, the kendama was probably the biggest hit with the man, as it gave
him countless combinations of patterns in which to try
and catch the attached ball. Small, wide, pin, wide, middle, small. Braden had taught him how it worked and it
served as a very useful distraction.

Until yesterday, when one new magus tried to take
it away from him. They said that it happened so quickly,
one moment, he was reaching for the toy, the next, he
was staring at a stump of an arm lying on the floor. If the
kids had not been there at the time, the magus would
have been dead. From what Ishtower reported later that
day, having a healer on hand in the Lion had been ben-
eficial, for the arm had been reattached and was already
beginning to get some feeling back in the fingertips.

The magi had wanted to treat the Butcher like a rabid dog after that. There had been screams and moans and yells and "should" and "would have," all of which were stupid man-speak to invite action. In the meeting that followed, Vie experienced language that was nearly completely incomprehensibile, but she did learn quite a bit about the way these magi thought and acted. Like most men, they tended to think either directly or absently—in other words, they always sought easy solutions. After about an hour of such nonsense, she had had enough.

"You're all being *stupit*! It wasn't his fault; it was the magus who tried taking his toy."

Ishtower had immediately rallied behind her, citing his own observations over the past several days and chalking the whole situation to impatience. He clearly and carefully explained that the injured magus had suffered simple impatience. He said that only the one hurt should be held accountable for his mistake. He then made an interesting example of putting one's hand in a bear's cage, which inevitably led to one being bit.

Despite the reality presented to them then, the magi still deliberated the issue for the rest of the afternoon. Vie had no patience for their childish bickering. Eventually, an irritable Ishtower finally came back to her with news. "It takes us a while to accept facts before us, but we usually come to the right decision. We'll leave things as they are now. They've decided to keep a few of us around just in case something should happen, but with me in charge, hopefully nothing bad will happen. There is a proviso, in that we will study him, but attended. With his attention span and lack of self-knowledge, there's only so much time we'll have to work with him, but perhaps in watching, we can learn a little about who he is."

"Do you think it's the right decision?"

Ishtower had looked at the big man learning the slappy game from Bon. After a while he said, "Yes. It's the only decision, really. That sword of his reeks of arcana. I'd bet my life that it's the sword that kills, not him."

Sword or man, Vie had barely slept since she had broken into the Apocryptein because of worry. What would he do to her kids if left alone for too long? Would they be able to control him in any situation? What would prevent them from getting hurt? What would happen if they decided to show him the worst parts of their beings, the willful disloyalty, the dangerous curiosity? For now, he captivated them, filled them with the wonder that came with a new pet. But children were children. What would happen when her kids grew bored with *him*? Or had they so thoroughly accepted him into the family that it created a bond that could not be broken even by irresponsibility?

In addition to worry about the Butcher, there were things that needed her attention. Top of this list was Galym. The man was like a pricker of worry in the back of her head. What she had successfully kept secret from the magi thus far was that there was a reason she was in the Apocryptein that night. And that reason was Galym. While the man was a bizarre mix of ambition and desire, she knew that it was only a matter of time before he came inquiring about the job. As she had never failed in anything Galym had hired her for, she had no context for his reaction concerning her failure at the silver tower. She could not—would not—escape her responsibility to him. He had been too good an employer over the years to just ignore now that she was facing the end of the world.

In addition to Galym, there was also the issue of her

dragon form, a detail that she had been utterly unable to devote any time to. What did it mean? Was it different from her mouse aspect, which she could shrink into at will? Was she actually a dragon, or was it just another skin that she could take on? And what about Yue? Had she found a new place to stay while the Stout was being repaired? And, of course, there were the other eleven Cataclysms. There were too many questions about them, about everything, wearing her down and, despite her public face of absolute trust in her children's faith, this man-child filled her with worry.

"By lookin' at him, ya wouldn't fink he'd be one of de most dangerous people in all existence, woodja?"

"Squite!" Vie said, getting up to hug the stooped ancient magus. She gave his withered cheek a gentle peck. "What are you doing here?"

"Just came wif de Skeleton Key, who wanted ta talk to his lordship and Ishtower himself. And, to be honest, check up on you." His bushy old eyebrows twitched upward in concern.

"I'm fine," Vie said, looking away from the friendly old man toward her children.

"Are you now?"

She could not bring herself to lie, nor did she want to admit her fears and concerns, nor the uncertainty that had given her the deep dark bruises that she could feel gathering about her eyes. She chose to watch her children rather than answer.

"Fought not." Squite creaked into one of the wooden chairs around a sun table. "Far be it from me to tell anyone what to do, so I'll just put dese big old ears of mine to work if you need dem."

"What if I have nothing to say?"

"Den, I'll wait until you do."

"No offense, but what if you're dead before the words come?"

Squite chuckled. "Den at least I'll have more reasons to hunt you out afore I'm dead. Gives me somefin' to look forward to, yeah?"

Vie took his gnarled old hand in hers.

"So a dragon, huh?"

Vie sighed. It would have been so much easier talking about the Butcher. "That's what they keep telling me."

"Can't say I know what that's like. Rheumatism? Arfritis? Tooflessness? Lots have experience wif dat. But bein' a mighty bein' from anofer realm? Well." Vie did not like where Squite was going with this and started withdrawing her hand, but he held it fast. "You look at me, now, old and wrinkley and ugly as I am. Dere's gonna be problems. Big problems once word o' dis gets out. But whatever happens, you stay true t'yerself. You stay true to dem'uns. You stay true, and if you forget dat, if you need any help, den dere's at least one old man who'll be dere for ya. Long's I can be, any which ways."

Vie sniffed back the tears she felt coming on and clutched the old man's hand tighter than ever.

"Can I ax you a question?"

"Sure."

"Why are you here?"

"What do you mean?"

"You could have just left dis all behind, taken them kids back to Sludge, or gone wherever, and left us. Hamza's said dat wifout de Choker of Sorrow, dat you're free. If you broke clear o'dat before, dere's no way we can hit you wif it again."

"Does he want to?"

Squite gummed his jaws as he stared out at the kids playing in the lake. "No. Dere ain't nofing in it for dat. Four Hells, I don't know. What can we do if you were? Kill you? Dat'd do no good. If you really are a dragon, den that'll be just as bad as havin' a big fight with de Butcher. No, I think it's good to have you on our side for now. But you ain't answered my question yet. Why'd you stay?"

"Because I need to find out what I am. You magi are my best chance at that."

****

That night brought on the balm that often came with spring. Once summer hit, the Singing Bay hummed lullabies of sweltering humidity, but springtime air carried the cooler breeze from the oceanic north. The Singing Bay was nearly an ocean of itself, but it was open enough that it brought people from all avenues of life—sailors and traders from all parts of the world, even some of the strange people with their peculiar gods from the far west and deep south. Here in the Gilded Lion, Vie was without the hustle and bustle that was always riding in on the tides. It left the place and her with a seclusion she was unaccustomed to, but it also meant that conditions were perfect. After making sure the kids were tucked into their large single bed, Vie crept down to the immense gardens of the hotel.

Over the past couple of days, she had brought her children and their charge exploring. At first, they had followed the stone walkways painstakingly set out along paths to help walkers find the key places of interest: the bubbling waterfall, the rose garden, the animal-shaped plants, the small temples. With the boundless energy that the children had, it soon became much more of a real exploration of what lay beyond the paths and what lay hidden behind the trees. Here, they were able to find a small maze of hedges, a tiny village of brick and plaster buildings in which the hotel staff lived, and even some sculptures so ancient that the totems they had represented were completely unidentifiable. Vie had convinced her children that such explorations would be interesting, especially since she had never spent any time in a mighty hotel like this, and that it was good for the kids to be able to explore a clean garden. And, although the kids took to the task with gusto, the reality was that she wanted to find a place where she could explore herself.

The night's sky was clear yet dark, black but twinkling, despite the glow of the city beyond the gates of the Gilded Lion. It was late enough that the lanterns in the garden had long been put out, which gave her even more privacy. Crossing over one of the hand bridges to the island that she had chosen, Vie glanced down into the water. The sky reflected perfectly in its gentle ripples.

Toward the far end of the island, where a wide yard of sand led out toward a buoyed, covered pavilion, there was a stone statue of an ancient god that Vie did not recognize. Nevertheless, she used the small covered brazier beside the statue to light three incense sticks and set them before it. Being from Sludge, the act of prayer was an act of defeat. Those she knew would chide her for her weakness and tell her that a person's actions in this life were what chose their fate. Of course, they said this, knowing full well that none in Sludge had the means to rise above it. It was a petty game of scorn and social sabotage and, sadly, it had taken root. She would not pray but just being here, in the silence of the night, she felt a strange feeling of spirituality wash over her. To not light the incense would be inappropriate for what she was doing. She slipped off her robe and stood naked, the cool breeze stirring her exposed nipples. Were it not for her anxiety, it might have aroused her.

She strode into the middle of the sandy clearing and turned her senses inward. The scent of her familiar mouse was readily evident, a sweet little creature with twitching whiskers. She stroked the soft fur of this form and stepped past it, down a darker corridor, where dwelled emotions and responses she rarely gave mind to. Here were darkened sacks of hatred, of rage, and shame. There were glimpses of the mistakes that she had made in her life, of a hidden ghost who would haunt her every time she looked in the faces of her children if she let it, and also of the faceless phantoms that were all she remembered of her parents. It had been so long since she had been abandoned in Sludge that she could not even remember.

Moving deeper into herself, she could feel the three collars she had been forced to wear. The first was when she was a child, slave to a sex house until she had found her freedom with the help of Yue and the discovery of her mouse form. The second was possessed for such a short time yet led to such an important phase of her life. Then, more recently, the collar given her by Lord Haphenasis. Her neck was still bruised and scabbed over from this, an ugly green black that was now beginning to fade into a gross mustard yellow. Yet the pain was still there. Pain of shame. Pain of insult. Pain of slavery, of knowing that control of her actions had been stripped from her.

Slavery came in many forms. There were slaves who could not earn coin, as she had once been; there were others who could earn coin, but were so swallowed by debt that their entire lives would be an uphill battle that they would never surmount. She had heard stories of people who became slaves to their family, sacrificing their very beings for the sake of husband or child or parent. But those were only physical manifestations of slavery— the easy lives. The most dangerous were those of the soul. True slavery came to those who embraced it. These were the people who said, "I cannot change this situation or my life or the people around me, so why bother?" These were the ones who gave up the fight and embraced the miserable tragedy of their lives. True slavery was a choice that people made because they stopped caring. True slaves were people to be pitied because they could not—or refused to—see any alternative.

Vie shuddered to think how easily she could have wound up like these others. She had seen depressed mothers trying to drink an escape from their babies that ran naked in the street. She knew the indifference bordering almost on yearning that a horse would crush the child underfoot. She had seen grotesques rage their anger in the streets of Sludge, so full of hatred for the world that they were only happy taking out their frustrations on others. These were the true slaves—people who resented their imperfections. Hatred of the world around her, of herself, was a lifestyle that she could easily have embraced. A lone woman of eighteen with three mouths to feed. There were women who abandoned their lives for less. How easy would it have been to give her own children up, leave them to the elements to die? On her worst days, she told herself that it would be easy to do. But once those moods passed, she knew she had been fooling herself. In truth, it had been a real consideration only once.

Malek Izzard had left her months before. But he had left her comfortable. In his apartments, he had items of value but little food. He never had been good with food. He enjoyed a raw onion as much as he had a piece of chocolate. His appetites had always been larger, more sexual in nature. So when he left her halfway through her pregnancy, she had to waddle to the markets, pawning what she could for the food her babies craved. Izzard had been gone too long, the most precious of his collection had disappeared, leaving only valueless knickknacks and bare essentials—eating utensils, sheets for the beds, her own limited wardrobe. She knew that she had been abandoned by the only man she had ever loved, and with that realization she had fallen into a depression.

Because of this depression, she had barely noticed when her water broke. Wet, terrified, nearly lost to her own abandonment, she surprised herself by delivering all three children in solitude. A day and a half later, when all was done, she was sprawled in the bed of her children's father's home, exhausted, blood, shit, and afterbirth everywhere, wanting only to curl up and die. Were they even breathing? They had been quiet so far. Did babies usually stay so quiet during their birth? If they were dead, all the better. It meant that death had arrived already. All her effort was for nothing, just like her life.

And then Bel cried.

It was an annoying sound that pulled her back from

the exhausted doze toward which Vie had been drifting. Insistent. Demanding. So demanding that Bon soon picked up and joined in. Her breasts throbbed then, as if they were begging to satisfy these whimpering beasts. She crawled to the other end of the bed and pulled her children to her.

They drank heartily. Bel and Bon, greedy, insatiable, while the third just shuddered and moved on its side, helpless, yet already strangely patient. She stared at this third child, her Braden. He was quiet, his eyes closed, but he was smiling. She found herself resenting him, thinking he was mocking her trouble. What are you smiling about? If she had the energy then, she would have carried them outside and left them on the street. It was a flash of desperation and panic. But that resentment quickly faded beneath the power of that little face. As she stared at him, his siblings softly pressing against her chest, she felt her muscles soften. The more she watched, the more her tensions eased. What matter that Malek had abandoned her? Before he had left, he had given her these three beautiful children. This boy was smiling for the first time ever, and she, his mother, was there to witness it. For the first time in weeks, perhaps months, she found herself relaxing.

Their first day alive and already they were improving her world.

It was then that she decided to accept this. Her children were hers and that while taking care of them would be difficult—especially now that her funds had about dried up—so long as her children were a part of her world, she would be fine.

She found herself smiling at the joy they brought her,

and as she thought of them, she found what she was looking for: the trigger.

She wrapped herself in her children and squeezed. She savored the transformation, exulting in the comfortable tightening of her muscles, the pressure of her tail pushing out above her ass, the tingle of her wings as the skin of her back extended. She stretched outward until she could go no more.

Just as it did when she hugged her children, it felt right.

Vie, the dragon, stood in the sand and closed her eyes. The air was still cool but comfortable on her scales. Like it had her naked glory, the wind now tickled the thick hairs of her chin and swirled through the horns behind her eyes and caught in her outstretched wings to slip down beneath them. She could hear the gentle gurgling of the carp in the lake, the peaceful music of the leaves rustling on the edge of this sandy courtyard. There were even the pips and peeps of small nocturnal animals in the trees, no doubt scurrying for food. A subtle glint of incense smoke found her nostrils, and from the walls surrounding the palace, came the odd funk of human waste and pleasant aroma of dirt, sand, and sap.

At last she opened her eyes and gazed down at the reflection of herself in the waters below. She was both ugly and beautiful, immense and mighty and awkward. It was strange to move her arm and see the dragon reflecting back do the same. She felt as clumsy and ugly as she did when she was pregnant with the triplets. Back then, near the end of her term, she had to maneuver around carefully to avoid banging her gigantic belly against tables or corners or people. Walking became a difficult waddle

that made a duck's walk graceful by comparison. Though
she had refused to look at herself in a mirror or any kind
of reflective metal, she did so from a sense of false con-
fidence. But this was different. Walking around in the
sand was awkward, certainly, but only because she was
not used to her long thick tail or her leathery wings. She
knew the feeling of four limbs and a tail but having two
wings in addition to everything else was quite a bit different. For the first several minutes, she found herself for-
getting her legs if she tried concentrating on her wings,
or she'd forget the wings and they'd twitch as if on their
own. The walking was strangely comfortable, almost as if
she had been doing it all her life. The instinct was there,
but she just had to feel it out.

As she walked around, one of her feet splashed down
into the edge of the lake. A fish glinted over her toe as it
rushed to escape. It gave her a silly idea, though. She waded into the water until she was completely covered. Once
under the water, she took a deep breath and ducked her
head. She stayed there for a long time, testing just how
long this big body of hers could go without breathing. After what felt like quite a while—at least far longer than she
could normally—her chest began groaning for air. Cursing herself for her curiosity, she opened her mouth and
let the water fill her up. She wanted to scream and cough
it all out, but as the water entered her body, it felt oddly
agreeable, almost as if this were no different than walking. What was even stranger than being able to breathe
water was how clear her vision remained through this experiment. Enjoying this new ability, she swam about under the water for some time, chasing the golden fish who
lived here, doing somersaults, and testing the different

parts of this new body.

The oddest part of her new form, though, was the additional sensation. It was like a humming that did not touch her ears, a scent that she could not smell, a taste that was not in her mouth, nor anything she could see. Whatever it was, she could feel it with every part of her massive body. It was present both outside on land and under the water and was warm and thick and gentle and tingly. Was this the arcana that the magi were talking about? She had overheard Ishtower talking to one of his brothers about dragons coming from a world unlike their own, where the Veins ran far stronger than they did here.

If she could sense the Veins, did it mean she could use their power? If so, for what? How? Would it be a physical power or one of the mind? Was her ability to breathe underwater part of that power or was that just a regular feature of all dragons?

One thing was for certain: there was no way to get answers to all her questions out here by herself. Certainly, she could learn more about herself—how her body worked, what she could and could not do—but there were things that she knew nothing about, ideas that she would never consider on her own.

As the birds began their serenade to the pre-dawn, Vie shrank back down to her normal self and wrapped her robe about her familiar old body once more. She felt small and dumb. Compared to the wonder that was her dragon aspect, her regular self felt so limited and confined.

The incense that she had lit was nothing more than a stub as she started making her way back to her rooms. Two thoughts entertained her as she walked: the first was how much she had enjoyed this evening. The second was imagining how Ishtower would respond when she told him she wanted him to help her learn about this wonderful new body.

Chapter 20

OVER THE PAST SEVERAL DAYS, LORD HAPHENASIS HAD BEEN dividing his attentions primarily between two very specific functions: communicating with his brothers in the Order and arguing with his brothers in the Order.

While both might look like the same thing to an average person, they were two very distinct actions. The first was a one-sided requirement. The Skeleton Key, Hamza, had demanded that his lordship keep his brothers abreast of his progress in tracking down the Twelve in whatever form it took.

It was immediately *after* the completion of his duty had been performed that the latter generally began. The specifics of the interaction were something that coursed through his mind at random intervals in the subsequent days.

The delivery with Ishtower in the Keyhall was simple

enough: "I am pleased to inform my esteemed brothers that the first of the Twelve Cataclysms has been found and is now in our... custody."

After the expected and understandably jovial response of cheers (there were no back pats, a remission he attributed to his new title of Cataclysm) were dished out, Ishtower had cleared his throat. The big Yeganian could have given the subsequent message as well as his lordship could have, but he deferred the task, claiming that it was his lordship that had let the whole mess happen in the first place. Therefore it fell to him to enjoy all the glory and discomfort that came with the task.

"You have more to add?" the Skeleton Key asked from the Bough.

It was then he had explained the limitations involved with the "custody" that he had mentioned. That while the Butcher was technically in their custody, the circumstances of such were far from optimal.

"You are telling us that the Butcher is free?"

"Technically? Yes."

"And that he is free because a child says he should be?"

"Technically? That is also true."

"And you are not laughing in this child's face?"

"Correct."

"Because his mother, the thief, Vie, is a dragon?"

"Indeed."

While this admission did not get Lord Haphenasis kicked out of the Order for incompetence, it did manage to open the floodgates to discussion on how best to handle the situation. He quickly lost track of the varying suggestions for how they should resolve this problem, mostly due to the fact that each one was more idiotic than the first. During this discourse of horrid ideas, they yelled at him, they called him inept (among other names which were hardly appropriate for someone of his social standing and success), and they derided the situation as being untenable. They said he had embarrassed all that they stood for. Several had even gone so far as to attempt to work together to find a suitable solution to the problem, but for each idea that came up, Lord Haphenasis had found himself in the uncomfortable position of agreeing with the solution put forth by the burglar: they should leave the butcher to her children.

Even after the decision that the Butcher should remain in custody of the children had been ratified, a handful of his brothers came to him either separately or in pairs or small groups in the attempts to dissuade him from supporting this course of action.

"Look, they have some power over the Butcher. I do not know what, but so long as these children are with him, he is as docile as a kitten."

"You must never have had a kitten of your own, Lord Haphenasis; otherwise, you would know how naïve that statement is!"

"Regardless of my poor metaphor, the fact remains that there is logic in this situation. Unless you are here to inform me that we have found an alternative method of containment—one as effective as the Apocryptein was over the Riot—then I am afraid the only tenable solution is that the children oversee the Butcher's rehabilitation."

"Rehabilitation! By the aether! This is a Cataclysm we're talking about, not some common criminal. There is no rehabilitation to be had with this one."

"Perhaps not, but can you argue the reality? With the Butcher here, under the control of these children, we are presented with a rare opportunity of study. In our midst we have not just the Butcher, but also a dragon! How long has it been since a dragon has been on Traumanfang, let alone been in a position of experimentation?"

The larger arguments largely dissipated at that point, leaving only the smaller, mundane grumbles and complaints of who was to do what and how the studies would be done. An inevitable outcome of whatever their choice would mean that the Gilded Lion would play host to a variety of magi in the foreseeable future.

Lord Haphenasis, however, removed himself from all the deliberations that had to come in the wake of this. They could manage their own pastimes as they needed; he had more important things to worry about and did not trust his brothers to succeed in his role. Unfortunately, his tasks had to wait a day or two so that he could orient his brothers with the Lion and to introduce a number of them to the thief, her children, and the Butcher. But once that was done, he washed his hands of the whole nonsense and returned to his greater task: that of finding the other eleven Cataclysms.

Each of the past several days, when time permitted, he had resumed tracking with the hound, and each day another so-called "emergency" had cropped up, forcing him to delay his physical hunt. The first time was when a younger magus—a Theoretician, from the look of the sash—wanted to see how the Butcher would react to spoken commands. Lord Haphenasis had whisked him away from the Butcher's blade long enough for the middle child to calm him down. It took the next several hours to reattach the fool's right arm, though using it would be severely limited for the next several months. At least it helped to prove the theory that the Butcher saw spoken commands as an act of aggression. Now that they knew what triggered the man's belligerence, they could take steps to avoid setting him off. Despite this, the children were still best at actually commanding the man to partake in essentially safe activities.

Then, on the second day at the Gilded Lion, poor old Squite taxed his powers by trying to open doors to a delegation of twenty from four different parts of the world. Lord Haphenasis had to berate the foolish old man while he submitted a formal complaint stating that with all the Order activity, there should be no less than four Ventagists on hand, and to the hells with the one-Ventagist-per-region law. While the Order had still not made up its mind about the issue, the members relaxed so far as to summon Squite's nephew to aid in the transportation of magi. This the lord met with satisfaction; Yankee was a quiet giant whose greatest weakness was fine wine. The pair had spent many a night over the years sampling and conversing over the finer details of things like a Chartle reds '45 compared to a '47. Evidently, if the old man's flirtings with Vie earlier that day were any indication, despite the stress on his body from overextending himself, he was on his way toward a full recovery.

The one point that met with his total saitisfaction was that the two magi who had the wherewithal to work directly under him, Aziz el Hoeft and Georgan Waever, successfully managed to track down one of the Cataclysms. While neither had commanded their teams into the world yet, they had taken prodigious notes on their findings. When Lord Haphenasis had returned from the Innervein, the three met to discuss the notes. He was pleased to be able to compliment the two young magi showed remarkable skill with residual scents despite the fact that they were not yet up to par with the current vibrations. From their findings, they learned that the other ten were still in motion. It fit the theory that, as disembodied spirits, they would pick at and snack on whatever they could, but once they found a destination providing prolonged sustenance, they would settle down. There was little point in rushing after the fading scent until there was a certainty to strike.

"What about this one?" Aziz asked in his curiously high-pitched voice, tapping the notes on one of the vibrations.

"Has it moved?" Lord Haphenasis asked, reviewing the details.

"Only locally," Georgan responded. A pudgy man with more baby fat in his cheeks than most babies, he looked at everything with a wide-eyed look resembling constant worry. Despite this, Lord Haphenasis found his ideas to be quite astute. "Both of us ran our vibrations through the Hound. We have gotten in this habit. It reduces any potential mistakes. Be that as it may, whatever it wants is right here in Reservwyresport."

"Such is never a good sign," Lord Haphenasis mumbled.

"Should we launch the team?" Aziz asked.

"No." The apprehension of the Butcher had not gone as well as he would have liked, and he was pointedly feeling the pressure of failure. Everything he did this past week had seemed rife with errors. If he paid heed to such superstitious drivel, he might have attributed it to a competency curse. Unlike real spells, curses were more suggestive than practical. They could only succeed if the cursed believed in the cursing words. What he actually believed was what he knew and could touch; creating a running tally of failure that he knew had to be remedied by his hand alone. "No, I have this one. If they are getting impatient, have a pair go to Darkwoods. That place has long had a reputation of hauntings and corruption. More specifically, the Lich was apprehended near there. If she were to return, I have little doubt that she will return to the seat of power she had in life."

"Yes, milord," Georgan replied. "What about the Tinker? Should we also send a contingent north?"

"Tell me, Georgan, have you ever been to the Zeu'yan Valley?"

"None has. Zeu'yan is supposedly translated into 'the forgotten' in old Yeganian."

"So why would this valley be called 'Zeu'yan'?"

"Because nobody knows where it is," Aziz replied. "That's what I told him, too, but the dumbass didn't want to listen to me."

"Yet, the theory has merit." Lord Haphenasis scribbled down a quick note on a piece of parchment. "Holg Ank is an old acquaintance of my family's. More specifically, he raises Gergian sand snakes."

"He what?!" Aziz asked.

"You heard me. In their youth, the beasts are remarkably susceptible to human control. Very useful means of transport, I have heard. But they lose their functionality after their third or fourth year, when they become far too large to respond to the controls. Send someone to his home in Mustka'vee with this note. Unwieldy as they may be, those snakes could prove to be invaluable once the Tinker settles. I want to be prepared. Keep a team at station there."

"I know just the pair," Aziz said, nodding. "They're from the desert there, so it should be no problem. Hells, they may actually know this guy already."

"Sort it out. Now; if there is no more business, I must be off."

Once in his room, Lord Haphenasis pulled out his travel ruck to prepare for his investigation in the city. His assistants had placed the spirit smack dab in the middle of Sludge. He regretted the notion of returning to the seedy filth of Reservwyresport, but the solitude of the hunt was absolutely necessary. Without having to conform to the limitations of a group, he could focus the totality of his attentions to the task. In essence, tracking this Cataclysm was no different from finding an important tome in a library. A partner would have distracted him with simple physical presence or conversation but, alone, the task would take a fraction of the time. Despite this, he would be unable to bring a hound with him. Such devices were far too fragile to bring into a congested place. An errant bump or a jostle, could send it shattering to the ground. Rooftop vigils were also out of the question, as the upper levels of the district were far too crowded together to allow for a proper observation. He needed an alternative to these. It was all a matter of finding the damned thing from the pits of the ruck.

"Oh, for... just spit it out already!"

The ruck heaved once and the item plopped onto the bed where Lord Haphenasis had been working.

"Finally."

He picked up the small silver sculpture and played it between his fingers as he called up the arcane scent of the Cataclysm. Once attuned to the spirit's frequency, it would make tracking him down simplicity itself.

****

The smell of Sludge greeted Lord Haphenasis three streets away. It always came back to the stench; it had the peculiarity this morning of having some boiled laundry mixed in to the usual reek of waste and refuse and rubbish. He paused, leaning on his walking staff, a solid oaken thing that he had acquired in a game of wits and was blessed with a variety of runic tattoos, to refortify his determination to go in.

"Why Mayor Tobindon does not set this slum to the torch is beyond me," he mumbled and slathered himself in a Wet Nose, an arcane ointment that mimicked the smell-preventative elements of the common cold. Lord Haphenasis saw a runny nose a far preferable annoyance to the ongoing stench of the place. Despite feeling satisfactorily prepared to enter Sludge, he double checked his harmonic resonance. Arcane-sensitive could usually identify other arcane-sensitive, especially when certain high-arcana spells were being channeled. If the second Cataclysm were here, he did not want to take the risk of being sniffed out prematurely. Just to be safe, he rolled down another curtain of ephemeral silence. His raw power was such that anyone sensitive to the arcane spectrum would be able to hear him from a mile away. But with several curtains already rolled down, his arcane resonance would sound no different than any other low-class wretch.

That done, he set the mutt down on the dirty cobblestone before him and tapped it three times with his staff. The sculpture shuddered once and began growing. It stopped when it reached the size of a small Dalmatian. The mutt lifted its gleaming metallic nose to the air and sniffed. Not finding its quarry there, it set its nose toward the dirt, where it continued sniffing, beginning what was called the "searching" phase.

In a measured jog, it took off toward the morass that was Sludge. Lord Haphenasis summoned a cloud for speed and to avoid dirtying his boots on the baser of the unfortunately recognizable flotsam and jetsam in the streets. Happily hovering several inches off the ground, he set off after the mutt.

They pursued the target like this for only several minutes before the mutt slowed down to take deeper breaths. It zigged and zagged as it determined which direction the Cataclysm had gone.

"Oy! Get your stupid mutt out of the road!" a cart driver shouted, annoyed at having to pull his mule up short to let the little silver dog pass unharmed.

"Official Order business!" Lord Haphenasis shouted back, without taking his eyes off the mutt. "Just have some patience, and we will be on our way."

Sure enough, the mutt found its prey and took off at its original pace. It was only a matter of time before they were upon the spirit.

Excited to be near the end of his hunt, he rounded a corner and sped down the road after the arcane mecha. He could feel the Cataclysm but could not pinpoint it. Surely, the mutt had it.

As he caught up to the stopped animal, he threw out

a handful of Divining Dust (and ignored the complaints of the people nearby on whom it landed) and spread his consciousness through it. The minds of each person the dust touched opened to him, allowing passage into not just the superficial mundane thoughts of the person, but also their subconscious. There was so much to sift through that without the Divining Dust, just sorting out these fifteen people would have taken far longer, perhaps even an hour. With the dust and armed with the knowledge of exactly what he was looking for, he was done within a minute.

When he had left their minds, the walkers drifted back to the confusion that always came with an interruption of consciousness. They would not be aware of just how vulnerable they had just been but, nevertheless, none could escape the sense of remarkable power that came with such a mental touch. When he had been subject to its effects, back when he was a mere student, Lord Haphenasis had found it to be an altogether humbling experience.

If only this time it had paid off. The mutt had laid down at his feet and was whimpering, something it could only do in the event that it had lost the scent. So if the spirit wasn't in these people here, where was it? Lord Haphenasis looked all around him. He was on Back Row, known for pleasure houses, disreputable pubs, and cheap living quarters. Twenty or so people were in sight; countless others were probably there, hidden behind the walls and doors of the various buildings.

With no other option and not ready to be so easily dissuaded, he threw a protective shroud around himself. The mutt had failed, but he was not so easily defeated.

Even though he had told himself it was too dangerous for the hound here in Sludge, he nonetheless extracted it from his ruck. Once the hound got to spinning, it drew up a completely different part of the city, confirming the mutt's results, that the disembodied spirit of the second Cataclysm had fled this place. Grumbling, Lord Haphenasis put the hound away and looked about one last time in the useless chance of spotting the spirit. Mollified that there was no sign of it, he set out for the next spot, across the city.

Chapter 21

When the knock came on Lord Haphenasis's door, he got up and glanced past the light curtains to the open window beyond. There was only the barest grey to frame the trees outside his third story chamber. He puttered about on the thick bear skin rug for a few minutes, during which time he rolled himself a cigarette. The headiness that characterized Massasoit tobacco filled his nostrils and mouth. The weeklong eschewal of his fine smoke had ended yesterday with the delivery of a small drum of Massasoit, and the lord had found his appetite for the plant to be ravenous.

A cigarette later, he deigned to dress himself in just a robe and slack trousers with slippers on his feet. It was too early in the day to worry about dressing up. The footman had said that his guest would be downstairs in the ante hall, where many visitors awaited their calls. It was a fine room to wait in, spacious and decorated with a generous bookshelf of novels and periodicals. When he first had come to this hotel, he had learned that it had actually been a library for one king or another. Sadly, the hotel as it was now had nothing of true worth for him to read, but he found many people enjoyed sitting in the room with a news daily or novel in hand.

Stepping into the ante hall, he found Constable Erchak seated on one of the high-backed lounge chairs, sipping from a teacup.

"Constable Erchak!" Lord Haphenasis said, approaching the lawman with an outstretched hand. The constable hastily set the cup down and took the lord's hand. The pair then sat. A serving man poured a cup for the lord. Picking it up, he was pleased to find rich black coffee inside.

"Lord Haphenasis. Pardon the early morning intrusion, but it's your business that I came so early to speak t'you about. I had considered getting a message to you, but seeing as how I was on my way nearby already, I thought I'd stop up and tell you in person."

"Tell me? Tell me what?"

"The other day, you'd passed the message to me to keep an eye out for anything odd. And, while I don't know if this counts, I thought I'd report it to you."

"Spit it out, man; we haven't got all day."

"Begging yer pardon, Your Lordship. The fact is, sir, that there've been a number of murders in the last week. Well, not all murders, really: suicides, actually. Such things are pretty common, especially in Sludge, but they've moved up to High Water, Furnace Way, First Street, and Hawthorne Place."

"Exactly how many are we talking about?"

"On average, we do a weekly tally of deaths and generally look at a hundred or so. Mind you, sir, it's a hard business to track down all the deaths and disappearances that hit these streets, but here, we're deep in spring. The deaths usually fall off from here, if only a little. We've got some rains coming in soon but, until then, in this weather, we're talking about the best time of year. Lifts the spirits and all."

"So, you're saying...?"

Constable Erchak pulled out a small ledger. "Yesterday, fifty-seven cases of spontaneous suicide, eight of which were with family at the time. Witnesses report just a 'daze' hitting them and, next thing you know, dead. Two days ago, forty-three. One body was found in the Bakery District's well. Another jumped off a roof. A third ran himself in with a pitchfork. The day before that, twelve cases. If these numbers keep going up, we're gonna have a hard time keeping track of these dead. You see what I'm getting at, my lord?"

"Sadly, I do. And, sadly, I think this is exactly what I had called on you to maintain vigilance about. You said that you are on your way to a recent death?"

"Yeah, just happened about an hour ago. I had the night shift, which is why I'm here."

"Please do not go anywhere until I have returned. I will be dressed in a jiffy."

****

The body in question was masked in a dry red seal, as if someone had dunked the woman into a vat of wax and held her under until she had expired. Suffocation and burning together must have made for a horrible death.

Certainly enough, when one of the junior constables cracked the wax from her face and hair, even her blank eyes were swollen with burns.

"When was it found?"

"About an hour or so ago and, as you can see, the rigor mortis has already begun to set in."

Lord Haphenasis took the dead woman's wrist in his and lifted it. It required some effort to do so; then, upon its release, it lingered in the air where he left it.

"We've got a man over here, claims to be her husband."

"Yes, yes, a moment."

Lord Haphenasis took hold of the woman's wrist again and closed his eyes. He explored her being with his mind and body, pushing outward with his arcane powers until he bumped up against the woman's soul. The edges were frayed but, for the most part, it was still intact. That meant he had not arrived too late to probe for whatever insight he might glean from her death.

Hastily, he erected an Ouaja to trap her soul in place. When it felt the touch of the mystical cage, the soul moaned in displeasure.

"Enough of that now," he told her. "I am here as a friend."

"Leave me be," she moaned, her incorporeal self blinking into a hazy mesh that might have convinced a lesser magus that she was escaping.

"I will ease your suffering once you answer several questions for me."

"I will do no such thing!" she roared, bearing down on him with a fanged threat. This, too, he waved aside, knowing full well that souls alone could do no harm.

"Yes, you will. And to convince you to take me on faith, please accept this humble offering." Souls were testy, tricky, and astral; upon the severing of their bodily ties, most dispersed among the myriad paths of the Veins. They appeared to hunger for a total immersion in the Veins' arcana as a fish yearned for water. Despite the threat of giving away all one's connection to the Veins, Necromancers taught that a dab of the Veins' energy would satiate a wary soul for a short time. Too much, and they would come to possess the magus. Too little and they would offer no aid whatsoever. Lord Haphenasis balanced the amount perfectly.

The woman's soul moaned with pleasure. "I will answer your questions so long as I am able."

"Thank you. My first is... how did you die?"

"In life, I was a chandler whose fingers had long ago grown numb to the burns that my hot wax caused. In the mornings, before my husband and children awoke, I would come down here from the loft above our workshop to start the fires that would boil our wax. Today, when the wax began to melt, I found myself drawn to the pot it was in. I gazed down into it and saw something... It was not me."

"Please describe it for me."

"It was a man's face. Long, gaunt, and handsome but with terrible eyes. I felt myself drawn closer to it, like I was going to kiss it. When I did, I felt the burn but could not push away from it. My hands... I pushed off the pot, but could not free myself. He pressed me into the pot, pushing me down as my hands and face melted, as wax filled my throat and nose."

"Had you ever seen the man before?"

"No. Nor from in a dream. It was sudden, so sudden..." she began to gaze off past Lord Haphenasis. Her time was nearly up.

"Thank you for your help. May the Veins quell your sorrow."

With the kiss of arcana that Lord Haphenasis gave to her, the soul dissipated into the air.

"You all right, milord?" Constable Erchak asked.

"Yes. The spirit of this woman had not yet discorporated. She has been sent on her way now."

"You actually... spoke to her?" a junior constable asked, his eyes bulging slightly.

"Constable Erchak, I would appreciate it if you kept your charges' attention focused on more relevant matters than what I am doing."

"Oy! You heard the man: find something better to be doing, or I'll have you scrubbing the pots back at the precinct."

"Sir!" the constable said, running off to investigate the pot that the dead woman had drowned in. "Will you be wanting to talk to the husband?" Constable Erchak asked, lighting up a cigarette.

"No. All he would be able to do is give his own account of the situation, which will be far inferior to anything I could theorize."

"What? You got a problem with a magus working this scene?" Erchak shouted to someone Lord Haphenasis could not see. "Bloody leeches, always wanting to see what's what. This is gonna be in the dailies today, I tell you that now."

Lord Haphenasis ignored him. With the woman's confirmation that the Possessor had, indeed, struck her, his work had just begun. Over the past week, he had called forth the Cataclysm's arcane vibration so often that he could recognize it by touch. All it took was a little concentration and... there it was, the little devil! A tiny ripple of residue that curled about, trapped in the recesses of the body's trap. It always worked this way. Merging with other beings always left something behind, no matter how meticulous the separation was—like a person leaving behind a hair or fingernail or dandruff.

As Lord Haphenasis rubbed the Possessor's psychic residue under his astral nose, he got a stronger whiff. Through this scent, he got a very brief, very intense connection with the Cataclysm. There! He looked at the crowd crowd just beyond the constable line which kept unimportant riff-raff from intruding on the scene. It was a woman, who was staring intently at him. He had no doubts that the Possessor looked out from those eyes.

Seven spells welled up inside him. Four struck the woman, two more missed entirely, and the last speared the soul of the killer but only superficially. When Lord Haphenasis arrived at the woman, she was sobbing, confused by her sudden imprisonment. All that remained of the Cataclysm was a crust of psychic skin.

"Was that him?" Erchak asked, rushing up with two of his men, their sabers already drawn.

"The killer, yes."

"He get away?"

"Indeed."

"Want me to swear for you, milord?"

It was not a complete loss. While the Possessor had gotten away, he had come one step closer to him. Lord Haphenasis drew a small glass bottle from his ruck and inserted the psychic skin into it. With this, it would make tracking the Possessor a simple task but, more importantly, through this interaction, Lord Haphenasis now knew exactly who the Cataclysm had been in life. All in all, it was a tremendously successful morning's work. "Thank you, Constable. But that is unnecessary. It is only a short matter of time before he is ours."

Chapter 22

WHIRL'S LECTURE HALL WAS EMPTY SAVE FOR ISHTOWER. HE had been coming back here every day since they had set up base in the Gilded Lion. It had begun after he and Lord Haphenasis had given their reports on the apprehension of the Butcher of Fitch. He knew that his mastery of the vibrations was not at the level of the lord's, and so sought out this room for a private refresher. One of the most important parts of his rehabilitation following his wife's death was his assignment as temporary warden in the Apocryptein. The first six months went so well that it had become a recurring feature of his life for the next two and a half years—up until its destruction the prior week. In the time he had spent in the Apocryptein, he had been assigned guardianship over the twelve prisoners and commanded to learn their vibrations.

"Why me?" he had asked when Skeleton Hamza had personally given him this assignment.

"You were an acclaimed Martialist for over twenty years, were you not?"

"I was," he had replied.

"And when the 713th Skeleton of our Order perished fourteen years ago, it was your prowess in Martialist skills that inspired your application to the aethir for the position, was it not?"

"Do you even need to ask this? There were seven of us in contention for the role, one among us was *you*. We sat in the Keyhall for a whole week without sleep or food while the Veins tested us each in weird ways that I still can't even begin to express."

"I remember it well. It was horrid to imagine how different my life would be with eyes. It affixed limitations that I would hate to even consider."

"And I saw myself without Rebubula and the kids...," he had trailed off, remembering too well what her death had been like. The stabbings going on and on. Seven years after the fact and it had still been too fresh in his eyes. The bottle that he had drowned himself in had not been enough to kill those memories. Hamza's hand fell on his shoulder. He was brought back to the conversation.

"The hallucinations we endured at the appointing were horrible."

"You were not cursed to live yours."

"No, but you were. For seven long years, I have allowed you to mourn her, but just as the Veins gave you the horror of Rebubula's death, they have told me that your mourning period is over. I know not what it is they have in store for us all, but I do know that a Martialist of the highest caliber is necessary. The day you returned to us, sober after these long years, I knew you were who the

Veins had considered. They have chosen you, Ishtower. That is why."

It had been enough for him. For many long years, he hated the Veins for giving him the vision of his wife's murder, and for a time his faith in the Veins had wavered tremendously. When his wife's death had finally come, it had been infinitely more horrible than the Veins had promised. It had destroyed him. For seven long years, he had relived the day again and again, too distracted to practice his arcana, too absorbed to look after his own children, too haunted to do anything but drink until he passed out. It was a dark time of indifference that he finally overcame after great difficulty. Only after a violent confrontation with his son, Ulcher, did he start the long journey back. With Ulcher's aid and the rekindling of his faith in the Veins, he had finally gotten over the physical and emotional addiction of alcohol and rejoined the world. Since then, his faith in the Veins had been unswerving and almost obsessive. It was something he did not openly decry, but the trust and faith was there, guiding him through each day and encouraging him onward each time his memory recalled Rebubula's death.

So he had gone to the Apocryptein and learned. He learned the stories of the Twelve and he learned their vibrations. Maintaining a sense of who they were in life, each one evoked a different emotional chord in him: the Lich, for example, tugged out a thread of pity from the dirge that was her vibration; the Whim was terrifying in its absolute disregard for the world's laws; the Tempest threatened unintelligible violence. None, however, brought out the hatred in him the way the Possessor did.

As a bully in his youth, he knew a bully when he saw

one. It was only after being put in his place by a larger bully that he understood just how horrible it was to be a victim. Much of what had broken in him was his belief that he was bigger, better, and badder than everyone else. In touching the vibration of the Possessor, he recognized that same cruelty in which he had once reveled. Every time he touched this vibration, he felt hatred for the Possessor and for who he, Ishtower, had been. In recognizing this, he understood exactly why Hamza had called on him to be the interim warden. By giving him a firm comparison of what he hated, he was provided a glimpse of how not to live his life.

So why did he keep coming back here, to Whirl's lecture hall, to replay this horrible vibration? At first, he thought it was to prepare his senses for the next of the Twelve that he and Lord Haphenasis would encounter. It had been a clear point that first day they were in the Gilded Lion. Because the second Cataclysm was right there in Reservwyresport, they would stay until they had apprehended it. Despite this, he found himself coming back here, taking advantage of Squite's or Yankee's ventilation. And here he would stand, listening, reaching out with his arcana. For what, he could not tell. Was it just to be prepared should he encounter this Cataclysm? Had he become so obsessed with this taste of true evil that he could not let it go? Or was it something more?

"Ishtower," a voice echoed through the massive room to him. Yankee sounded a lot like his uncle, save for far more clarity his voice. Without his teeth, Squite was sometimes hard to understand, but Yankee's soft voice was always precise and clear. It carried the same gentle cadence that another of his children, Aaron, possessed, and it brought with it implications of backward thought and disgusting habits. Ishtower did not dislike Yankee but, if his suspicions were ever confirmed, he would lose whatever respect he had for the man. Tolerance of a person's faults and acceptance of a person's depravity were two completely different things.

"Yankee. What can I do for you?"

"Lord Haphenasis has been looking for you. My uncle thought you might be here."

"Mastering the vibration as I have all week. What does his lordship want?"

"That, he didn't confide in me. I was instructed to bring you to him."

"Hopefully, it's a lead," he said, savoring the horrible anger he felt at the Possessor's scent one last time. He then released it into the general orchestra and ascended the stairs to where Yankee awaited him. The two walked largely in silence to the nearest Veinway. What had begun as a thin zone of arcanic weakness had been bolstered into a permanent gap that facilitated the ventilation from dimension to dimension. As with all Veinways in the Innervein, it was a direct line to Traumanfang. Yankee activated it with a tap of his fingers and the two stepped through.

They found themselves in the massive garden of the Gilded Lion. Ishtower nodded in satisfaction. Lesser Ventagists could only ventilate onto the actual Veins, but Yankee was able to move, even to here, at a midpoint a league between two of the Veins, seemingly without any difficulty.

"Nice. Where is he?"

"In the mess."

"Dining hall," Ishtower corrected. "A mess is just that: a mess. If you've ever been a solider you'd know the difference. The Gilded Lion's got a feasting place fit for kings." He slapped the Ventagist's shoulder and set off, realizing, as he walked, that he could do for some food. In the Innervein, he tended to lose track of his own physical desires. The Veins always seemed to sustain him while he was there.

As soon as Ishtower entered the well-lit room through its glass doors, Lord Haphenasis saw him and beckoned him over. The table was modestly set, with only a few porcelain dishes filled with rice and different vegetables. A small river catfish was cooking away in a pan over a portable fire. It smelled delicious and, as he sat, Ishtower served himself a generous portion from the animal's backside.

"Squite found you, did he?"

"Yankee," Ishtower corrected, blowing on a large chunk of white meat. His mouth was watering such that he almost shoved the juicy fish in without even waiting for it to cool.

"I saw him today."

"Yankee?"

"The Possessor."

Ishtower's chopsticks parted, and the juicy lump of fish plopped to the floor. "You what? Where? How? Did you get him?"

Lord Haphenasis set a small vial onto the table. Through its smoky transparent glass, a wisp of arcana whirled lazily. "This is psychic residue left over from my encounter. We have been using Hounds but, with this, not only can we pinpoint exactly where he will be but, if necessary, we can summon him to us."

There was genuine excitement in the pudgy man's face that Ishtower had never seen before. No, he had probably seen it, if he had allowed himself to look. With the confrontations they had endured over their long acquaintance, he had just seen the fat man as an obstacle, worse, a target. It had always been so easy to do. The man's idea of conversation was a lecture, and while he always seemed to know what he was talking about, he always spoke down to everyone, as if his shit didn't stink. No, everything about the man had been positively begging to be ridiculed. It was strange to think of him now as a real brother, one with value. Indeed, he found himself actually curious about the whole incident. "Lord Haphenasis, tell me everything."

And so he did. While the lord spoke, Ishtower ate with a fervor that matched the speaker's excitement. He even shared his theories of what the Possessor's goals were, those of causing chaos and strife to fuel his regeneration. According to the lord, the Possessor was already responsible for hundreds of deaths around Reservwyresport. At the rate he was going, it would only be a matter of days—maybe a couple weeks, at most—before he were strong enough to reconstitute his body.

"How is it that we didn't just kill this guy when we had the chance?" Ishtower asked, stabbing the leftover rice on his plate with a chopstick. "I mean, this guy, whoever he was—is, whatever—sounds like the worst possible thing that has ever lived. Why did we not just kill him?"

"How much do you know of the Nine Realms? I mean really know?"

"In what way?"

"No, that is the wrong question. Perhaps the better one is how much do you know of death?"

"Oh, come on," Ishtower snapped. "What do you think I am, a newborn babe?"

"Humor me," Lord Haphenasis replied, scratching the back of his neck, where the short hair of his head met the thickness of his shoulder.

"Fine. It largely depends on what religion the speaker is part of, but we of the Vein have witnessed the truth of it. Our souls may linger for a while before they enter the Veins to be recycled. It's all a part of the symbiosis of form and spirit that is the aether."

"And, if the soul is full of corruption, guilt, sadness, and anger?"

"They are drawn to the Yin, where they suffer their problems for eternity."

"What about those of amazing peace and contentment?"

"Capo calls them, the place of eternal peace and prosperity. Such as one can attain in spiritual form. 'Course, if you ask me, I'd much rather be split up and reborn through the Veins. It sounds much more pleasant than either of the other two options."

"To me as well, but the point is that those two alternatives that you have just now mentioned are exactly why we did not just kill the Cataclysms."

"I don't follow."

"Think about it," he plucked nine vegetables from the white porcelain bowl and set them on his plate. "What are these?"

"Vegetables?"

"Exactly, just like Capo, Traumanfang, and the Yin."

Ishtower patted the lord's shoulder. "I hate to burst your illusion, but they're not vegetables at all."

"I mean, just as these are all vegetables, the destinations of our souls are all the different realms of the Innervein."

"Yes?"

"Maybe a demonstration will clarify it for you. This potato chunk is Traumanfang, the cherry tomato is the Yin, the olive is Capo, and the broccoli head is the Innervein. You with me?" Ishtower nodded. "When a soul dies in the potato, they either stay or go to these two other places."

"I'm still with you."

"But, as with water, what if a stone gets in the path of the soul's journey? Then, instead of going from the potato to the cherry tomato, the soul would veer off and reach this chunk of taro."

"If I'm following, what does the taro represent?"

"The Blue Realm."

"So the soul would go off into the Blue Realm?"

"Precisely!"

"How is that a bad thing?"

"A realm populated with winged mischief-makers and elves? I hardly think such qualifies as a positive result."

"It's not all that bad. I mean, it is the realm of Nymphos, isn't it? It's said that they consume men two at a time."

"You do know what *consume* means, do you not?"

"Absolutely, and it has nothing to do with what you think it means."

It took the lord a minute. When he finally figured it out, his face scrunched up with distaste. "Oh. That. I will never understand men's fascinations with that."

"What's wrong with a little procreation? It's great for relieving stress."

"Procreation I understand. But the act of denigrating oneself to the basest of intimate contacts with another person seems like far too much trouble to be worth any possible benefits. Take the final results of said interaction into account and you are just asking for a lifetime of trouble."

"How can you say that?"

"Look at the monsters that that woman we're burdened with has pooped out!"

"'Pooped?'"

"Evacuated. Whatever."

"Are you drunk?"

"Is that not the pot calling the kettle black?"

"I only ask because you just said not one, but two of the stupidest things I've ever heard."

"And here I was, thinking that I could avoid your abuse for once. Never mind. Perhaps my description was too complex for you to understand in the first place."

"Hold on a sec, you hypersensitive git!" Ishtower said, grabbing Lord Haphenasis by the wrist. "That came out wrong. Can I help it that ragging on you is easier than having a real conversation with you? What I meant to say was, 'Are you serious about what you said?'"

"What of it?"

"How old are you?"

"Fifty-two or fifty-three. What of it?"

"Are you really telling me that you really have no idea what a woman is like?"

"Having observed a variety of relationships over the

course of my life, I can honestly state that the whole process holds no interest to me. Look at how wasteful it is: there is a painfully prolonged courting period followed by bloody messes, gooey explosions, and screaming children, to say nothing of being bound to a nagging shrew for the entirety of your miserable existence. Prove to me that my observation of the whole process is incorrect and perhaps I shall reconsider any prior conclusions I have relating to the whole deal."

Ishtower leaned back into his chair and stared blankly at the candle smoking on the table before him. "Actually, that sums it up pretty nicely."

"I rest my case."

"But, in all of that, you've left out the most important part: the love."

Lord Haphenasis scoffed. "Truly, are the drawbacks worth the transience of the emotion?"

"Just ask Vie. You've seen her with her children, haven't you?"

"Sadly. Their displays of affection are quite ill-setting."

"That's because you've never had it."

"What would I do with it?"

"Experience it." Ishtower's mind went back to the blows he and Ulcher had come to. In that mighty arcane confrontation, he had been beaten soundly. It was mortifying to go from one of great Martialist renown to one so handily beaten by such a young, inexperienced magus. Yet as he sat there in pain, he witnessed his son's anger turn into pity and finally regret. He knew that his son had beaten him up because there was no other choice. For all that, he understood that this was the boy's last-ditch attempt to bring change to a loved one. He saw that the boy had become a man during his oblivion. It was sobering. "Trust me, the love of a family is the greatest magic I've ever known."

The two sat in silence for what seemed a long time. Neither were very good at talking about feelings, and the flush of pride that Ishtower had in his son had filled the two with a mutual embarrassment, as if this were a topic most inappropriate for them.

At last, with an awkward glance at Lord Haphenasis's plate, Ishtower remembered the vegetables. "So, the vegetables?"

"The what? Oh! Yes! Our souls might pass on to another of the realms. Just like in Sanhueza's *Song of Sirite*. Have you ever read that?"

"I've seen it in your library, but I never got to it."

"It was the biography of Sirite, a magus born in Domani, whose most notable experience was how he was befriended by dragons who had been living here at the time. With Sirite's death, his dragon friends captured his soul and returned to their own world with it. As the story continues, Sirite actually returns to Traumanfang to visit his old friends before returning to Lamytal once and for all. The amazing thing is that when he was reborn on Lamytal, he was born into a dragon form, along with all the benefits that come from it.

"Now consider how much trouble each of the Twelve Cataclysms has caused on Traumanfang. Imagine what would happen if each soul were released to be dispersed among the aether. If none from the other eight realms were paying attention, the souls would eventually disperse and everything would be copacetic. But what if someone were paying attention? They might be able to steal away the souls and bequeath on them the skills and powers of their native realms. Coupled with the inherent abilities that these monsters already possess, it would elevate a danger to the level of an apocalypse."

"So that's why they weren't killed."

"Exactly."

"Then we need to track this bastard down as soon as possible."

"As I said before, we have probably a week or two at most. But with this," Lord Haphenasis shook the little glass container like a bell, "Tracking Izzard will be no problem at all."

A mouthful of coffee exploded from Ishtower's mouth. "Izzard? *Izzard!!* Maketh-el have mercy upon us! No. Calm. It can't be him. He was sentenced to an eternity of crucifixion in the sun. Lord Haphenasis, please clarify something for me, since I could never uncover just who the Twelfth Cataclysm really was. The Possessor— who you've got a fragment of in that little glass there— doesn't happen to be Malek Izzard, destroyer of the Fifth Transport of the Yo Vein, does he?"

"As a matter of fact, yes."

"Son of a bitch!" Ishtower was on his feet, grabbing for his chair. The rage inside him made the world disappear for a moment and, when the spell passed, he had only a single leg of his chair in hand. The two tables before him were a shattered wreck of splinters and metallic fragments, with food splashed out in a radius from him. Despite this, he was feeling much better, far more in control. He pulled his long black hair from his face and turned to regard Lord Haphenasis. "I knew I knew it! I knew I recognized that damned vibration! Hamza promised me that he would be killed for what he did to me – to us. How is he not dead?"

"Ah yes, now that you mention it, I think I remember mention of your name in conjunction with his apprehension. The official story was that he had been sent to crucify in the sun, yes. The reality is that we could not let another dimension get their hands on him. That would be unfair to us and to the other Realms. You should have seen him when he came to me. He had been starved, beaten and tortured. His vibration rattled with disharmony, as if his very spirituality had been flayed and reconnected. To say he was a pitiable sight would under credit just how poor a state he actually was in."

"So what? You took pity on him?" Ishtower looked disgusted.

"On the contrary, I demanded to know why he had been brought to me. I wanted that foul creature near me no more than I wanted the pox or the Kassernian Flu. I demanded that Hamza fulfill the punishment he had promised the monster. But you know how he can get sometimes. He rooted in and said that the punishment that the council had decided upon was unrealistic. Even if we were able to bind him to the sun, it would incinerate him in a heartbeat and we would be back to where we were before, with Malek Izzard loose upon the Nine Realms. So he became the Twelfth."

"Then today, we will find and capture that son-of-a-bitch once and for all."

"Have you any theories on a method of capture?"

Ishtower felt a wave of true evil well up inside him. "I have had a decade to plan my revenge on him. So, yes, I do."

Chapter 23

Ishtower's list of revenge on Malek Izzard consisted of twenty-six methods of torture from A to Z. Sadly, many of them were merely rhetorical due to the impracticality of their logistics. Acquiring (and taming) a Gergia sand snake was impossible due to the simple fact that such snakes were so massive that they left dunes in their wake. The revenge part would come from feeding Izzard to one, and laughing as he were slowly ground through the spinning serrations of its deep-layered teeth. Other revenge methods were more practical but far less satisfying. Plan "M" hoped to track down a family member of Izzard and possess him. It would be a torturous death at his family's hands. Plan "L" was named because of the ludicrous nature of it: to flay Izzard one finger at a time until at last, there was nothing but a quibbling, bawling child, begging for his life to end. There were more passive forms, like Plan "X," which was a simple forgiveness, but such emotionally redeeming plans were far from Ishtower's agenda this day.

No, he wanted revenge. He wanted to hurt Izzard.

The first step of this was to sample the psychic residue that Lord Haphenasis had bottled from his earlier encounter. It was a complex scent, but one that had become familiar over the past week of study. The emotional roil came back to him. He could feel Izzard's mind seeping into his own, almost as vividly as he had on that fateful day so long ago. Time had not cured him of the Cataclysm's touch as well as he had hoped it would.

"Did you hear me?" Lord Haphenasis asked, breaking Ishtower's concentration.

"What?" He looked around. The evening sky was slightly overcast, threatening spring rain. In spite of the rickety quality of the shanties beneath their feet, he felt very sure of their footing on the flat pathway stretching from this abode to the next. Beneath them, raised torches illuminated a narrow street still filled with people in various states of coming and going. The tropical quality to this city made a more comfortable exploration than his home of Gimhae, which played host to mountains of snow for nearly half the year. Yet he found even this springtime heat to be restrictive. To balance it out, he had adopted a more freeing, open-shouldered robe, leaving his arms bare. As the robe tied shut about his waist, his hairy chest was covered—a fact of southern sensibility that he never understood. In the heat that comes from summertime, should the residents of Reservwyresport not be encouraged to wear minimal clothing?

"I said that the mutt has tracked him. Look."

The silvery totem glittered brightly as it hastened down the street. The two magi had been following it for the past thirty minutes, waiting for it to pinpoint the main bulk of Izzard's vibration. This part of town had been built at the base of the floodplain before it rose steeply into the gentle hills that marked the rest of the city. Because of its dropped location, the wealthier denizens of the slum had built their abodes into the roofs and alleys of those below. It made traipsing around after Izzard a bit of a challenge but, with the mutt's shiny body, easily recognizable to them even from a great height, it was not beyond their ability. Before the hunt began, Ishtower had blessed it with a ward that prevented the more value-oriented denizens from absconding with it.

As the more physically maneuverable of the pair, Ishtower took the lead, racing across the rooftops, under awnings and wooden ladders, as he chased after the mutt. The clouds that Lord Haphenasis used could be quick on a straightaway, but in the labyrinthine levels of the rooftops, it had nothing on his own maneuverability.

For a moment, Ishtower thought he had lost the totem. He was at the crest of a roof, where one side of it angled down sharply over a short porch. Creeping toward the edge of the crest, he peered down. Three levels straight down to the street and there, trotting along, reflecting the orange glow of the lights, was the mutt.

Something about it was different. It wagged its tail once, twice, and sat down facing a doorway.

A literal alarm went off in Ishtower's head.

"There he is," Lord Haphenasis said, breezing up to him. "You feel that, do you not?"

"Nice modification to its enchantment."

"How do you want to take this?"

"You're asking? Well. Isn't this a day just full of surprises?"

"I failed once. Let us see if you can put one of your plans to work for us."

"Most of those plans, sadly, require him to already be in our possession. But there are one or two that don't require that. Since he fled from you earlier, it's a safe bet that he is recognizant of danger. That means a certain degree of self-awareness."

"Of which we are aware if he has been manipulating these deaths that Constable Erchak was bringing to us."

"Right. It's likely to assume that he would recognize you if he saw you. Which means I take the direct route. You come in from the back or roof, or whatever this place has. Try to set up a soul net. But do it quietly. If he hears you, he'll bolt."

"Should I tell Yankee to get backup ready?"

"No. Hold off on that for now. It could take a while to drive him out. Whatever it is he's doing in there might distract him enough for two of us, but if we call in a remote party, he'll know it and will be gone before we can even corner him."

"On that note, are you sure you will be able to distinguish him from the other patrons?"

"Yes. One doesn't forgot someone like him easily." *Screams... movement...* "Besides, if you were to take the entrance, you'd stick out like a sore thumb."

"May the Veins guide you."

Ishtower nodded and descended.

The mutt turned its panting face to him as he lifted the hood of his sleeveless cloak. This place was as seedy as they came, halfway between nowhere and despair, right around the corner from desperation, and wedged between isolation and oblivion. It was a place he had known all too well just a few years ago. His body longed for the physical memory of that time, where a night began with a sip and lasted until the sun beat down on his face and he slowly came to. It was an easy role for his body to slip into.

The room was low and dark, with large wooden benches jutting out on one side of the room, across from a long bar on the other. The base of a stairwell lay just at the edge of vision behind a spattering of men drinking away their lives. Stepping through the doorway, he heard a dull thud coming from upstairs, no doubt where he needed to go. However, none who came here ever reached the back rooms without first paying the entrance fee.

When the bartender looked up at him, he would see just another bum, the weight of experience and loneliness bearing down on him. The stagger that carried Ishtower across the room was a drunk's walk and his words struggled to make the sounds he needed.

"What was that?" the bartender asked.

Ishtower dreaded the words he had to say. Having one so close, one that he had actually paid for, might undo the years of therapy his children had set him down. In a place like this, where he had to fit in, there was no option. One did not simply order a mug of water.

"Beer."

The wooden pitcher set before him stank of sweat and memory. In the dim lighting of the place, it was a dark amber with a thin line of foam. Stale and bitter. There was only one way to deal with this; a brother warrior had once described *quaffing* as a drinking art form where one spilled more down their shirt than they got in their mouth. It was a more colorful description of the art than just throwing back a pint.

Ishtower took a deep breath, opened his mouth, and quaffed the drink until his body was soaked in the stale stink of the drink and his lips were just barely wet. The bottom of the pitcher, however, was empty of all but dregs.

Forcing a burp, he flicked a copper chit at the bartender and asked for another.

Then he could get started.

This jug took longer to go "down." Plenty of time for him to close his eyes and feel out for the vibrations. The whole process was made more difficult by the thudding that came from upstairs, but it was clear that Izzard was not in this room or even on this floor.

"Loud night," he grunted to the bartender.

"Got a problem with it, go somewhere else."

A woman screamed. The bartender frowned.

"No problem, just wondering if you got any more girls up there."

"Cost you five for curiosity."

"How much up there?"

The bartender said nothing. This was standard business for dives like this. They set the trap and come what may, whatever business was or was not transacted upstairs, a profit was still to be made. Ishtower grumbled as he set down five copper chits and rose from his stool. Beside the stairwell, in a small alcove, a bouncer flipped cards to entertain himself. He glared at Ishtower as he stepped past and up the creaky steps to the second floor.

At the top a pudgy woman in a nightdress read a narrow book. She was marginally attractive under the painted eyes and blushed cheeks. Below that, her small exposed breasts looked out of place between her thick arms and double chins.

"Eyes down, son," she said. "Why bother with a face when you've got nipples meeting you?"

"What've you got?"

"Depends on your mood."

Another crash set the entire building to a minor shake. A scream and a tittering chuckle followed. Ishtower cocked an eye at the hostess.

"Business as usual, I reckon."

"Is it a problem?"

The hostess looked him over.

"If it was, what would you do about it?"

"This happen a lot?"

A flash of pity flickered in the corner of her mouth.

"How often?"

"Business is business. They always come for her."

"*They?*" This took Ishtower by surprise. "How many we talking about?"

"Two. Brothers. Tried them once, but they didn't like me for one reason or another. Can't complain, though. I seen how Wesselle looks after they're done with her. They got some odd tastes, those ones."

"How much and how often?"

"Thirty per visit. Few times each time they're in port. Last time was two seasons ago. Sailors, I reckon."

Ishtower reached into his robe and withdrew two silver coins. "Payment for the next year, if one is who I'm looking for."

The hostess's face lit up and fell at once. It was really quite charming. "Um... you a hunter?"

"In a manner of speaking."

"Just make sure they're out b'fore you hurt them. There's only so much she can take."

Ishtower nodded, not entirely sure what the woman meant. He started down the hall. Doors lined the narrow hallway. A few quiet moans and grunts rocked several of the most nearby rooms. The show was in the fourth room on the left. Ishtower paused at the door to try for Izzard's vibration. There was no doubt. One of the three in the room was him.

"Rebubula, this is for you," he whispered.

The door exploded into the room and Ishtower rushed in closely behind it, ready to strike any or all of the three. He took it all in at a glance. The place reeked of feces and urine and he did not even want to think of the wet floor. The woman, bruised and teary in face, was on the bed, her legs spread wide, two hands deep inside her. One brother—narrow, thin, wiry—at her crotch, working himself into her, the other—also wiry, but the type that was the pure muscle beaten into a slick form—hammering away at the first brother from behind. The sheer oddity of the scene made Ishtower pause.

For a fleeting moment, all in the room had the look of startled deer, unable to comprehend what was being seen. Then Ishtower moved with all the speed he could muster. He was at the first brother's side, pressing finger-tips into pressure points, collapsing him to the ground with barely a grunt. The second brother would be more trouble, what with the awkwardness of his exploration of Wesselle, but a couple of jabs made his arms as supple as a cloth. Slowly, so as not to injure the girl—for she looked to be barely older than his youngest daughter—he extracted the man's hands from her insides. He almost vomited when he realized how the man's hands were inserted.

"Are you all right?" he asked in order to push back the bile he felt creeping up his throat.

The girl's eyes were wild as she stared at him in shock and a certain revulsion. She was trembling from head to toe.

As one, all three groaned and writhed. Ishtower stared, confused. Then the girl was on him, scratching, biting, and beating, the way an animal would attack.

"The Four Hells?" he swore, pushing the girl off of him. She landed hard on the smaller of the two brothers and they grunted as one. The man was immobilized, trapped in his own body. It meant that Izzard was also trapped within. He had him, so why was the girl flipping out? "Girl, I don't have patience for this. You're hurt and bleeding. I have money for you."

Her eyes showed no understanding of his words. She leapt up with a shaped wooden rod in hand and struck Ishtower across the face. Stars danced in his eyes as another blow hit his back. The blows hurt! A prismatic shield prevented the next blow as he got his bearings and kicked the girl's leg out from under her. She fell with a soggy thump. Before she could move again, he bound her in an arcane mesh.

"Stay there, you crazy kid."

The bigger of the two brothers was completely coherent, staring at him with murder in his eyes. There was no doubt. He was staring at Malek Izzard.

"Do you know who I am, monster?" He drew up a glowball to illuminate his face.

The man's expression did not change.

"Are you self-aware enough to remember who you are?"

"Yesssss," the man hissed.

"Do you remember where you were for the past decade?"

"Trapppped."

"Yes, you are. Pressure points. They trap you in these bodies. And this, this is just the start." Ishtower pressed a finger to the man's forehead. "Even if you don't remember me, I remember you. This charnel house is nothing compared to what you put me through. And I know what works against you. I know your manipulations and how to stop them." To demonstrate, Ishtower blasted the man with concentrated mental arcana, dangerous to the mind and soul, but harmless to the body.

All three screamed as the larger brother's head whiplashed backward with such force that it cracked against the floor. They squirmed on the floor as if three large fish were thrashing about for their very life. It was then that Ishtower realized his mistake. Izzard was not limited to just one brother. He had split his consciousness between all three.

The girl was getting to her feet. Ishtower lunged for the girl and nailed her pressure points, dropping her to the floor once again. Standing over the girl, he looked over his opponents and considered his options. The brothers were still thrashing, but the girl was sobbing in a way she had not before.

Ishtower drew a circle in the air and spoke into it. "You'd better get in here. Second floor. Fourth door on the left."

The girl was helpless to push him away as he inspected her eyes. The madness that had forced her frenzied attack against him had fled. Instead, there was only agony. To her cries of pain, he picked her up and set her back down on the bed, where he covered her in the cleanest part of the single filthy sheet in the room.

He knelt down between the two brothers and flipped them over so that they could look at him. "You're in pain. Good. Now we've just begun something here. Unless you want to suffer an eternity of agony, you'll pull all of yourself back into these bodies."

"I knoooow yoooo..." the smaller brother whined through a gap-toothed mouth.

"I'm glad. I'd hate for you to wonder why you're being tortured." Pressing his thumbs against both men's foreheads, he blasted them with another massive shot of psychic energy. They screamed. "Now pull back."

"Nooo."

Again he hit them together. Each time was a rush. The frustration he had felt at the bar, so tantalizingly close to his old habits, had been redirected. For so long, there had been no hope of extracting revenge, but here he was —Izzard—in his grasp. He hit them again. A shudder of satisfaction crept up his spine. Another. His breathing became heavy, as if he had been working outside, shoveling snow, chasing after prey. Again. The two brothers were barely conscious, their eyes glazed but for the glimmer of horror that was Izzard.

"You like that?" Ishtower spat in their faces. "You like this?"

He pressed his thumbs against their heads again. One more shot might be enough to knock these elements of Izzard's persona out. They were already trapped within the bodies, but he hesitated. It was an instinctual response, one borne from having to step back from one bottle too many. During his convalescence, he was taught that anything overly fun needed to be looked at from a distance. As a Martialist whose focus was shatterpoints, he could not hold himself separate from the rest of the world. If he truly deserved his title and powers, he had to look at himself as intensely as he looked at anything else. What he saw shocked him: he was erect, unleashing vengeance without consideration of the host bodies with an almost lustful passion. There were waves of energy coursing from him to the naked, bloody, broken brothers before him.

"You son of a bitch," Ishtower said, pushing his will against the Cataclysm to get up. "You've been feeding off me!"

"You have no idea how lovely you taste," the smaller of the brothers moaned, his voice far clearer than it had been earlier.

"What have I done?"

"Far worse than that cold spring day so long ago," the other brother said. "You've aged, Ishtower."

"No."

The brothers panted in unison, their bodies effecting the almost sexual satisfaction that came from the absorption of Ishtower's energy. He stepped back from them, disgusted. He had done his part in trapping this chunk of Malek Izzard's soul in these two. It was only a matter of time before these two larger chunks of his soul summoned the lesser parts to it. This was only a brief respite. He would ask Haphenasis for aid in the capture and containment of the third part.

Just as he resolved to do so, he heard a heavy step in

the hallway. The floorboards squeaked and he saw the lord's shadow fall into the room.

"Glad you made it. Let's wrap these two up and..."

Crack!

It was not Lord Haphenasis at the door but the bouncer he had seen earlier. A heavy metal cudgel flashed in the candle light as his head struck the floor. With unconsciousness beckoning, Ishtower wondered how he could have been so careless as to be bested twice in one day by someone who had been dead for over a decade.

Chapter 24

VIE'S TRAINING WAS MAKING PROGRESS. SHE HAD LEARNED TO identify some of the different vibrations of life and had begun to summon them into her body. It was not a comfortable process because so far it left her with a dire need to pee, but she assumed it would improve with time. Ishtower said that was what always happened when you filled your body with arcana. It created a pressure within the body that was initially identified in the bladder. Over time, she would learn to spread that pressure out over the entirety of her body until she could use it for whatever purposes she wanted.

"Because you are a dragon, however, the means with which you channel and release this energy could be a manner none of us had ever thought to use before."

It was not very reassuring.

This evening, she was practicing how to channel the energy in her body into different parts. Of course, nothing she did seemed to work very well. The energy burned down her arms, but then it fizzled out without anything to show for it save for a faint glowing of her silvery blue-black scales.

"Where are you, Ishtower?" she mumbled into the darkness. The day's activities were fast creeping up on her and her tiredness was beginning to make her as grumpy as her daughter had been that morning. The poor thing had finally reached the end of her stir-madness, and as such things did with the girl, it came out in a verbal explosion.

"Momma, if I don't get outta here, I'm gonna *asplode*! It's not fair that the boys can all go out and have their fun; I need to get out, too. So can we go out, Momma? Please, can we?"

Vie had given her half a dozen suggestions, and to each, the girl had patiently explained in the specific detail that she was so good at that they had already been done. She had set a magus' foot on fire. Another she had entertained with a half jillion questions before the magus accidently released an enchanted wombat into the hotel that doubled again each time it ran into something. At least chasing them all down for the magus had given the boys and the Butcher a great time. And at the end, a small group of magi had personally come to Vie, dragging a screaming Bel with them.

"Your child has been rooting about our quarters," a bespectacled magus said from a bushy moustache so thick that his mouth was completely invisible. "You'd be wise to keep her better udner wraps, lest something horrible happen to her."

"Is that a threat?"

"No," came the answer from the bobbing moustache. "It is a statement. We deal with the great mysteries of existence and it would be a shame if your child were lost to them."

Vie had thanked the group of magi and after they had departed, explained to Bel that theft was something that one should only do when there was no other option.

"Is that why you were in Lord Haphenasis's tower in the first place?"

"Partially," Vie had admitted. "Your Auntie Yue said she could look after you but I was sick of never having enough to eat. I'll be damned if you have to suffer through your childhood like I had. To that end, I was hoping to make enough to get out of Sludge."

"We're gonna leave Sludge?" Bel asked, awed by thte notion.

"And are we not living out of that dungheap?"

"Yeah, but that's different."

"The means are, but the results aren't. Trust in your mother, girl. She knows what's about."

"So what was your plan?"

So Vie gave in to her girl's request to wander about. A short time later found the pair dressed in the fine clothing that they had found in their closets, two ladies made beautiful for a day of exploration. As they walked around the city with a sense of casual indifference, they talked about everything, from Vie's hopes and dreams, and of finding a small country home, to Bel's revelation that by the time the magi found her this morning, she had already swiped a silver snuff box, a deck of painted cards, and a glass sculpture.

Vie was proud of her daughter's skill. To steal three

items before getting caught was a sign of a future expert. Of course, she did not tell Bel this. Instead, she told the girl that she could sell them.

"Can I really?" she asked, her black eyes growing large with excitement.

"But it's up to you how much you get from them. Pawn sellers aren't easily won over. You gotta be smart about it."

Bel got more for the cards than Vie had expected but in the other two was out-haggled by the seller. Still, it was a victory for the girl and as a reward for the job well-done, they had spent the whole morning shopping—not street shopping, but real, in-store shopping—and giving their critical opinion on everything they came across, whether for sale or on display. It had been nice to not need to worry about what they would scrounge up for dinner. In fact, they had actually splurged and purchased food when they became hungry: on a pork pie for lunch and a pair of apples that were so juicy, Bel let it dribble down her chin and pretended to be a dragon feasting on a cow.

While they were out, they walked down to Sludge and checked on the repairs of the Released Stout and to see if Vue had returned yet. Most pleasure houses would be allowed to fester or be taken over by people with power, but luckily the Stout was a place of its own power; of the kind that certain people would mourn if something permanent happened to it. Vie was not surprised to see a labor man standing out front with a sawhorse and a saw. Next to this was a stocky man with massive fists.

"How go the repairs?" Vie had asked of the pounder.

"Slow and cheap," he replied brusquely. Then, looking at who was actually talking to him, his attitude changed a bit. "Hello! Haven't seen you around here before. Are you one of the ladies who lives here?"

"I have spent the night from time to time."

"Really? To work or to sleep?"

Vie smiled back at his pleasant flirtations. She knew how beautiful and classy the clothing and cosmetic powder on her cheeks and under her eyes made her look. "Does it really matter?"

"I ain't no dunce, ma'am. I know what this place is. All I'm saying is that a pretty lady like you? Yeah, I think I'd start coming here regular-like if you were working here."

"Pretty? Me? You silly, kind man! But if you think I'm good on the eyes, you should see my friend, Yue."

"Wanna tell me about her?"

"Oh, she's a bit taller than me and is a little plumper, but in the right places. She's never been a mother, like I have, and is as sleek as a virgin."

"Do tell!" The man had completely lost interest in his work. The laborer who had been sawing stopped to overhear. A third man stood at the door.

"If you see her, you would recognize her. She's got a thin slip of golden fur."

"And just where does she have it?"

Vie let out a snort of feigned shock. "You naughty man! You'll give a lady a heart attack with talk like that."

"No disrespect meant, m'lady."

Vie smiled broadly to let him know that she was just teasing him. "Well, if you're gonna be all cute about it... Yue's got that lovely fur all over her body, she does, except for her head, which she keeps long. When she is at work, she sometimes lets it fall. It's like a golden waterfall."

"She sounds amazing."

"You haven't seen her around here, have you?"

"Someone like that, I'm sure I'd recall."

"That's a shame. If you see her, would you tell her that Vie is staying at the Gilded Lion and that she should come visit me when she can?"

"Lady, it would be a pleasure. And what are you all looking at? You never seen a pretty lady? Get back to work!"

Vie joined her daughter where she had been playing with a street kitten. "Auntie Yue's not here. I have one more stop to make. You up for it?"

"Yeah. I got what I needed." Bel slipped her hand in her mother's. "Guess what? I found out from Suki that that man with those little wings that don't work, that her mother's been letting stay with them, jumped out a window."

"Really?"

"He's dead. But Suki said she's not sad. He never talked to her, but just looked at her strange, like she was a strange little duck.

"Can I get one of those fried bluefins? Since we have that money from earlier, I know you love them, too. Thanks!

"But even that's not the strangest thing. I mean, what's the greatest things in the world? For people, that is?"

"Fried bluefin on a stick?" Vie asked, taking a bite of her river fish snack.

"Dogs. At least that's what everyone says. Dogs are girl's best friend, and I think they're right because, if all dogs were like Dell's bulldog, I think all of them would be fun and smooshy-faced and cuddly and amazing company. But that's what makes this so strange. A couple days ago, Dell's dog disappeared and she was downright depressed."

"Well said."

"Thank you! I been practicing. She thought somebody had taken the dog, maybe one of those gross sailors like that one there— see how skinny he is? *Bleagh*! So she went down to the docks to see and what do you know, but no one knew anything about it. So she went down to the beaches to see if maybe he decided to go fishing there and had no luck there either, so finally, she just started walking. She got distracted by a seagull that was squawking at a cat and as it flew away, she looked up. Do you know what she saw?"

"Tell me."

"Her dog! But it wasn't just hanging out, panting like it does 'cause it's too hot here for it. It was downside-up, speared like this," she said, holding up the remains of her bluefin on a stick. "It was on one of those weird weathervane things that show which way the wind is blowing. Isn't that crazy?"

Vie agreed with her excitable daughter. "Now, listen, honey. I have to go into a store near here. I need you to stay here. Will you be okay for a little while without me?"

"Mother, please. You forget who you're talking to."

Vie kissed her daughter. "No, I didn't. I just wanted to make sure that nobody switched you for a changeling."

Despite her brave words, leaving Bel alone on the street had been an uncomfortable experience. Bel's tales of the oddities going on were not the only ones she had been privy to of late. Something was certainly hitting the city, and it was something that she did not want to think about. She knew that Bel was a resourceful kid, streetwise and so used to commanding others that she had no fears when she could use her tongue to her advantage. Still, the sooner she got this taken care of, the better.

Galym was the man who had started all this. An unimpressive man to look at, he was a master of numbers and coin. He had carved for himself a sizeable import/export business in Sludge and while he had some political influence over the shipping orders down at the docks, he was not one to push his business over onto others. Instead, he let the bigger fish battle it out while he quietly benefitted from the dregs that both left behind. The man seemed to know of everything and everyone, while actively participating in nothing. It was this deception that made him so potentially dangerous. While others were busy engaging their political squabbles, he was sneaking in and taking whatever he could find.

That was why it was no surprise when he had sought her out. The first theft was a simple burglary, one that impressed him, not just for how well she did it, but also with the value of the item. He promised her then and there that she would have work whenever she needed it. Since then, it had been the odd job that never pushed her too deeply into any bad situation. Because of his connections, her cat burglary went largely unnoticed yet was well-compensated.

Until this last job went so horribly wrong.

Vie took a deep breath before climbing the steps toward his third-level apartment. She had never failed him before and, while he had looked out for her in the past, there were always limits as to the generosity of a certain type of employer. One thing that encouraged her to take the slow steps up was the satisfaction at how well things were progressing with Ishtower and her dragon aspect. It was insurance that this meeting go the way she hoped.

Galym's majordomo, Tylire, opened the door when she knocked. The little man's pug nose and birthmark around the eye made him look remarkably dog-like.

"Miss Vie!" he said with his customary high-pitched squeal. "Isn't this a pleasant surprise? After you left us the other night, I feared the worst. I trust you are well."

"Quite well, Tylire. Is Galym home?"

"With an apprentice, I believe, but when has that ever stopped your beauty's welcome?"

Closing the door behind them, Tylire waddled off down the comfortable sitting room of the apartments, toward the back, where Galym did his business. The "office" was a wide room with an opened patio that looked out onto the river below. From here, one could look out at all the goings-on of the riverside ships and across the river toward the farmlands opposite. Facing west, it also made an ideal spot from which to enjoy a sunset. Galym was exactly where Vie expected him to be, cross-legged on his couch, with his fingers resting on a soft pillow, comfortably held by a manicurist. He was dressed in a bathrobe while his long pink hair was invisible under a bathing cap, his face covered with rejuvenating mud, his eyes hidden behind cucumbers. Plain as the man might be (despite the hair), he certainly had a taste for the finer pleasures of beauty-making.

"Master Galym," Tylire said, entering the room. "Miss Vie has come to call."

"My dear! Come in, come in. You'll forgive my preoccupation, won't you? Hmm? Do tell me you are well."

"I am, thank you, Galym."

"Oh, this is such a pleasure to hear your voice. When word of the tragedy up on the hill reached us down here, we were so worried. All I could think of was your beautiful face, those wonderfully mournful eyes of yours. It would be so horrible if you were unable to return to us."

Vie settled down in one of the easy chairs spread throughout the room. Galym's preoccupation with pleasure made him an ideal host, one who always saw to the comfort of his guests. To that end, a servant was almost immediately beside her, pouring her a tall crystal goblet of white wine.

"It was... an experience," she admitted, taking a small sip of the beverage. Bitter yet with a hint of fruitiness. She liked it.

"And what of that beastly magus? Did you have to reckon with him? Perhaps you brought about his end? Hmm?"

"Galym!" Vie laughed. "No, there was no violence like that. Though, I have to admit, I understand all too well why you warned me about him."

"Those magi are dangerous people. I hope you'll have no more dealings with them in the future."

"That's unlikely."

Galym sighed. "More's the pity. They are such a nuisance. But enough about them. I can only assume that you are here now, so late after the job, because you had no chance to slip away previously."

"Yes, that is true."

"And what of your responsibility?"

"Are you asking me what happened?"

"My dear, you insult me! Of course I know what happened. I merely ask about your responsibility to me for the item we had discussed."

Vie pulled a large ruby from her pocket. It looked nothing like the crystal that Galym had shown her the day of the break-in, but its appraisal today had set its value upwards of a small cargo galley. "The crystal you wanted is gone. The circumstances of that night destroyed it. I brought you a gift in apology, however. It's not the same as the gem you wanted, but it's large and valuable and special."

"It's not so unique that it will indict me, is it?"

"I doubt it. Its former owner has probably never been to this part of Reservwyresport."

"Dare I ask where you found it?"

"One of the magus where I am staying was a little too careless when he called me in to interview."

"About?"

Vie held her tongue. She had never really trusted the man seated across from her. When she first had started making the plans to leave this city behind, he had been her first choice for the means. Assessing her decision, he had come up with the single job. He had given her an image of the crystal he wanted from the Apocryptein and had provided her with the details of the magus'—Lord Haphenasis's—departure that day, and she owed the man for all the help he had given her but, despite all that he had done, she could still not bring herself to tell him of her recent discovery. To his credit, he was smart enough to let it drop.

"Well, I'm sure it's lovely," he said, still indifferently blind behind the cucumbers. "I thank you. But a gift does not excuse the small problem of the artifact that I had commissioned stolen. That crystal was priceless."

"Was it really that valuable?"

"To a collector, each item is of endless value."

"I meant to you."

Galym withdrew his hands from his manicurists and plucked the cucumbers off his eyes. He carefully set them down on a small silver tray beside him and shooed the girls from the room. His pale silver eyes stared hard at Vie. "Are you asking if I wanted the item for myself or a client?"

"There are no clients, Galym. Everything I have ever stolen for you has been for you. I've seen you wearing those golden occlot earrings I stole three years ago. The yycrab silk robe has been worn by a girl or two of yours. You're even still wearing the dragon-crowned ring I first stole for you."

Galym's smile was not the embarrassed, caught-in-the-act one Vie had expected from normal people. This was more a smirk of satisfaction. The palms of his hands came together in a dull clap that kept the newly beautified fingertips apart. "Oh, aren't you the darling with eyes more precious than platinum. Well said! Yes, I've been enjoying the results of your labors. I have for years. You have always had such exquisite tastes that it would have been a shame to merely pawn them off on a philistine with no appreciation for real beauty."

"So answer me something. In all this time, with a few exceptions (which were pretty safe), you've more or less let me pick out my own targets. Why the sudden change? What was so important about this crystal that you justified sacrificing me to get it?"

As Galym stared at Vie, she realized that her voice

had risen as she spoke. She was furious in a way she had not even expected. So much had happened that it was not until this moment that she knew all this could have been avoided if he had just stuck to their previous arrangement. Just as Lord Haphenasis had tried taking out his anger by making her a scapegoat, she felt the urge to claw out this man's eyes for unleashing hell upon the world.

Galym took her anger with the same irritating deliberateness that he took everything. Rising from the deep velvet cushions of his couch, he poured himself a tall glass of wine and stood over Vie. Every step was perfectly placed with the utmost grace and dignity. Most other men she had seen, who carry themselves with such appreciation for the finer details of life, tended to enjoy other men's company, but Galym was different. He was a dandy whose desire for women was virtually insatiable. As he stood above her, delicately sipping his wine, she felt tremendously self-conscious, as if he were evaluating her for a sale. It was an old, familiar feeling that she had long ago hoped to leave behind.

"Come join me outside, dear."

On the porch the air was scorching hot, but the uncharacteristically cool breeze dulled the potency of it. Galym stood out by the banister that separated the porch from the streets below. The general noise of this part of Sludge was far weaker than that of the rest of this dump; it created a certain illusion of privacy despite there being none to anyone who opted to look up. Vie lingered by the door, as far from this man as she trusted to come, lest she give into her desires and scratch his eyes out. His entire presence felt so different from every time before now.

In confirmation, he pressed two fingers to his lips and withdrew them. A small sprig of blue energy uncurled above his hand and disappeared with a snap.

"You're a magus?" she asked, startled.

"Oh, please. I have as little interest in those self-aggrandizing holy men as they would have in what I do. My small skills come—quite literally—from another vein, gifts passed down from one generation to the next. My luck with coins is something different—an unexpected gift of this lifetime."

"This lifetime?"

"Indeed! I was someone of an entirely different character in my homeland. Nowhere near as handsome. Nor have we such wonderful distractions as you have in Traumanfang."

"What are you telling me?"

He turned and looked hard at her. In the darkness of his eyes, waiting beneath the silver that was their irises, she saw something completely inhuman. For a moment, Vie wanted to ask him all about his home, where he was from, how he came here, what his world was like... all the things that she had wanted to know about herself and how she could have been born to a human. It was the unease she had always felt with him that stayed her tongue. Instead, she stuck to the facts. If she needed questions, she could sick the magi on him.

"So why are you telling me this?"

"Because in all my years here, no other cat burglar showed the promise you did. My only hope of getting the crystal lay in your skills. So I encouraged your growth until such a time I could wait no longer. You know what the crystal is, don't you?"

"Yes."

"Tell me what you have learned."

"The crystal is one of twelve. Each one is a prison to an unspeakable evil."

Galym nodded. "Would you be surprised to learn that one of the Cataclysms was from a different dimension? I doubt it. You know as well as I that evil can come from anywhere. What you would call 'unspeakable evil,' however, is such an everyday concept for my family. Would that I could forget that I was a part of them. I would do anything to excise myself from their reality. But family is something one can never escape, is it? I had hoped to leave them behind, but they found me here and set me back on task. Did you know I was originally brought here to track down one of the prisoners and return home with it in tow?"

"Why is it so important that the Cataclysm is returned?"

"To wage a war, I can only assume. My family is about as boringly predictable to me as the Order of the Vein, or any of those other silly orders out there—the Harmonists, the jungle people of the Adalain. They seek power for the simple sake of possession. My lovely cousin is absolutely instrumental to our matriarch's power play, however. So here I am: back on the scent of our little black sheep. It took me a long time to find this prisoner, and I had hoped to return the undamaged crystal to our family. Sadly, that was not to be the case, was it?"

"No. All twelve prisoners escaped."

"Wouldn't the old folks back home be thrilled at how this has played out?" Galym asked, almost mockingly.

"You agree with them?" Vie asked.

"Dearie me, no. I think it is the height of tragedy. I dread how the Cataclysms will change things for us all. There is so much of value here. And all shall be wasted by those tasteless boors."

"In Sludge?"

"My dear, as I am certain you already know, even Sludge has its little gems. But I fear it will soon go, like the rest of this fair world, to the blights." Galym sighed and flicked a hand toward her. "Your gift truly is lovely, and I appreciate your generosity in returning to me with an item of value, even if the result of our endeavor was lost. I hope this does not prevent us from pursuing further business in future, though I fear that we shall never again be partners."

As Vie turned to leave, Galym said her name quietly. She turned and regarded him.

"While I am sad this did not work out as we had planned, I am pleased that you got your wish."

Vie left his apartment shaken and unsettled. Even now, under the moon's light, Galym's revelations weighed heavily on her. The Butcher's presence was one that bespoke no evil until aggravated, but Galym's sorrow was real. He spoke as if from firsthand knowledge. She regretted not asking him which Cataclysm was his cousin or what they could expect when dealing with it. At the time, all she wanted was to escape him, almost as powerfully as she had wanted to escape from Sludge. If there was a silver lining, it was the fact that she had, indeed, escaped it. Today, she had felt a lady, or at least a dragon in disguise as a woman in disguise as a lady. Waiting for Ishtower, she resolved to tell him about Galym's involvement with the Cataclysm and maybe reveal just what her role in the destruction of the Apocryptein had really been.

If he ever decided to show.

Ishtower's delay rankled. She needed to pick his brain about this. Swallowing back all her frustrations, Vie waded into the waters of the pool. It took a moment, but finally she let herself relax into the swirling energies of the water. Here, submerged, her channeling powers seemed a bit stronger. The nimbus of light that had been little more than a flash on land was becoming a series of streaks over her body. It made her feel as pretty as she had in the dress. She closed her eyes and let the magic play about her, enjoying the gentle ebb of the waters around her.

When she returned to land, she found Ishtower in a heap on the gazebo. The sharpness of his stench reminded her of the alcohol distillery upriver from Sludge.

"Pretty lights," he mumbled.

"What happened to you?" Vie rumbled.

"You've mastered that indoor voice of yours. Great."

"What happened to you?" Vie repeated, more vehemently this time.

"I got drunk, woke up, got drunk again. I'm better now."

"You reek."

"I probably do," he said with a sniff of his dirty cloak. "Can't smell myself, though."

"What brought this on?"

"I captured the Cataclysm, got beat up by him, woke up, and remembered everything I tried to forget. I hadn't had a drink in almost four years. I thought I was over this. Good things, are thoughts."

Vie shrank down to normal and wrapped herself

in her robe. Her bare feet were silent as she joined the magus on the gazebo. Sitting down on the bench beside him, she stared at him, waiting him out. Even in the darkness, she could see tear stains on his cheeks.

"So, what's your story?" he asked abruptly.

"I think it can wait." She ran a hand across his back. He winced at her touch, but left well enough alone.

"When my wife... died... it destroyed me. I entered a bottle and it was my home for the better part of a decade. Two days ago, Lord Haphenasis told me that this Cataclysm we're tracking is the one who killed her. All I wanted was to take out my revenge. I just..." Ishtower's words faltered as a sob wracked his body. "It didn't work! I hate him! And that's... that's all I have... But that just fed him. It just gave him more and more and it made him stronger, and he escaped because I kept giving him more and more and all that revenge—all my plans—were worthless against him. It was because of me that he slipped through Botch's traps."

Vic smiled. "Don't let him catch you calling him that."

"Screw him."

"No, I think that would be even more impossible than recapturing these Cataclysms of yours."

Ishtower snuffled and wiped his nose with the back of a hand. "This was more than I could take. What he was doing to those people... It's like before. He hasn't changed at all, and I just... I needed to forget for a little while. I'm better now. I've stopped it. It won't happen again. But that fear? That fear right here, right smack in the middle of my chest? That is real. If I meet him, will I just be another dish at the buffet? He's free because of my hatred and... and I can't stop that! I can't just close it off like that. The things he did... he has to be stopped. He should have been killed in the first place, not locked up so he could escape!"

"Ishtower, I'm sorry. I had no idea. It wasn't anything I could control."

He waved it aside. "Nah. Don't blame yourself. What's done is done, and what was done by you and *Botch* were accidents, but this... What Izzard did to us, that was deliberate. That was just... inhuman." Ishtower drifted into silence. His quivering face showed he was crying again.

Vie felt as if she had been slapped. The name hit her with waves and waves of memory, of countless nights, awkward moments, pleasure and pain, freedoms and hatred. Could Ishtower really have said what she thought he had said?

"What was that name?"

"Izzard. Malek Izzard." Ishtower spat and looked at her. The look he gave said it all. "What? Did he ruin your life, too?"

"No." It was him. It was really him. "No, no, no, no." Vie rose and pressed her hands to her head. It was impossible. He was gone. Out of her life. He had abandoned her before she could share the joy she had borne with him. He was gone, dead. He had to be dead. That was the only explanation.

"Vie?" Ishtower asked, concern plain in his voice.

"Malek Izzard. Tell me, magus. Are you serious?"

She could hear his teeth grind. "Not tall. Lanky. Eyes like ruby gimlets. Dangerous, dark, perverse. Dressed well.

"Four Hells!" Tears of rage and anger and sadness poured down her face. And then she was laughing. There was no transition, no chuckle, nor titter—it was just a full-on roar of hysteria.

"Vie? The Hells?"

Her insides were cramping. But the fit was subsiding. She wiped her face. "Ha. Oooh, my sides. It had to be. Would it be anyone different? If anyone was to become one, it had to be him."

"Vie, you're making no sense. What does Izzard have to do with you?"

She forced a smile, uncertain that the magus could even see it in the darkness. "Now I know. After all these years, I finally know what happened to that bastard. You see, I was pregnant. I thought he was just the typical man from Sludge, fucking and running from what came afterward. But, no, turns out that he had to go unleash hell on the world. Just my luck."

"Fatherhood?" Ishtower asked, aghast.

Vie nodded. "My children were born from his seed."

Chapter 25

Useless. Every single book in this library was completely useless. Lord Haphenasis had scoured the shelves at the Gilded Lion five times already. He knew that the bright blue cover of *Lovelorn Lord* had a dark coffee stain across its edges. He had already flipped through *Coulculations* and had come to the conclusion that the unfortunate spelling of the book's title was not in jest. The author really was a complete idiot.

How he missed his own library. He yearned to grab any of his 4,690 books (only ten away from 4,700!) and trust that whatever the topic, there was something fresh and valuable to glean from it. He had all the greats: Poe,

Knickersaugh, Id Akin, Sharin Da Groot, Weeka Fuff, Mie Li Soong, The Llama of Urano Kai, everything that Cong Hui had ever written (even though she had been a woman, her brilliance of theory and wordplay was unrivalled even by Illim Fuego). He had all four original copies of the *Buh Nohr Bible*... but not anymore. There were copies of the copies out there somewhere, but the only four originals in all of Traumanfang were gone.

Standing in what the Lion called "the library" was depressing. Lord Haphenasis would have loved to be somewhere—anywhere—else. But where? His rooms? Where there was nothing to do but stare out the window? The cafeteria? He had already eaten his fill and was too bothered to properly gorge. The gardens? Lovely, certainly, but he had never been an active fan of wandering through trees and fields unless he had a problem to ponder, then he found the quiet of a well-maintained plot of land to be both helpful and relaxing. He already knew what he needed to do, he was just not certain how it was to be done.

"Magus Ishtower and Miss Vie are here to see you, Lord Haphenasis," a footman said from the edge of the room.

"What do you want?" he asked of his two guests.

"Where've you been? I've been looking for you all day."

"You all recovered from your apoplexy?"

"Lovely way of describing it. Thanks for the whiskey."

"It was clear that you needed it."

"I did. Much as it set me back from four years of sobriety."

Ishtower took a seat while Vie wandered over to the

window. She looked different from how she normally did. Her hair had been layered, half down while a silver clip held a small bun into place. The green dress, Lord Haphenasis had to admit, suited her, hugging her skinny frame well, while possessing enough flare to suggest the curvature that was in fashion these days.

"Please close the door behind you," Ishtower said to the footman. With a gentle clicking of the doors, the three were left alone in the library.

"To what do we owe this privacy?" Lord Haphenasis asked, taking a seat and removing his cigarette pouch.

"Fate, it would seem."

"What do you mean?"

"Malek Izzard has made some bitter enemies in his life."

"The Fifth Transport is no small number of people, nor were the inhabitants of Yega, nor the entire Ganymeade Region. The numbers he appears to be racking up since his liberation are nothing to be sneered at either. Recent figures from Constable Erchak put the death toll at nearly two hundred. All in the last week. "

"That's not what I'm talking about."

"So, then, what?"

"You. Me. Her."

"I can only assume that you are referring to me as his past jailor and yourself as a victim of his practices both recently and during the time of the Fifth Transport's massacre. You have me at a disadvantage, however, in regards to the woman."

"I guess that's my cue," Vie began, continuing her vigil at the window. "I've never really been in a good situation, but fourteen years ago, I got in something that was worse than normal. I was a claims runner for a bookie in Sludge. That means that I got to collect money people earned. I had other jobs at the time, but this was the big one. One night, I was called down to the shore, where a bare-handed boxing match was going down. The winner liked what he saw with me and pulled me back to his room. I saw it as a way to earn a little extra on the side before I had to turn in the winnings cash. While we were sealing the deal, a goat-horned bastard busts in with a couple goons and starts pummeling the boxer.

"Turns out the boxer was supposed t'have dived in the third round. The goat wasn't happy to lose his money, and me being there with the winnings of a competitor, well... let's just say he was pretty happy."

"Did you escape?" Lord Haphenasis asked.

"Tried to. I went mouse but got caught sneaking out through the window.

"'You'll bring me a pretty coin,' Goat-head told me. I was tossed in a tiny metal box so I couldn't get out and me and the boxer were taken to a slaver. A couple miserable days later, we had our big day at the auction.

"For six hours I stood there, completely naked, as a number of traders and scum poked me, prodded me, pinched my arms or nipples or ass. They groped about in my mouth to see if I still had all my teeth. One woman wanted to have sex with me to see if I was worthy for her pleasure house. I don't even know how many people looked at me. It didn't really matter, really, once *he* showed up."

"Malek Izzard."

The woman nodded.

"Not the tallest person in the world—a little bigger

than me, really—gaunt, a huge smile, and beady red eyes. He was dressed well in a silver suit with silver hoops in his ears, but not finely. He stank of something I'd never smelled before. Not a horrible smell, just strong: a little like smoke, but of a different type from what everyone else was smoking. He simply stared at me for a few minutes, staring in me, it felt like.

"Then he approached me. He stood out even more because, unlike everyone else, he didn't touch me. He simply walked around me, studying me, then he stood up next to me and sniffed. One long sniff.

"'You do not belong here,' he said with a smile. 'Shall we leave?'

"I don't know how much he paid for me. But I was his.

"For a year, he kept me as his for whatever he needed me for. In a way, I didn't mind much. The food was good and readily available. I got to travel a little, see some of the world. If I had to give him my body several times every day. Well, there were worse fates, all things considered.

"And worse is what he brought down on me. As the first year wound toward an end, he started doing things to me that I won't repeat here. Sometimes, he worked alone, other times, he brought in friends to play with me, but one thing is for sure. He never let anyone else fuck me."

She paused as if expecting one of the two magi to speak.

"That was when he started showing just how cruel he could be. Never to me, though. I was party to his perversions but never to his cruelty. Sometimes, he'd just bring in people off the street and skin them alive, or worse, sit back with me at his side as he had them skin each other alive. It was…"

She brought a hand up to her eyes. "I'm sorry." She sniffed.

"He was—is—a possessor," Lord Haphenasis said softly, so utterly absorbed by her tale that he had let his cigarette burn down to his fingers. Disgust barely even began to describe his feelings on the situation. "IT is not just exploring people; he enters people's bodies and forces them to do… hideous things before letting them go."

"Which he sometimes did," Vie continued. "He'd let them go and leave them to deal with the horrors that he had made them do.

"And then he released me. Well, that's not the most accurate word for it. He came to me, sniffed at me like he always did by way of greeting. It turned him on, you know. Sniffing me was the biggest arousal for him. More even than hurting others. But sniffing me… I couldn't figure it out. I never could.

"'I will be back,' he told me. 'There are errands requiring my attention. A man's work is never done,' he said with a laugh. But he never came back. For several weeks, I was all right in his house, but I was getting bigger. I didn't know what was happening to me at first, but it made sense. By the time I realized that he wasn't coming back, it was too late. I was alone and the kids were born."

"Are you trying to tell us that that… monster is their father?"

The woman turned. Her dark eyes were as hard as diamond in their tear-reddened shells. "He must be and he is, for I had no other man in the two years before they were born."

"I need a drink," Lord Haphenasis said, leaning back in his chair as if he had been slapped.

"That was my reaction, too," Ishtower agreed.

"Interesting fact, nonetheless," Lord Haphenasis continued, his mind racing with this deluge of new information. "His possession abilities might live on in your children. That could explain why the Butcher is so docile with them. But, by the Veins, if any of that man's madness lives on in your children, they will be Cataclysms all on their own!"

"They will not," the woman said quietly.

"But how do you know? Can you read the future, woman?"

"My name is Vie!" she snapped. "I am sick and tired of all this disrespect. I am no 'woman'; I have raised three children on my own. I have endured two years of Izzard's perversions. I have endured far more pain than you could even imagine. And I am a mother-fucking dragon! So, the next time you call me 'woman' like I am nothing more than the shit you wipe from between your toes, you'd better be pretty goddamn sure you want them to be your last words."

Lord Haphenasis struggled with the violence of her response. No doubt, it was just her venting the memories of her short time as his slave, but in spite of it, in the cadence and the tenor, there was something in her he hadn't noticed before: her poise. Whether borne from her recent discovery that she was a dragon or from a lifetime of having to be responsible for herself, she carried herself with as much—indeed more—dignity as any noble he had ever known.

"I meant no disrespect."

"Of course you did. I can see your bitterness every time I look at you. If you're gonna keep that bitterness, then own it. Respect me. Respect what has come before you and learn from it. Don't just bitch and moan like a little boy. I swear, you can act like more of a child than my own kids."

Ishtower merely watched the pair, quietly taking no side. Looking to his loathsome brother for either aid or support was a confusing thing to the lord. To maintain as much dignity as he could, he relinquished himself to her passion. "You are right. We would appreciate it if you would continue your most compelling rationalization."

"Fine." She then sighed herself back to the issue. "Your doubt about my kids isn't misplaced. They're mischievous little shits, that's for sure. About the only thing I can trust them to do is cause trouble, but one thing's for damn sure, they're not evil. Not like Malek was. I've made sure that I got at least that right. It's not been easy, and I've had to slap them upside the head often as a sailor cusses, but I swear that so long as I'm here, they'll leave this world no worse than they found it."

Lord Haphenasis would have liked to argue the point more, but just then, a tentative knock came on the door. "Enter!"

"Sounds like I missed summat," Squite said, hobbling into the room on the arm the tall Ventagist that was his nephew.

As they entered, Vie crossed and kissed the old man's cheek. The last week had aged the old man.

"Thank you again for your aid the other day," Ishtower said to Yankee.

"I was disappointed to not be of any actual help. Nasty bruise you got there."

"It's healing," the Martialist said, reflexively prodding the large welt at the back of his head. It could have been much worse had Lord Haphenasis not arrived to harness his arcana into a flesh-binding.

"Heard the place burned down."

"Just about that entire part of town was built with wood. There is no creativity when it comes to effecting an escape."

"So he did get away, eh?" Squite asked, easing down into a large armchair with the largest pillows in the room. "Ah... dat's de one. Good fin' we came prepared. Yankee, show 'is Lordship what we brung."

"You have it?" Lord Haphenasis said excitedly.

"Yes, sir," Yankee said, pulling a large book from under his arm. "As you requested. My uncle wanted to be here when I gave it to you. The fickle old man's getting antsy in his old age."

"Boder to dat," Squite said as he handed the dusty old volume to Lord Haphenasis.

It was the only remaining original copy and even just getting it here to study had cost the lord not one, but two favors of the head librarian back in the Innervein. He had had a copy of his own but, like everything else, it had been lost in the Kremsek's fire.

"What is it?" Ishtower asked.

"It is the answer to a nagging question that's been bothering me since Constable Erchak woke me up the other day.

"If anything is to be learned from that fiasco in Sludge, it is that Izzard's power grows daily. Just his interaction with Ishtower alone was something that significantly amplified his powers."

"Damned leech," Ishtower said.

"That kind of animosity is exactly what fed him. He is like a parasite, feeding first on latent energies, but as he grows, he will start exerting more and more control over people. The night he broke free from the Apocryptein, I might have been able to trap him all by myself, but that is no longer the case. His casual escape from both Ishtower and me is proof that he is wily, crafty, and highly dangerous. After knocking Ishtower out, he used his remaining host to burn the place down. If I had not been concerned with saving lives, I likely would have been able to trap him then and there. He is highly mobile and painfully slippery. That means capturing him will require some unorthodox methods.

"The only way do so is through preparation. And that is where this book comes into play. It is known as the Necrocommunique and copies of it are banished from almost all collections. Technically, even possessing it is a crime, as it was written by one of the Twelve, but in its pages is the Soam Ule. It is the only spell I can think of to summon all of Izzard here. But once here, we will have him, trapped and at our mercy."

Chapter 26

ALL THE NECESSARY PREPARATIONS WERE MADE. THIRTEEN veils had been strung about the room, two of which were already closed and the rest would need to be closed when the time came. Mullet's Cloak was hanging on a coat hook, ready to be used if they needed it. Candles were spaced evenly around the room, allowing them plenty of light and to provide them with enough material for Smoker's Shield. A pot of mud was simmering on a brazier that had already begun stirring itself. A lone crystal, purified by the fires of Mount Devos lay waiting to be filled. It was time.

Lord Haphenasis considered the three other men in the room with him. Two Ventagists—Squite and his nephew, Yankee. Ishtower, a master of brute force. And there was himself, the brains and commanding presence that would lay the villain low.

"Are you ready for this?"

"Let's get it over with. There's only so much hate I can protect myself with."

"I still think I'd be the better choice," Yankee muttered.

"Shush, boy! We need ya for bringin' him here."

It had made too much sense, Lord Haphenasis thought as he bound the heavy rope about Ishtower's wrist. With a summoning of this caliber, one that could recombine a soul after even generations of dissipation, having two Ventagists on hand to fine-comb the soul was of absolute importance. One would be suitable but, with his age, Squite might not be able to handle it all by himself. Whereas Yankee lacked the precision that Squite wielded his powers with. Lord Haphenasis double-checked the knot at Ishtower's right ankle. It would hold.

With Lord Haphenasis as the executor of the summoning, that left only Ishtower to play the role of receptacle. Once Izzard was brought here, he would have to host the soul while they properly aligned the resonant energies of the crystal to Izzard's arcane vibration. The veils were there to bolster the crystal's power. Even then, Lord Haphenasis would have to rely on Ishtower's rage to prevent Izzard from calling forth the captive's powers.

"How do you feel?"

"Uncomfortable, but this is nothing compared to training with the Ghong Venn mercenaries." His arms were spread across a heavy metallic bar over him. His ankles were tied from the substantially heavy bedframe to a metal pipe running up the corner of the room. Despite his bravado, he was already sweating from the pressure of the arcane vise that they had built about him.

"Is the vise too tight?"

"Let's just say that this coupled with having that bastard in my head will be my excuse for not doing anything for the next three days."

"You can still feel the Veins?"

"Feeling them but can't touch them."

"Good. Squite, Yankee?"

They nodded their readiness. Lord Haphenasis set his hound on the table beside the chair he was sitting in and let it wind up. Izzard was in no less than fourteen different places. His lordship opened his mind to the two Ventagists, and together they attacked the first of the fourteen elements.

The sliver of Izzard screamed its indignation across the Astral Plane as they dragged it back and threw it into Ishtower.

They did this again and again, a painstakingly exhaustive task. After five attacks, the hound revealed that he had recombined all of his being into one person, almost as if waiting for them to come.

"So this is to be my return to form, is it?" he mocked as they surrounded his soul. They responded with a psychic blast that numbed him for transportation back to Ishtower's body.

Ishtower strained at his bonds as Malek Izzard's soul filled him up. He roared and shouted bloody murder, fighting to be free of the possession, but his greatest means to escape—his link to the Veins—were denied him.

"Ease him," Lord Haphenasis commanded of Yankee, who blasted him with the numbing calm of the Morpheus Charm. Ishtower's body went limp, his head collapsing onto his bare chest. The most immediate problem taken care of, Lord Haphenasis then set the hound to spin one last time, just in case they had missed anything.

"Whaz yer name, li'l magus?" Ishtower mumbled with a voice not his own.

"Can we assume that this is all that you are, Malek Izzard?"

"We c'n. No mor'v me ou' there. Since you know me, c'n I say t'same?"

"I am Lord Sesellebach tel Haphenasis. I was warden of your prison in the Apocryptein and I am your captor again. These men with me are the Ventagists, Squite and his nephew Yankee."

As he spoke, the two Ventagists and Lord Haphenasis sealed the room. Within moments, the place was completely disconnected from the outside world. Air, currants, thoughts, nothing could enter. As the air in the room would run out before long, an unseen timer had begun. Their window for imprisoning the Cataclysm had begun closing.

"Charm'd, I'm sure."

"If you would excuse us, we have the trivial matter of preparing your new prison."

"This isn't my new prison?" Ishtower asked, scouring his body with semi-conscious eyes. "Shame. I like't. Strong."

"Which describes you well," Lord Haphenasis said, trying to distinguish between the vibrations between his brother magus and the soul trapped within.

"Yesss... recovery's goin' well. Lots'v hatr'd here. Kill a few. Feed. Good f'r soul. Long time b'tween meals."

"Yes, we are aware."

"I know you. You're th' one chasin' me 'roun' the city, aren't you?"

"You saw me the other day after you killed that poor chandler."

The crystal was aligning quickly. When they pulled Izzard into it, it would be done with no discomfort to Ishtower. Lord Haphenasis reached out to the two Ventagists. They were with him, adding their energies to his. Together, they pulled.

"Whoa!" Ishtower said, jerking against the pull of the crystal.

It was working. Tiny slivers of the Cataclysm were peeling off.

"Stop that!" Ishtower screamed.

"No. You are going back."

"Please, no! I can't bear it!"

"Your freedom is done."

"But it hurts so much. I can't stand—iiiiiiaah ha ha! I'm so sorry. I couldn't keep that up any longer."

This time, Lord Haphenasis caught the inflection. He was not slurring his words any more. His existence was seeping into the prison crystal but something was wrong.

"You feel it, do you not, little *wizard?*" A smile spread across Ishtower's face.

"Do not stop!" Lord Haphenasis shouted at his two assistants. "Hasten the process! Suck him all in now!"

"That will not work, you smelly man. Yes, there it is... it's there. Right there, the loveliest scent I've ever known. I thought I smelled her on Ishtower the other night. On you three now. It was only a matter of time before I found out for sure."

"Pull him!" Lord Haphenasis reached out a meta-physical hand and grabbed Izzard by the ectoplasm. He pulled with all his might, stuffing layer after layer of the malleable soul into the crystal.

"He won't let go of Ishtower!"

"Time is not on your side, my friend. With the deal I made before nudging all this, it would take ten of you and I would still have plenty of residue left to escape. Think on that tonight as you slip off to bed. You had hoped to catch me, but you failed, Sesellebach tel Haphenasis. And, soon, I will have a wonderful new body once again."

Ishtower's body flicked his fingers toward the crystal on the table. As if struck by a powerful bolt of energy, it ruptured and shattered. The backlash was explosive, blasting the magi from their chairs. An imploding *Whomph!* shook the room as every barrier and veil they had so painstakingly set up evaporated in a swirl of smoke. Air blasted into the room, battering the four men around.

Coughing, his body aching, Lord Haphenasis struggled to his feet. He no longer felt Izzard's presence anywhere nearby. "Squite? Yankee?"

"Oh, dear Veins, no!"

"Squite?" Haphenasis staggered over to the other side of the room where Yankee crouched over his uncle. The ancient man was shuddering, his hand clutching his chest.

"Let me at him! I can fix it."

"Nnn—nuh... Iss time, kid... Tell... th' girl... tell her...."

"Uncle!" Yankee cried, gripping his uncle's hand and pulling it close. He waited for the old man to say something witty but nothing could be said, not from Squite. Not ever agian.

Chapter 27

V IE LET THE TEARS COME. S HE WAS TOO SAD, AND BOTH HER hands were full of her kids' hands. Squite lay on the bed before her, as peaceful as if he were taking a nap. His big hands had been folded across his chest, and he was dressed in the same robes he had worn the whole time she had known him. His feathered cloak was wrapped around his shoulders, maintaining the old bird's avian appearance.

"Does he have anything else to wear?" she asked Yankee, who sat in the chair by the bed.

"What?" Yankee asked, looking up at her as if he had not even noticed her enter the room.

"Be good if we could dress him up."

"Like Mag Hoffle," Bel said. "When she died, her mother had to scare up whatever coin she could to buy a new dress for her. But I don't see why. If people are just going to be buried, why spend money on a box or on nice clothes?"

"It's a way to show respect to our loved ones."

"Not me," Bon said. "When I die, I'm gonna have no friends so that, instead of burying me, I'll get to lie there naked and make everyone run away."

"Don't say that, Bon," Vie scolded him. "You have no idea how wonderful it is to have friends. There are too few as it is."

"Couldn't Lord Haphenasis have saved him?" Braden asked.

"There are some injuries that no magus can fix," Lord Haphenasis said from the doorway. His face wore a few new cuts on it. Vie was surprised to see it, as he had been so quick to heal himself earlier. "Old age and heart problems like this are a couple. When the crystal prison exploded, it lodged fragments in his chest and neck. The shock of it... his heart... it was too much for the old man."

"He was your friend, wasn't he?" Bon asked.

Lord Haphenasis's brows arched up. He blinked a few times. "He and I go back a ways. More of the flesh than of the mind, he still had nothing but my respect. He was a fine magus. I feel like this is all my fault."

Bon stepped over to the fat lord and took his hand. "Shit happens."

"Bon!" Vie snapped.

Lord Haphenasis took his hand back and looked at the boy with an oddly, curiously, out-of-place look. "Excuse me, please... I... excuse me."

"Of course," Vie said.

The magus left the room with a hunch in his shoulders.

"What have I told you about your language?" Vie snapped at her middle son after the Lord had left.

"That I'm 'not to fuckin' use it less it's an emergency.'"

"Hey!" Vie said, cuffing her son across the head with the palm of her hand. This scored a giggle from the naughty boy.

"He's dead?" the Butcher asked. He had been standing by; a strange fascination of the dead magus had taken him over.

"Dead as a nail, *wham!*" Bon said.

"When will he wake up?"

"No, you big silly, he's dead," Bel explained. "When you die, your soul leaves and you join the Veins and your body just lies there, until you're put in the ground."

"Or burned!" Bon added.

"Or burned. But if you're put in the ground, then little worms and ants and grubs and mice and things come and eat you up until there's nothing left of you but bones, and, even then, that might disappear, too."

"That sounds horrible. Hey, old man, come back. Don't let the little beasts eat you up. Hey! Do you hear me! Don't let yourself die. Come on!" The Butcher had started poking at Squite.

"Hey, leave him alone! Show him some respect!" Yankee said, rising from his chair.

"You will not tell me what I can and cannot do!" the butcher said, pushing Yankee back with such force that he tumbled over the chair he had been sitting on and struck the wall with a mighty *whack*. Bon and Bel were by his side in a flash, trying to calm him down.

"Nobody will die like this today!" The Butcher had drawn his sword and was getting ready to stab it into Squite's body. "If they do, I'll kill them!"

Braden grabbed one of his arms. "But killing them

means they'll be dead."

"What kind of nonsense is this?" he snapped at the small boy.

"If someone dies, they're dead, right?"

"That makes sense."

"And if you kill someone, they're dead, too, right?"

"Yes..."

"So if dying and being killed are the same, that means that people are dead in both cases. That means they're the same thing, then, right?"

"Huh," the Butcher said, lowering his blade. "So this man is dead?"

"Yes," Braden said.

"Who killed him?"

"Someone horribly evil," Vie said, taking his hand.

"If I died or were killed, I'd want to go after the person who did this and cut them up."

"But you'd be dead. How could you come back?"

"I..." he looked lost for a moment as he stared at the darkness that was his sword. "I don't know. But I do know that I'm hungry! Anyone want to go and find some food?"

"What are you thinking of?" Braden asked him, with a glance at his mother that said everything was all under control.

"How about dog?" Bon asked, running toward the door.

"Bon, don't be silly!" Bel nagged, following him to the door. "You know as well as anyone that now that we're living up here like kings and queens that we don't need to eat dog anymore. Besides, they're too cuddly and cute to want to eat."

"I like kings and queens," the Butcher said as they reached the door. "Do you know any?" And then they were gone.

"I'm sorry about that," Vie told Yankee as she helped him up. "My kids seem to have him under control, but around anyone else...." She shrugged.

"Sleight-of-hand, if you ask me. Distract him from whatever's got his anger up, and then he's just another kid hanging out with them."

Vie left him alone after giving the old magus a kiss on the forehead. She would miss the dirty old man and his flirting. Moreover, she would miss the kindness that he shared. With him gone, the whole world seemed a little less bright. She considered following the kids and their puppy downstairs, but she wasn't feeling up to it. Instead, she found herself ascending to the next level where their suite was. As she walked past Ishtower's room, she paused and knocked once to a bleary grunt of acceptance.

As the evening had begun to fall, the room was awash in reds and oranges. The magus was seated at the small desk by the window, a bottle of liquor in front of him. His hair was disheveled and a beard was coming along on his chin. His bed was unmade with his winter's cloak tossed over it. It was clothing the man would never need here. Even in the coldest of winters, the temperature seldom fell to freezing. He sat with his broad chest bare. His symbolic tree tattoo of the Order rippled as he lifted the bottle to his mouth. As the light hit his wrists, she saw how red and raw they were.

"Pay your respects to Squite, did you?" he asked her.

"The Butcher learned what happens when people die. He was quite threatening about it all. He said he'd kill anyone who dies on him."

"Think he'll remember this tomorrow?"

"Not likely, but one can hope. Every day it's like he has to start over again. Whatever he learns, he seems to forget a few moments later. If his mind worked then maybe we could figure out who he was and who did this to him."

"You looking for another kid?"

"Three is more than enough, thank you very much!" Vie sat down opposite the big Martialist and nodded to the bottle. Ishtower passed it over to her. White rum. It felt good going down. She passed it back to him.

"You're doing right by them."

"I hope to all Four Hells that I am, but knowing who their father is... I sometimes can't wrap my head around everything that he's responsible for. I honestly had no idea. It explains too much."

"As does your certain skill," he said, wiping his mouth after his sip. He winced as the alcohol seeped into his raw wrist.

"Has this happened before? I mean, dragons aren't from Traumanfang, are they?"

"Not that I've ever heard."

"So, if they're not, then how was I conceived?"

"A friend dies and you start thinking about birth?"

"It's a strange cycle, isn't it?" She took another sip.

"Better birth and death then horror after horror playing out in your own head."

"What did he show you?"

Ishtower glared at her.

"Sorry." She took another sip and let the sunset fill the silence left in the wake of her apology.

"Rebubula—my wife—was not beautiful," Ishtower said softly. "She had a big laugh and the front teeth of a donkey. Stocky, even before our kids. But the things she'd say... she could jump from kindness to lewd to stony to resolute in a second. That girl had fire! She was a nurse. I was a soldier. About a decade ago, we were serving the Fifth Transport—a regiment that saw to the maintenance of roads and major thoroughfares. We got a call of some problem. The whole Transport was summoned. We found a massive uprising of locals trying to destroy the road. It made no sense, but as a titled Lieutenant, it wasn't up to me to question their motives, it was to stop the loss of life. As we're pushing these people back, Malek Izzard strolls through the battle, hands casually in his pockets, whistling.

"He looks at me and asks if I'm in charge. I tell him I was and to get under cover, lest his head get cut off. He gives me this horrible smile and waves his hand. The soldiers behind me fall on each other with their weapons. Within moments, they were all dead. I'd never seen anything like that. I was dumbstruck.

"He then tells me to relax and enjoy the show. Like what I'd just seen was only a warmer. And it was. The Fifth imploded. And I mean the whole regiment. Absolute madness. Every single one and the rest of the people... they just lit into each other. I tried to stop them, but I couldn't move, couldn't touch my arcana. I could only stand there, a dumb witness while they destroyed each other. When most were slaughtered, he brought Rebubula forth...."

Ishtower grabbed the bottle and slugged back several large gulps.

"The Fifth was 600 men. The community that started the uprising was almost that. Add the train to the army and we're talking sixteen hundred people. Only a hundred were left. Bound like this, unable to close my eyes, I was helpless to do anything but watch as the hundred remaining members of the Fifth had their way with her."

"They had their way...?"

"They fucked her!" Ishtower said with a fury in his face and madness in his eyes. "Even long after she stopped fighting, long after she stopped screaming, they just kept coming. One after the other, sometimes two at a time, sometimes three. The only thing I can thank Maketh-el for was that by the time they were all done with her, she was dead. If she were not, she would have begged me to kill her. And I would have. Veins help me, I would have."

Ishtower slumped into his chair and took another drag from his bottle.

Vie's lip quivered in horror of this. In all the time they were together, Izzard had shown signs of depravity, but nothing like this. No vendetta could even begin to touch the evil that it would take to do something like that. She did not understand it. All she felt was rage. Bitter. Total. This was an unforgiveable crime. What she had been able to learn earlier about his total crimes was nothing to this type of violation. She looked at Ishtower with both sympathy and respect. Most men she knew would have been utterly shattered by an experience like this. But Ishtower had managed to pull himself together once.

"No wonder you lost yourself in a bottle."

Ishtower's jaw clenched. "He showed me everything. I thought I had dulled the pain of it all. It's still there. Every thread of disgust. Every piece of revulsion. Every spark of guilt. It's all here again."

The sun had sunk behind the distant hills before Ishotwer spoke again.

"For a little while, I was able to forget all my hatred, but the whole time he was there, searing my scars with a hot iron. I was able to do it once, but two of them... my kids... they still won't speak to me."

"I'm sorry. Sometimes I think that Izzard's not human. Not like how I'm not, but in things he does, the way he acts, almost like he's as new to the world as the Butcher. He's contemptuous of everything but is endlessly curious about it all, too."

"You talking about Lord Haphenasis or Izzard?" Ishtower's lip curled into the barest of a smirk.

Vie snorted, relieved that even through the darkness of it he was able to bring a little humor to the conversation. It gave her hope that Ishtower would be able to recover from this, too. "They are a match made in the Blue Realm, aren't they?"

"Pretty deserving of one another."

The two sat in silence for a minute. A pair of ducks took off from the pond below. Behind the hills, the sun's fire was cooling into a rich pink with purple trails.

"That was rude," Ishtower said. "He and I have never been friends. Never been good at seeing eye to eye, either. He's an aristocrat from big-city civilization. I'm the son of a common soldier who was lucky enough to be found. I rose above the uncertainty of a military life. I've done well for my kids... for Rebubula. He was born into it."

"That doesn't forgive him his attitude."

"Nor did his attitude deserve the endless shit I gave him in our youth. But, push comes to shove, I'd want him on our side. See, people he doesn't understand at all, but arcana?" He lifted his hand and a small stream of fire rose up from it.

"It's nice."

"It's me: all brute force and flex and contract. But Botch? He'd light the thing up, make it dance, throw it around until he got bored with it. Then he'd just let it hover in the air around his head. I've never known anyone with the skill that he's got. Makes it crazy that Hamza called him a Cataclysm. But it's working. He's doing what he can."

"So what happened today?"

"That's the real question. After the whole thing went down, I didn't want to talk. But he made me, so we talked —Lord Haphenasis and I—compared notes, such as they are. Izzard's recovering from his imprisonment too quick. He was always powerful, but this...? He was in my mind. I saw his and you were there. You and your kids. It's only a matter of time before he knows where we are. He wants you and them."

Vie said nothing. She took a big slug from the bottle. There was not much left.

"Then we better be ready for him when he comes." She offered the bottle to Ishtower.

"All yours. It's dulled the aching. That's as good as it's gonna get for me."

"How are you doing?"

"Honestly? I feel like snow that's been ground in the mud and thrown in an oven. I'm steaming. This was failure in a big way. But I tell you, girl, it was sound. Damn him to the Four Hells. It was sound."

"You should go to bed."

Ishtower rolled his head to get a glimpse of the bed. It was no more than a couple feet away.

"Too far."

"Come here, then," Vie said, taking him by the armpit. He groaned as she pulled him to his feet and guided him the great distance to his bed. It took some rolling and getting into bed with him to finally settle him decently onto the bed.

"Thanks," he said but, with his face buried in his pillow, it sounded more like a muffled "Fnz."

"You're welcome." She hovered over him for a moment as his pain and misery dragged him to sleep. He was a handsome fellow, all right. She ran her hands through his hair, kissed his temple and said, "Sleep well."

She then threw the bottle out the window and left.

Chapter 28

A WALK TO CLEAR HIS HEAD WAS ALL LORD HAPHENASIS REAL-
ly wanted.

It was supposed to be only a short nighttime walk,
one which took him to a diner for a seedier meal than
he could have found at the Gilded Lion. The pressures
of dealing with the Cataclysms would call him back soon
enough, he just needed this time away. Every once in a
while, he just needed to forget everything and enjoy the
simple things, watch the world like a normal person, with
normal-people problems. What he found was neither.

The diner was little more than a nighttime tea house
not that far from the Lion, but far enough that he felt
comfortable in its distance. After the confrontation with
Izzard, he needed to get away from himself and any ac-
cusatory stares that anyone at the Lion would cast upon
him. His brothers would argue it away as something that

came with the territory of being a magus, but they would still blame him for letting Squite die, for letting Izzard get away, for allowing the Twelve to escape in the first place. They would glare at him with and, in their heads, little voices would whisper, Cataclysm. It was for that reason that he used such a small group. These were men he trusted and—yes, he had to admit that Ishtower was fast proving his inclusion—respected. So he pushed everyone else away.

Leaving poor Squite to suffer the consequences of his self-consciousness.

"Earl Grey, with a dram of whiskey," he told the serving girl.

"We haven't got whiskey here, milord," she said.

"What have you got?"

"Honey? Maple syrup? Syrup'll cost you extra, though."

"I could use something sweet in my life right now. Hopefully, it will wash away all the bitterness that I must contend with."

"So which'll it be?"

"Honey."

"Very well, milord."

Lord Haphenasis bridged his fingers before his nose and pulled forth a mirror of memory. He watched himself the night that Vie had broken into the Apocryptein. Tall, fat, arrogant, comfortable. That last detail was the biggest change he had endured since then. There was no comfort in his life any more. Not in the way he was used to. So, then, was it really comfort?

No, it was complacency.

When he left home to join the magi, his father, Lord

Lincoln tel Haphenasis, had pulled him aside for a last snippet of advice. "You are better than the rest, and do not forget it. You will live what they learn and show them that your blood, the blood of nobility, is a better conduit then their layman's blood. You go there and make us proud."

He had. Every waking moment he had. He had lived and breathed the spells that others conjured. He was alone in being able to feel out the arcana that he or others could call. Just as Izzard could command other people's souls, he, Lord Haphenasis, had managed to exploit others' spells. They were all just a finger's breadth away. It only took a slightly different vantage to see it, and a subtle call to make them his own.

He was unrivaled!

But then he had gotten the assignment at the Apocryptein.

"Here y'are, milord," the waitress said, setting down a small porcelain pot of steaming water before him. With measured, deliberate movements, she lifted the pot above a small tea cup. With two hands, she steadied it and poured it into the cup. The stream was steady, not too quick and not too slow, just enticing enough to lure his eyes into the action. When that was done, she lifted a ramekin and dipped a tea spoon into it. The honey was thick and golden. It dribbled off the spoon, but she rolled it, caught the dollop, and rejoined it with its body. Then, as quickly as a hare, slipped the honey-coated spoon into the cup. Stirred until the spoon had no honey left on it.

It was ideal. Soak up the honey. Sit. Collect. Soak. Stir.

Is that was this was? When Vie broke in, was she

there because he needed to stir up this life he had created for himself? Was his decision to use the forbidden Osaizi's Cant hubris or was it chosen as a means to test his own abilities?

He had no answer, but feared the latter.

This whole ordeal was far too similar to an exploration of his curiosity. The thesis: how effectively had he absorbed the potential of the five Veins beneath him? Osaizi's Cant had been his gateway. It was a spell that no one else had dared use, which made it perfect. It was the potent coil of absolute chaos that would have allowed the test to come to bear. It was the platform on which he could evaluate his potential, his intelligence, and his blood.

Yet he could not help but feel he had accomplished nothing with it. The woman. Her dragon form. The destruction of the Apocryptein. Ishtower. The release of the Twelve Cataclysms. The continuing freedom that the butcher enjoyed. Squite's death. Malek Izzard. Malek Izzard's manipulation of him. Nothing was what he could possibly have envisioned. Nobody was fitting the mold that he might have hoped to create. The only thing he had were these thoughts, spinning around and around, but unlike the honey in his tea, unable to be dissolved.

"You are as wise to the ways of people as a pig," his mother used to say about him.

But he did know himself. He knew what he could do, what he was capable of, and what he was willing to do. So perhaps, that was where to start. What was he willing to do? Whatever it took to prove himself the best. So what did that take? What was he missing if he were to take down a manipulative psychopath like Izzard? One thing he always taught in his classes was that the right question was half of the method. Once you had that, the answers came easy, just as the idea came to him now. Izzard reveled in destruction, confrontation, and fed on agony, frustration, and difficulty. Who would be most at stake in these confrontations with him? Vie and her children. Ishtower. Himself. What were his assets? Skill, a lack of traditional morality, scientific curiosity. Had Izzrd not also gloated of a deal that protected him? Yes, whoever it was that had aided him could be found, coerced to switch allegiance. It would only require some bribery—everyone had their price. So then the question was: who might gain from an allegiance with Izzard?

The complexity of Izzard's trap began to unravel once the lord brought Izzard's ally into consideration. The ally had been powerful enough to erect psychic shielding. Either it was a natural-born telepath—which was one of the rarest of the Blessed's gifts and so would be easily tracked down—or it was an arcanist. None in the Brotherhood would ally themselves with Izzard of their own free will, and precautions had been erected among all brothers that protected them from psychic manipulations. The way Izzard had spoken, it was as if his protection had been given freely, which implied a previous relationship, one that dated before his imprisonment in the Apocryptein.

"Could she...?" he wondered, tea steaming before his mouth. No, that is unlikely. She had no power like that. As he thought about the arcana more, he realized that it was unlike any barrier he had previously encountered. It was arcana, but whose resonance was way off, almost like an entirely different language of comprehension. It did the same as spells from Traumanfang, but was unrecognizable. So what could have created such power?

"Oh no," he said, setting down his delightful tea. "He is not alone."

"What's the matter, milord?" the serving girl asked.

"I must go," he said, reaching into a pocket for a copper chit.

"I'm sorry, but we don't take change."

"Then how...?"

"How are we paid?" she asked, smiling gently. The smile stretched across her face into a gross caricature of the expression. Her eyes began tearing up as panic and madness filled them.

"Izzard."

"Hello, dear friend," the man sitting beside the server said, casually sipping his own tea.

"Did you think we would just let you go so quickly?" chorused the two women in spring dresses to his right.

"Izzard, let these people go."

"Or what?" the server asked, taking a butter knife from the man beside her. She flashed it slowly in the gentle candlelight of the room.

"Or I will not be responsible for whatever harm comes to these people."

"Oh, aren't we generous. But you see, I know you are not responsible for what happens to these people. I am." The waitress stabbed the butter knife into her cheek, cutting straight through into her mouth. "Pletty, in't thee?" she asked as a stream of blood drooled from her lips.

Lord Haphenasis stared in horror at the poor girl. Then his mind switched on. He slammed his walking staff on the ground and a murder of crows burst forth, striking all the people in the room. Izzard screamed as he lost control of his powers.

"Take her to a healer at once," Lord Haphenasis commanded to the man beside him. He then hastened toward the door.

Out on the street, every eye had turned toward him. Forty people if one. There was no way his crows could purify all in one shot. It would require something different, an Irony. Distract them with a wave of irony, bind them in the morass of their own consciousness, and they would be incapable of action.

"Yowlp!" he shouted as something heavy struck him upside the head. The pain was excruciating, dulled, thankfully by the shields he had hastily placed about himself. A reactive push and the assailant flew backward into the waiting crowd. But another was there, a feathered fiend with a knife. The blade cut into his side, minimal pain, deflected just in time. His staff flicked out, igniting his assailant's face in a blinding light, knocking him back. But there was another. And another. Hitting, beating, kicking, knocking the magus down to the cobblestone of the street.

He did not want to hurt them, but he needed them to back off. Doing so required a delicate spell that had to contain but not kill or crush. Noticing a hanging vine dangling off the building that he had been backed up against, he had found his tool. The vine grew exponentially, animated by his touch, until its tendrils roped around the crowd. They were yanked back away from him as he groggily staggered to his feet. His face was tender, his breath was labored, most likely the result of more bruised or broken ribs.

"What now, wizard?" a man jibed, leering at him.

"Why not just take me over, like you have done these people?" Lord Haphenasis shouted.

"Where is the fun in that?" asked a little boy with blood trickling down his brow. "Besides, the concentration it would take to possess you would distract me too much."

"The revitalization of your body, perhaps? With your world-mate's aid, are you not powerful enough to realize that yet?"

"Ah. You are the smart one, aren't you? Yes, very dangerous, indeed."

"Who is it?"

"Oh, my dear lordship, you amuse me. Why should I tell you that my guardian is none other than a cousin who joined me in this this bright little realm of yours as a failsafe? Why should I tell you that? Why, when it would accomplish me nothing?"

"So why are you telling me?"

An aging woman with her hair stacked elaborately on her head laughed the haughty laugh that Lord Haphenasis had been hearing his whole life. "Dear boy, is it not obvious? I can say whatever I want and still get anything and everything I want."

"Like your body?"

"My body? That old thing? Why, that was never anything more than a shell for who I really am. Besides, like this, I can enjoy such freedom that I never could in just one limiting body of flesh and blood. No, little blubbery lord, I am after something far greater. Imagine what the children of three worlds could do."

He knew. Lord Haphenasis did not know how, nor did he care, but Izzard was aware of Vie's Otherrealm origins. He could not let her children fall into his hands. Even as he pulled in a cloud to carry himself off, he knew he would be too late.

"I wouldn't do that!" forty voices shouted at him, staying his departure. "If you do, you would be killing every person here. Oh, that would be fun, but is the life of a single woman worth those of forty innocents?"

Lord Haphenasis looked at the faces of the people around him. They were innocent, only a part of this drama because they were in the wrong place at the wrong time. He thought of Vie, protected by Ishtower and his other brothers staying at the Lion. Perhaps they could stay this psycho's hand where he could not. He had control of only himself. "But this," he heard Hamza's voice coming back to him, "is where trust comes into play."

Lord Haphenasis folded his legs, spread his staff across his lap, and put his trust in his brothers.

Chapter 29

Vie awoke with a start. There was silence around her, save for a slight rustling. A hand on her arm.

"Who?"

"It's me," Ishtower said. "I thought about pounding the pavement, looking for him, but he'll be back for us soon enough. I can't sleep."

"Why?" Vie asked, alarmed to find him in her room. Darkness had fallen, and the wood frogs were singing outside.

"It's like the calm before a big battle. Tension's building, but I don't know where it'll come from. I needed some company."

"Bad dreams?"

"That's part of it. I was watching Rebubula again. They came at her... they fell..." He started sobbing. Vie reached for him, pulled his head to her chest. The instinct

298

was part maternal, part affection. Ishtower responded by pulling her tight around him, wrapping his arms about her. He then sobbed until he could sob no more.

She wished she could do more for him. She wanted to make his bad dreams go away, but the only thought she had was what she used with her own children, what they had mastered so well with the Butcher: distraction.

"Tell me about your children."

"My children?"

"Are they little shits like mine?"

He snorted wetly. It may have been a chuckle. "Worse."

"How so?"

"The oldest, Ghai, was a nagging wretch. She excelled in her role as matriarch, always telling me to eat, to shave, to stop drinking. If she weren't here, after Rebubula's death..."

"Who is the youngest?"

"Poluw. He's the quietest of the bunch. Smiles more than is right for a kid. He's sixteen and likes being around his friends. Speaks softly when he does and sounds like a girl. It's from my being absent. He was just a boy when his mother died. He needed a father's firm hand, to show him what being a man was about—not this girly stuff he's so interested in."

"Does that bother you?"

"Yeah, it bothers me! I should have been there, not swallowed up in a bottle. The boy's gone soft in the head. I blame it on myself."

"The burden of being a lone parent," she said, smiling wanly.

"Dealing with little shits for the rest of our lives."

"And never time for our own wants or needs."

Ishtower's hand was on her leg. She could feel the warmth of it, the warmth that was filling her up.

"Ishtower," she said, knowing that it would be wrong now.

"Do you deny it?" His hand moved upward. His hand was on her hip.

"Do you always use misery as a way to get the girls?"

"Only when I need to," he said as his mouth closed in on hers.

She met his tongue's exploration and wanted more, but, "No," she said, pulling away. "It's time for you to leave."

"Are you certain you do not want me to stay?"

The way he spoke was all wrong. The inflection, the voice. That smile.

"Malek!" she gasped.

Her hands snapped up above her head as she was thrust flat on her back.

"Hello, dear," Malek said in the voice of Ishtower. "I told you I would be back. Even if it took longer than anticipated."

Her legs, bound by some unknown force, were spread. Izzard pulled the covers off her. Although dressed in a nightshirt, she felt painfully exposed before his lecherous needs. She tried to concentrate on her other two forms, but the mouse ran away and the dragon would not come. Tears of helplessness began to roll across her face.

"It is always fun to possess a magus. They are so arrogant to think that they are immune to my powers." He removed the dark tunic and folded it. "Some are right. I might be able to possess that stuffy snoot, Lord Happiness, or whatever his name is, but doing so would probably exhaust me." Next came the belt, which he casually rolled up. "But this body and I are old friends. Not just from earlier today, either. I remembered the lovely taste of his anguish as his wife was raped to death." Beneath the trousers, he was naked and erect. "Did he ever tell you what happened then?" With the trousers folded and set aside, he stood above her, letting the gentle glow of the night's stars wash over him, highlighting the strong beauty of the man's body. "Once she was dead, he cried for her. I let him. I am not evil after all." His hands caressed Vie's hair, his lips played across her bound arms. "I let him go to her." A blue blade of arcana appeared in his hand as he cut away her nightshirt. His lips brushed her nipples, the hair of his unshaven chin tickled her belly.

Vie screamed.

"Shush, shush, shush," Izzard said, flicking the blade away and pulling down a bubble of silence over them. "You don't really want to have company do you?" He hovered above her, lay down over and between her. His eyes were closed as he inhaled deeply over every part of her. "Oh. Oh, yes. Oh how I have missed that lovely smell," he panted. "You were always special, little Vie. But you knew that. It is such a shame that you never could understand just what you really were."

"Leave me alone!"

He kissed her ear in response, gently nibbling on her lobe. It was as exquisite as it used to be. Despite her rage, her fear and hatred of this man in her friend's form, she could not stop her body's response to his touch.

"I do not want you!"

"Of course you do," he whispered. His lips on her

ear were agony. "But my tale is not yet over." He nuzzled
her breasts. "When Ishtower took his dead wife in his
arms, he was not satisfied." His hands cradled her shoulders—strong, mighty arms that felt so familiar despite the
wrong body. "No." She felt his hand along the small of
her back, hooking around one of her cheeks, pulling her
leg up and to the side. "Can you guess what he did next?"

She was helpless to fight him. All she had was a word
and knew it was insignificant. "No."

Izzard rubbed Ishtower's cock against her.

"Yes. Oh the places this has been. And where will it
go next? I think we both know that."

Vie screamed.

She screamed Ishtower off of her. She screamed the
bubble of silence into broken pieces. She screamed herself into a dragon that burst the arcane cords that had
bound her wrists. She screamed as she backed through
the wall, too large to be contained within her one room.
She screamed as she beheld the faces of her three children.

"Well now!" Izzard said, awed by her mighty new
form. "My beauty has finally revealed herself to me. And
her children."

"You will stay away from them," she growled.

"Mommy?" Bel asked, terrified sleepiness in her wide
eyes.

"Stay back."

"You know that you cannot protect them from me.
Give them up." He was standing there, flickers of arcana
dribbling off him.

"Over my dead body."

"If you wish," he said. Ishtower's body collapsed as if

it had been a marionette with its stings cut.

Malek Izzard was then there, in her head, penetrating her as foully as he had hoped to do a moment ago. Every sick, depraved thought that he had stabbed her repeatedly. Every indiscretion, every desire, and twisted want. For the first time in her life – past the stories – past her imagination, she felt everything that Izzard actually was. She roared in defiance of his evil. In doing so, she realized that while she could feel the twisted morass of his thoughts, she was still herself inside it all, fighting for freedom. She was being beaten, battered bloody by his wretched mind, but she was fighting.

With the realization that she was still in control, she lashed out with her tail. Two strikes and the wall to the exterior of the building burst. She dropped into the courtyard with a heavy thud. He was still there, right with her, but at least now she had space and her children were not at risk from a stray strike. Izzard gloated as he mocked her, threatening the truth, that without a body of his own, he was not bound by such limitations as breath or hunger, just her. He would never, could never, let her go. Above her, she could hear her children shouting something.

"Help her! Please, help her!"

The Butcher, his sword ever-present in his hand, was there, looking confused.

Fear clutched at her but it was not her emotion. She realized with a start that the emotion came from Malek Izzard. He looked upon the big man and his big sword and was terrified. It was a moment of authenticity in a creature of lies. He started to pull away from her, whether to ensnare the Butcher in his grip or to simply get away, but she would not let that happen. His violations of her had pushed her far past anger and into a strange clarity of vision. If he were scared to be here, then here he would stay. "You wanted me, bastard, then you'll have me." She wrapped herself so tightly around him that Izzard could not escape.

"Kill me!" she then roared at the Butcher.

Anger flickered over his face. But her children were right there, placating him.

"Leave him be!" she roared again to her children.

"Stop that!" the Butcher shouted at her. "Leave them alone!"

"Then come and get me, you coward!"

Bel screamed her name. Bon grabbed at the butcher, begging him not to give in. Braden? Sweet Braden simply stared at his parents in his mother's body, confused, but brave as the two fought for control within her. Her beautiful babies. Her reason for living and her reason for death. Whatever she could do for them, she would.

"I love you," she whispered to them.

The Butcher leapt.

Vie leaned back, spreading both arms and wings, exposing her heart to the Butcher's black blade.

Malek Izzard howled inside her.

"You're the one who wanted to be fucked," she whispered to him as the black sword plunged into her chest.

Chapter 30

LORD HAPHENASIS'S CLOUD SPED ALONG IN A WAY THAT NO cloud should. If propelled by a free wind, it would be moving on a hurricane's pace. As such, it required space to blow. It needed freedom to vent, which required altitude. He had never flown so high. If he bothered to look down, he would have been horrified by the distance between him and the ground below. His current elevation put him well higher than the tallest building in the city, the Temple of Higher Truth, whose steeple could be seen from all throughout the city. Lord Haphenasis did not look down because he had more important things on his mind.

His meditation back in the square had been a ruse. He trusted that Izzard would be unable to hurt or kill everyone in the square, but he also could not leave his brothers alone to battle him. It was not through lack of trust, it was more through a refusal to give in to the homicidal terror's demands. So he had sat down and split his mind, half remaining where he was, the other half going back to the Lion, where certain wards and guards remained, watching after Vie and the others. It was an easy trick, and one to which he knew Izzard would be oblivious. He had arrived back just in time to witness the dragon unleashed upon... Ishtower?

Of course. He would be the most likely lackey for the villain. The two had known each other from before. Add to that the fact that earlier they had invited him into Ishtower's body. Sadly, it was another area in which he had failed.

"Over my dead body," the dragon had said.

Ishtower dropped like a puppet with its strings cut. Izzard had projected himself into Vie's dragon form. Lord Haphenasis felt horror at the thought of a dragon possessed of Malek Izzard's mind. The level of destruction would be unimaginable. Even in his astral form, he managed to cast a protective bolster in the dragon's consciousness. It was the least he could do. It was the most he could do. The spunk she had shown throughout their brief acquaintance had been a bother, but for once, he hoped that Vie's force of will would be enough to stave off the attack.

The arcane vibration that Izzard gave off dwindled. It concentrated entirely around the dragon. The people in the square who Izzard threatened to kill would be free. Trusting that the dragon could hold off Izzard's influence for a moment, he had returned fully to his own body, blasted all the people in the square to sleep, and summoned the cloud.

The Gilded Lion was below him now. He looped

around to the western side, where their suite faced. Lights had been left out, illuminating the area outside. Similarly, from seemingly every room, there were freshly-lit candles. It was not surprising considering the ruckus made when the dragon knocked through the wall. Everyone wanted to see what the commotion was about.

The dragon roared something at the people in the chamber above them. What was it? With the wind howling in his ears, Lord Haphenasis could not make it out.

The Butcher. He leaped off the edge of the building with his sword in hand.

"No!" Lord Haphenasis screamed, casting half a dozen spells to keep the blade from the dragon.

The aura from the sword deflected them all and plunged smoothly through the glittering silver of her chest. The force of the attack knocked the dragon over onto her back. The Butcher stared down at her body, grimacing, seemingly almost cognizant of what he had done. Lord Haphenasis landed running and called on the winds to blow. Zephyr, Aeole, and Currant struck the Butcher enough force to blow him off the body of the dragon. The sword did not budge.

No matter. Lord Haphenasis panted up to the dragon and probed. Alive. Barely. The sword had severed her artery. She would bleed to death in moments.

"Botch?" Ishtower called down weakly from above. He was sweating and could barely hold himself up by clutching the ruined wall. A distant part of him wondered what he was doing naked. "Izzard?"

Lord Haphenasis searched for the familiar vibration. There was no sign of it.

Foul language was something used by the lower class,

but right now, here, there was something gutturally satisfying is such a lowborn oath. "Shit!" he screamed. There was no way he could have arrived too late. Why had he not used the winds first? It would have stopped the butcher. It would have knocked him away from the dragon.

Another voice within him spoke up then: What is done is done. Second guess yourself after the work is complete. It was the voice of reason, the voice that had always helped him through his studies, the abuse, and insults back at the Academy. It was the voice of logic, reminding him that emotion was useless here. Focus.

He had three options before him: The first was to rage and wreak vengeance upon the Butcher. The second was to track the spirit of Izzard if he could, an odious task, considering his inability to detect even the faintest glimmer of the Cataclysm. The third was to tend to the dragon, whom he could feel slipping away.

If he saved the dragon, he would have to touch the sword and risk a reversal of roles. The Butcher would wind up on the dragon's chest and he would be a dead, desiccated corpse. That was clearly no option.

Malek Izzard's soul was invisible to him, which meant two things: it was already dispersed into the aether or it had fled. If dispersed, it was out of reach. If fled, it would be weak, and there would be no better time to trap it, weakened as it was by the ebony blade. Unless it had been captured within the blade itself. Was that even possible? The threat of the weapon gave it such an air of mystery that he feared that any of its secrets would reveal themselves.

If he decided to take vengeance upon the Butcher, it would accomplish nothing. It would be only emotional satisfaction in lieu of emotional duress.

If he were alone, whatever decision he made would be the wrong one.

But he was not alone. There was a thump on Vie's belly as one of the children landed. There followed two more. A scream and the cracking of a bone came with the last thump. From the third story hole-in-a-wall they had jumped from, Haphenasis was not surprised that at least one of them was hurt.

"Stop griping. We're doing this together," snapped the girl. "Whine later."

"On three," said the smallest.

The children spread out onto different sides of the bleeding Dragon's chest. The middle child stood on one leg while the other two supported him.

"Ready? One."

"Two."

"Three!"

As one, they grabbed the hilt of the sword. A moment of change rippled over them, a dull flash that struggled with the contrast of the three individuals.

"Pull!"

All three screamed as they struggled to extract the ebony blade from their mother's chest. As it rose, the three children's forms blurred from one to the other, and to the Butcher. When it was free from Vie's chest, Lord Haphenasis summoned the three winds again and blasted sword and children away, separating all. The kids collapsed to the ground as the blade clattered well out of reach. The Butcher, he was happy to note, had not replaced any of them.

"Ishtower! See to the kids!"

In making their choice of action, the kids had given Lord Haphenasis his own path. Pressing his hands to the dragon's side, he could plunge a variation of Tactile Recall into her. In a heartbeat, he could feel every movement within the large body. He was no healer, but he knew arcana. The arcana of the dragon and the arcana of the sword were beyond his experience, but how different could each be?

The sword first. It had left a residue inside her cut, one akin to the secretion from a bug. It fought him as if with a mind of its own, but he commanded it out. It rose from the dragon's chest and was wrapped up in an arcane jar to be set aside while he concentrated on more important things.

Lamytal was a realm where arcana ran purer than in this one. That meant for all he knew, as at least part-denizen of Lamytal, she might be composed almost entirely of arcana. He thought of a craftsman that he once had the pleasure of watching. The man had deft skills that could mold clay into a number of forms. The way his fingers worked were as if he had had no eyes. It was those fingers that knew which shape was inside the clay, so finely adept at the craft that they only needed the man's imagination to set them working. While there had been no arcane manipulations in the man's action, Lord Haphenasis nonetheless recognized magic when he saw it. This was the example that he had to emulate if he wanted to reconnect the dragon's heart to its valves.

It was hot, warm, bloody, disgusting, and wonderful. The fibers of Vie's being struggled against his will, much like a body fought against a virus. Each attempt he made brought him up short. Like a living thing, the arcana in

Vie snapped at him, gouging away at his wards despite his efforts on her behalf. When he finally was able to draw one vein of her body together, another seemed to snap, releasing an extra bout of blood that spat upward in rebellion.

He pressed harder into her side, feeling the sharp scales cutting into his fingertips and palm. Ignoring the pain, he wove himself through the ventricles of her heart. Its beating had begun slowing. Slowing. Yes. That was brilliant. Drawing coldness from the air, he spread a layer of ice over her chest, hoping it would slow her heart down more. This was a tricky maneuver, as he did not want to slow her heart too much. If it slowed beyond a certain point, there would be no getting her back. The blood leaking into her gaping wound congealed and slowed.

The next step was to split his consciousness. One part would concentrate on returning the dark oozy red back into her veins. The rest would concentrate on resealing the hole. With the icy compress on her skin, it should keep the broken parts close enough that he could reconnect them with little problem. Strings of arcana appeared inside her, reaching from one end to another, drawing them close enough for him to weld them back together again. It was made the more difficult due to the peculiar aspect of her being. Arcana here in Traumanfang was a wisp, a tease at the ends of consciousness that made its mastery all that more difficult, but the arcana in Vie was so densely packed that it was hard to tell just how much pressure to put. The force required to manipulate the material of her body was nearly five times as much as he was used to. It was much like making a transition from cutting butter to cutting the more elastic part of tripe or an overcooked crust of bread that crumbled under his touch; there was no middle ground.

Three times he found himself cursing the inconsistency of her body. But he was making progress. Half of the organs had been successfully repaired. All that was left was one last piece of her heart. It was while pressing his consciousness into the heart that a spasm wracked Vie's massive form. The shuddering of her flesh shattered the icy poultice that he had set across her chest. A chunk of what he had done burst apart. Not all, thankfully, but he was running out of time. The dying usually suffered a rattle before their last breaths kicked in, and he feared that this was her final shudder before passing on.

"Do not do this to me!" he heard himself growling, a million leagues away, where his body was. The distraction made him acutely aware of how painfully he was trembling. As he shifted his view from the mundane to the arcane, he saw what was happening. Vie's body was acting as a sponge that was soaking up all of the arcana that he had stored over his long years inhabiting the Riot. At the rate he was going, he would be dead long before Vie was. Dragon or not, he was not about to let that happen.

Slowly, he began drawing what he could back to himself. Defeat came to everyone. It was time to let it go.

Just like he let go of the Apocryptein.

The thought hurt. He wondered if he might have been able to do more at the time, maybe one spell or another, but nothing was coming to mind about that; his head was too clogged up with a simple idea. It was what he had done when he blew the upper levels of the Apocryptein up. Grounding himself, he tapped into the two Veins closest to him and after only a moment of concern that the Lion was too far away for him to tap them, could feel Dei and Wn around him, but they were sluggish – was this a result of the tarnishing? Whatever the case, arcana was coming too slowly to be of any good; if he were to correct the remaining wounds in Vie, he would need more.

Lord Haphenasis took a deep breath. What he was planning could not take thought for the damage might be irreparable to him. Each living creature had an instinctual barrier that protected himself or herself from the full torrent of the Veins. In a way, it was like skin, protecting the body from the elements while simultaneously keeping the self inside and intact. One of the first things that all initiates learned is not to open oneself completely to the Veins. In essence, it was not unlike poking a hole in a dam. So long as the hole was properly reinforced, a safe quantity of water would push through, and the magus or Heart could use the arcana as they saw fit. However, if that delicate balance was shattered, so, too, would the levee. A river of arcana would blast forth from the Veins and crash through that person's body with such force as to create a total discorporation of both soul and body. So, without considering the more fatalistic aspects of such a strategy, he popped all his defenses and let both Veins flood through him.

The first moment was orgasmic. Both Veins were intimately known to him, and their rush of arcana filled him with a heady draught that left him weak in the knees. But just as suddenly as the pleasure started, it moved past and into a dangerous level, he felt himself being swallowed in the torrent of energy. Another few moments and he would drown.

Luckily for him, he was still connected to the dragon. Acting as a pipeline, he pushed the rushing tide into her. It hurt—of that there was no question—but this was tolerable agony. Already, he could feel Vic's aura increase, though her heart rate did not change. He had bought himself some precious few moments, possibly with his life, and he got to task.

At last the wound was closed. Somehow, he knew not where he found the strength; he turned the spigot onto the two Veins and felt the blissful silence wash gently over him. His body quivered as if it were a giant bell that had been struck by an endless series of blows from a mallet. He blearily rose from the dragon's chest, stained nearly head to toe in her blood, which, now cooled, brought a chill to him. He cared little for this. All he could think about was the woman, the dragon, Vie.

"Are you alive?" he rasped through parched lips.

The dragon sighed its response.

That done, he looked up. Dawn's light was creeping across the sky. Only in the western horizon did the dark trails of the night yet linger. In trying to climb down from the dragon, he tumbled and fell with a thud to the grass. Only stubborn pride forced him to not give in to the oblivious then and there. He found himself rising and looking around. Nearby, Ishtower was leaning against a tree, all three of Vie's children clutched in his arms. The Butcher lay huddled nearby, his attention completely engrossed with a pinecone. In addition, Constable Erchak stood off near the building with a handful of his troops, pushing guests back.

"Wha... what?" Lord Haphenasis stuttered.

A constable handed him some tea. The hot liquid

was blissful on his lips, though he could not even taste it. All he could tell was that it was warm and nice and wet. Ishtower had risen and came over to join him.

"You saw all the important stuff already. The kids didn't want to leave their mother."

It took another cup of tea to get him to the point where he felt he could try speaking. His throat was as hoarse as the rest of his body.

"How did they know to try and pull out the sword together?"

"We've been spending lots of time with him," Braden said. The other two had run over to check on their mother. "Learning about the guy who switched with him got Bon wondering what would happen if more than one person touched it at once." Large tears began falling. "He hurt our momma. We couldn't just do nothing."

Lord Haphenasis creaked downward onto his knee and stared the boy in the eyes. His hands clasped his shoulders. "You saved her life."

The boy's hug was the first one he had received in Veins knew how long. It was exactly what he needed.

Chapter 31

THERE WAS A LUMP, A BIG HEAVY LUMP, THAT TOOK UP THE majority of the bed. The thin sheet was almost completely doing its job for the lump, but not for her. Such was life with children. They invaded your life and took over, leaving you with nothing but the edges. They were uncompromising in their takeover, too. Even though a sword had plunged into her chest and left her laid up for two days, all three children still came in every night to join her in bed.

Vie sighed and, wincing, pulled herself upright. The tightness in her chest would be there a while, Dane Wunds had told her on the special trip he had made to check on her. Her body was still struggling to adapt to the oddity of having to reconnect some major parts that that sword had cut through. She stumbled to the luxurious full-length mirror that the room had been decorated with and removed her nightshirt. Slowly she unclipped the bandage and unwound it from her chest. The exposed scar had puckered into an ugly red slit just above her heart, marring the top of her left breast. It was a ghastly reminder of how brave she had actually been, of how much she had been willing to sacrifice.

Numbly, she thought about her choice. When he had disappeared those many years ago, she had cursed Malek Izzard for abandoning her. In the naiveté of youth, she had imagined the pair of them raising the children together, two young people from the rough part of town, overcoming all odds and raising three perfect children. But then he had left and she had been forced to raise them all by herself.

In the mirror, she could see them, one on the other, together and close. Bon lay closest to the wall, almost completely wrapped up in the cover. Only the leg that he had broken when the other two landed on him stuck out. His snores were a lovely racket. Braden was nothing but a white mound buried between the two, as well as it should be. He was smart enough to use the others as a buffer to the world. He would feel no pain, but when it fell, it would hit him hardest of all. And Bel. She had become so somber lately, but thankfully, no less inquisitive. It had broken Vie's heart to think of leaving her with the responsibility of the other two. And though Bel hadn't mentioned it, her eyes showed she knew how close they had come to that.

A sob rose in Vie's throat. Not wanting to wake them, she stifled the sound but let her tears fall. They had told her what they had done, told her of how Bon jumped first, then tried to catch the others as they fell, but that he had landed badly, which is how he broke his ankle. But he saw it through like a right little soldier, and together they gripped the blade. They had told her how they had talked about it before.

She was proud of them. So proud. So proud that they had none of their father's sickness. So proud that they were not lost and alone the way she had spent so much of her own life. Like she was again.

Learning that Malek had been imprisoned in the Apocryptein had revived emotions that she had thought long buried. Part of her had wanted the fantasy. Part of her yearned for his touch as she once had known it. That was why she had to know. From Squite, from his nephew Yankee, from Ishtower, from several of the other magi who had been here in the Gilded Lion, she had to know what he had done. They told her story after story, horror after horror. She had listened, disgusted, unwilling to believe them, yet knowing full well that they had been true. Everything had to be true.

Malek's choice at using Ishtower had been deliberate. She could see past his justifications. She knew he had known of her attraction to the magus. It had been a deliberate stab that isolated her from the people around her. She had seen Ishtower only once since then, when he came to express his apologies. It was him, free of Malek's influence, but she could only see Malek, teasing her, taunting her as he prepared to rape her. She had wanted to offer her condolences about his wife—the true horror of what Malek had forced him to do—but the moment she saw him, it had taken all her willpower to keep from screaming. When he had left, she rolled over and trembled herself to sleep.

This agony was Malek's legacy. It was the only way

he knew how to love. It was disgusting, but it was his way of looking after her. While he was inside her head, he had offered to give Vie her dream of them living together to raise the children, but she could see past the offer. If he had stayed with her, he would make excuses to take over her body or force the children to commit evil things, and the corruption that defined him would soon destroy them. No, they were far better off with him out of their life. There had been no choice. After everything that he had done, everything that she had learned, he could not be allowed into their lives.

Even if it meant killing the only man she had ever loved.

Vie blew her nose on a kerchief. She would not cry for Malek Izzard. She would not cry for the father of her children. He had lost the privilege of her pity long ago. Besides, she was from Sludge. Tears were for weaklings. Now it was time to get dressed.

Slowly, painfully, she wrapped the bandage around her chest and clipped it into place. She walked over to the wardrobe and looked at the clothing she and Bel had purchased during their outing. The green dress would not do, as it had a low-cut top that, with a more endowed woman, would show off her bosom. To wear it would be to display bandages. Her travelling clothes were worn and she did not want to give the wrong idea. That left the silver one with the white netting that framed her neck and head. Vie slipped it on and tied up the laces up front and the sash. She looked at herself in the mirror.

"You're pretty," Bel said.

"Want to do up Mommy's hair?"

Bel leaped out of bed at the notion. The pair sat in silence as Bel formed two layered braids and wrapped Vie's long hair around the two silver chopsticks that she had so often wore in her hair. Below this was a thin layer of free hair that hung about her neck. It was a very inspired and interesting hairstyle.

"You look like your dragon," Bel said proudly.

Vie pulled her daughter close and kissed her head. "One day you will understand what I did."

"I'll never let you go."

Vie eventually released her only daughter and wiped away the girl's tears that were falling despite her locked and set jawline. "Good. I'll kick your skinny little butt into next week if you do."

As Vie tucked Bel back into bed, Braden stirred. "Where you going?"

"Breakfast. You wanna come?"

He yawned and nodded. Throwing on a shirt, he was ready to go. They slipped down to the foyer where Lord Haphenasis was finishing a breakfast of rice, fried pork, egg, and coffee. He jumped when she called his name, chopsticks clattered on his plate. His eyes were lined and he trembled slightly. He struggled to rise. Vie waved him off and the pair joined him at the table.

"Vie, I had not expected to see you out of bed so soon."

"Two days is too long. There's lots I have to do."

"Quite," he sniffed and looked at her. "The... the silver... it matches... your hair... I... you look beautiful."

The compliment came as a complete surprise. Vie felt herself smiling at the fat magus. *Has he lost weight?* "I have you to thank for the fact that I'm even alive to dress up and make an ass of myself."

"No," he shook his head. His body creaked as he leaned toward her. "It is I who has been the ass. I have lived alone too long. I had grown complacent and miserable."

"You did find me stealing from you."

"I was annoyed at having a quiet Mundus interrupted."

"I did burn down your Apocryptein."

"Do not push my good will. I have been told that I am a powerful man."

"One with a bigger heart than he would credit himself with."

He folded his arms over his chest. "Best not to let that get out. If the other Cataclysms learn of it, they might assume I am just another pest out to bother them."

"Yes, just another common pest who brought a dragon back to life."

This seemed to brighten him up. "That is a fair credential if I may use it?"

"It is your deed."

"Vie... I. You must know, after I healed you, I looked for him – for Izzard."

"You couldn't find him."

The lord shook his head. "No. His soul was—is—gone. He is dead."

Such words could have once cracked her heart. Instead, they brought her relief. A nightmare had concluded, and the dawn was washing away even the faintest shadows. She ran her hands over her arms to try and catch the warmth that shot throughout her body. Yet, for all her satisfaction, Lord Haphenasis looked worried.

"What's wrong?"

"The Twelve were imprisoned so that they would never die. They would be trapped forever."

"Was there really any other choice than to kill him?"

"I have lived my life on the assumption that there is always a choice. I do not believe in no-win scenarios. In working alone, I always have won."

"After having worked with others, does this feel like a loss?"

"Not a loss, no. But not a win, either."

"You made a decision in defense of life."

"Yes, well. Your children had a hand in making that reality possible. Anyway." He finished off the last of the fried pork on his plate. "We must not allow the time to tread on too hastily. Despite your eagerness for mobility, I would recommend avoiding the front door. We have set out two of our brothers to keep the nosier of the paparazzi out of your hair, but be wary anyway. They will either want to ask you a million questions or kill you. I am afraid that you have become a bit of a celebrity."

"I can never return to Sludge. How tragic."

"Quite." He wiped his mouth with a napkin and took up his walking staff. Even getting to his feet was a chore; Vie signaled Braden to help him to his feet. "Thank you," he told the boy.

"You did the right thing, milord," Braden told him.

****

What is it about children and their need for making their opinions so known? Lord Haphenasis looked down at the wide-eyed child. Is he expecting something? At least the boy had gotten the honorific correct. There might be some hope for him yet. Still, the two stood a short step apart, for an awkward moment that seemed to drag on far too long. With the bulk of his weight supported by his staff, he reached out his other hand toward the child. He did not know what kind of contact was requisite in a social situation like this, so he hesitantly touched the top of the child's head. It had to do. He nodded at a job well done and took his leave.

His body ached through and through, and he had developed a twitch that did not appear to be going away any time soon. Walking was a chore, and even just the act of standing without his walking stick was virtually impossible. Dane Wunds said that he would be watching to see whether or not it was a permanent consequence of opening one's self completely to the Veins. Sadly, the Healer had no point of reference; Lord Haphenasis was the first to have done so and lived. Nevertheless, the healer had given the lord a number of painkillers and arcane medicines.

Exiting through the glass doors of the cafeteria, he saw Ishtower coming toward him from the other end of the hall. Just like himself, the Martialist was bearing signs of defeat. His face was drawn and dark under his long black hair. Usually well-shaved, the beard that he was developing gave him quite a savage look. Still, Lord Haphenasis found himself unable to dredge up the choler he had once had for this man.

"There you are! Come on, Hamza wants to speak with us."

As with everything in the past couple days, the walk to the annex was painfully long, and made longer by the worry that was assaulting him. Word had no doubt reached Hamza's discerning ears about what has become of the Possessor. With a deep sigh that strained his bruised and battered ribs, he entered the room to find Hamza sipping tea with his two assistants, Aziz el Hoeft and Georgan Waever, as well as another magus whom he did not recognize.

"You found him," Hamza said. "Good."

Lord Haphenasis began before Hamza could say anything. "Skeleton, about the Possessor, we did what we could—"

Hamza held out a hand to cut him off. "This is not about him. While it is tragic that he died, we can only hope that the Butcher's blade soaked him up or that his soul has already dispersed through the aether. I am not here today to discuss an unfortunate circumstance of our war."

"Then to what do I owe your visit?"

"News is always best heard from the source, is it not? Have a seat."

With a groan of necessity, Lord Haphenasis did as the Skeleton Key bid.

"First, the good. Mican Bracamonte has gathered a group to begin reconstruction of the Apocryptein."

"This is most welcome news, indeed."

"Don't get excited yet. His figures put its completion at two years. Manpower is scarce compared to what it was when the tower was first constructed. There is money in working like this, but the blood sacrifices will be harder to come by. We may have to strike a deal with Knockni in order to get the quantity we would need. It is not a thought I revel in, as they will likely try to ensure that it serves a double function as a temple to their bloody god. I loathe considering how well such sacrifices will be taken by the local judicial branches. But that is not your concern. Just you take whatever solace you can that it is being worked on. The other bit of good news is that so long as Vie is here, recuperating under the care of Dane Wunds, the Butcher will also remain here. Those are two concerns you had expressed worry in. Now the bad. Aziz?"

"Yes, Skeleton," the assistant said in his characteristic high pitch. "Milord, you see, we've been working toward finding the others, and well, you see, we think we're getting pretty good at it."

This did not sound like a very promising start. By his glance, Ishtower seemed to feel the same. "Go on."

"So over the past couple days—well, it's been more of a week, really—Georgan and I found it."

"So we took the liberty of sending a team. See, we've really learned a whole lot—"

"And thought it best to just go ahead—"

"But we didn't expect this—"

"Which is why Rhone's here. He's gonna tell you just what happened."

Lord Haphenasis leveled his gaze on the stranger. The look on the young man's face was all that he needed to see. There were only the smaller of the details, like which one he had found. "Are you certain that it was one of the Twelve?"

"Most certainly, milord," Rhone replied, plunging his hands deep into the pockets of his red robe. "We—that's Selva and me—followed the scent, just like Aziz and Georgan said, and well... we tracked it to this place in the woods north of Koein and, well... there were lots of dead animals. Something was there. So the Hound pointed us into the woods, right in the path of all these dead beasts.

When we got to the clearing, there was a woman."

"A woman?" Lord Haphenasis asked, not liking where this story was going. He had enough understanding of the Twelve to guess who it may be, but he wanted to hear for himself.

"She was old, like you, but really pretty. Maybe not so old, but the silver hair made me think so. Heavy-set with the biggest, most ripe..."

"Go on!"

"Sorry, milord. She looked at us and waved her arm. Selva exploded right there. No time to think or even do nothing, he just... popped. Didn't even look at me, though. But I didn't stay. I can't channel that kind of power. I was scared for my life."

"Was he a Blessed?"

He seemed surprised by this. "Yeah, he's the one with four arms—was the one with four arms. Does that—what's that got to do with it?"

"Everything." So soon. With a second of the Twelve fully reconstituted, it could well be a signal of the pace of events to come. There was no more time to catch their breaths. All they could do now is fight to stay ahead of the game. As Lord Haphenasis struggled to his feet, Ish-tower also rose. The lord's life of solitude was over and he was happy for it. The way he was feeling, he was thankful for whatever help he could get.

"Do you have a plan?" Hamza asked.

"Yes, I do. We will pack up, leave my two protégés to their hunting here in the Gilded Lion, gather a team together, head west, and hunt the Cataclysm down."

Epilogue

THE MAIGRE SAT UNMOVING, AS IT HAD BEEN COMMANDED TO do. Its black cloak had long ago merged with the darkness around it, a chamber that was no chamber for the darkness that filled it. It had become like a living thing, creeping and crawling over the cloak up and over the maigre's body. Until all that remained were four gimlets of blue fire. The maigre's eyes continued to stare, unblinking, uncoverable, at the small circle before it. From this circle there hummed a tiny orange light like a tranquil pond upset by nothing, perfect in its dormant silence.

A prickle of motion set a single wave across the surface, so small that the eyes of the maigre nearly missed it. The darkness surrounding the maigre shimmered and grew four tendrils that shuddered off the heavier obsidian, revealing arms ending in taloned claws. The claws gripped the edges of the circle as another ripple—larger this time—hit its surface.

Drop after drop struck the circle, a rainstorm striking a puddle as the maigre leaned forward, a red cavity opening up inside its darkness. The red glow pushed forward around the edges of the circle. As each beat struck the circle, the maigre hummed and the red glow expanded inside and back from the circle.

The rippling came faster now. What began as a drizzle had begun a torrent, splashing with violent force with each strike. With each splash, the maigre expanded more and more. Finally, there was a large booming sound and the rippling ceased. The orange glow faded. The room was silent once more.

Replacing the orange was the swollen red balloon that the maigre had become. Rocking onto its four clawed legs, it lifted its four-eyed head and crept along the darkness. Clicking resounded in the hallways of the gloom. It passed through the traffic of lesser paths, ignoring the music that played below, where the slave masters played with the bones and bodies of their beasts of burden.

Up and up it crawled, past the divining pools that dripped blood into storming cups. Past the Stables of Fell, where the Master kept the beasts of war. Past the rows of impaled. Beyond the sea of skulls, and through the villages and towns, all the while ignoring every wretch, soul, beast, and creature. It had its purpose and it would fulfill it and receive the Master's accolades.

At the obsidian door, it tapped a single claw against the booming black iron. The doors lifted, permitting it access to the immense chamber beyond. Here, the Vigil watched the world around them from viewing circles. It was from here that the Master learned of the proceedings of this realm. All around, the diligent eyes of the room absented themselves from work to turn toward the maigre. And there the Master was, enthroned, pleased, and watching all that happened.

"You are here," the Master spoke in a voice as oily as darkness.

The maigre had no voice to speak with, but it skittered up onto the dais beside the throne, where a mechanism of flesh and carapace awaited it. It settled down, pressing its claws into the four cavities beneath it. Claws met claws as a prying rod punctured the shell of its flesh. The rods were sweet agony as they plundered the flesh through and through until they emerged in the swirling spool of red energy in the maigre's sack. A current shocked through the tips of the rods, igniting the energy.

It swirled slowly, then with more violence, until it had taken on the visage of the soul that it had trapped.

"Malek Izzard," the Master said. "After so long, you finally return. Welcome home."

"Thank you. It is good to be home."

"You were imprisoned."

"I was."

"Thanks to your cousin, you are now free."

"Yes, but I was not expecting to return home again so soon. There was still so much fun I had hoped to have in Traumanfang. It's a tourist's dream."

"Do tell. And withhold nothing of this world of man."

A wicked smile crept across the face of the soul. "Mother, it will be a pleasure."

The story will continue in

The Twelve Cataclysms, Book II: Epitasis

Glossary of Terms

10-sided Riot – n.c. a Riot which is the connection of five different Veins.

Academy of Concept – n.c. one of the three main colleges of the Order of the Vein found in the Innervein. Its focus is Priber arcana, among others.

Academy of Time – n.c. One of the three main colleges of the Order of the Vein found in the Innervein. Its focus is Tentagist arcana, among others.

Academy of Touch – n.c. One of the three main colleges of the Order of the Vein found in the Innervein. Its focus is Martialist arcana, among others.

Aethir – n.u. elemental plane of existence where arcana lies. The Veins are points of potent Aethir collection.

Apocryptein – n. singular. Also known as *The Silver Tower*. This is a massive tower built by the brothers of the Order of the Vein to contain and stifle threats to not just life, but to all life across the face of Traumanfang.

Arcana – n.u. official term for all magic in Traumanfang and in the other eight Realms

Arcanum – n. name for magic in use.

"He created a bubble of arcanum that surrounded his prey, preventing the prey's escape."

Argun – n.c. 3rd day of the calendar week (Tuesday).

Blue Realm – n. One of the nine Realms. This one is known for its odd creatures and human-like Fey, sociable winged sprites, and the peculiar women known as Lysos.

Bowie – n. According to some belief systems, Bowie exists in the western world beyond the False Sea. It is believed that miserable souls retreat here upon death. Bowie has been identified by both Hearts and magi as the Realm known as The Yin.

Capo – n. Capo is the opposite realm to The Yin in that upon death, it is here, to Capo, that blessed or exemplary souls go.

Cataclysm – n.c. title given to threats extending beyond life on Traumanfang and into the other Realms. There have been twelve named as such.

Copper chit – n.c. the least valuable of all currencies in Traumanfang. A copper coin stamped with different images depending on location.

Crystal Dragon of the Magi of Ulster – n. For the past 200 years, The Crystal Dragon of the Magi of Ulster has been awarded by the Order of the Vein to the magus who shows tremendous capability with Arcana. It is a lifetime gift, and can only be awarded upon death of previous possessor. The item itself has many capabilities such as size-shifting, semi-sentience, and in flight, can carry the full weight of a grown man.

Emak - n.u. a high-ranking member of the Sisterhood of the Heart.

Fifth Transport of Ulster - n.u. A military convoy responsible for the maintenance of certain roadways stretching from Yega to the Ganymeade region. The Fifth Transport is responsible for apprehending and halting, roadside attacks, mugging and crime in general.

Festival of the Mother - n.f. Spring Festival Holiday which celebrates birth and vibrancy of life. It is named for The Mother, founder of the Sisterhood of the Heart. In Reservwyresport, it is celebrated as a water festival. Other cities have their own variations on the theme.

Four Hells - n.c. These are the less beloved of the Realms connected by the Innervein. They are Darkness, The Yin (Bowie), The Dreamscape, and Fracture.

Hessian nana - n.c. Slang. an insult which implies one smells really bad, thanks to the stinks Hessians create to camouflage themselves from the creatures surrounding Hess.

Hannut - n.c. 4th day of the week (Wednesday).

Ha Vein -n. previously, the only Vein to be corrupted and tarnished. Done so by Skeleton Key Feliz Durawk.

Hooselberries - n.c a type of berry that grows near Reservwyresport. Green with purple veins. Crunchy seeds.

Hound - n.c. Mystical device with whirring gyros and a

miniature globe of Traumanfang that can track people across the world.

Innult – n.c. 5th day of the week (Thursday).

Jose's Blade –n. A mythical weapon used in the beheading of the Black Dragon of Yournit

Kakak – n.c. title given to a third-tier Sister of the Heart.

Kasserninian Flu – n.u. originating in Kassernine, in Dagna, this flu is not fatal in and of itself, but it does permanently sterilize any who contract it. It is rumored to only be spread from its source, the Cataclysm known as The Plague.

Knokni – n. ancient group of people who offer blood sacrifices to their god. Sacrifices are not limited to animals.

Lamda – n. God to Lamdonnoleans. Wears a dark cloak and has the face of a child.

Lamytal – n. One of the Nine Realms connected by the Innervein. This is the realm of fragmented earth where Dragons make their homes.

Lysos – n.c. female denizens of The Blue Realm who reportedly feed on the sexual energies of males. Shape-shifters.

Magus – n.s. pl: magi. Title given to male scholars of the Order of the Vein, users of Arcana. Official title for nearly 1,000 years.

Maketh-el – n.u. The Charling who first channeled the power of the Veins (El Vein), worshipped as a god by people along the El Vein. Ishtower is included among such people.

Martialist –n.c. profession of magi whose focus is on martial/ physical manipulation with attention to strengths and weaknesses.

Massasoit tobacco - n.u. a heady smoking tobacco that Lord Haphenasis loves. Flavorful and full of potency.

Mecha - n.u. shortform of "mechanical being," mecha are apparently living creatures formed from metals, glass, ceramics, and wood. They have clockwork parts and run on arcana.

Mulnus - n.c. 2nd day of the week (Monday).

Name day - n.c. day when a child is named. Not necessarily the individual's birth day, but important for the day that the child becomes a real person.

Norm - n.c. elitist term used by the Blessed or those with Arcane capabilities for normal people born without such skills/ elements.

Order of the Vein - n. scholarly order of magi devoted to the study of the Veins and the creation of arcana. Limited to men. Their headquarters is located within the Innervein, one of the Nine Realms.

Otherrealmer - n.c. a denizen of one of the other 8 realms.

Pavlode - n.u. The most common language on Traumanfang. Named for the ancient country from which it originated, Pavlodar.

Plasmats -n.u (plural) a special type of arcane plasma material that can be molded and hardened to create a long-lasting arcane item. These can take on any shape, limited only to the skill of the magus creating it.

Priber -n.c. one of the main focuses of arcana, one that concentrates on the mind, soul, and connections between energies. Also the title given to one who has mastered the Pribing arts.

Reality Convergience – n. a theoretical event during which all arcana from all nine realms is stripped. Doing so, it is theorized, would bind Traumanfang, cutting it off from the other eight realms.

Reservwyre – n. The "Old" city that was first founded at the base of the Singing Falls sat the base of the Reservwyre.

Reservwyresport – n. The "New" city that was started at the mouth of the Sing Wing River due largely to its proximity to the Apocryptein. Different from Reservwyre and one of the most modern cities of the Traumanfang.

Resonant aura – n.c. vibration of existence that all living things possess.

Riot – n.c. an intersection of 2 or more arcane Veins.

Rippling of the vein – v. / n.u. an action which can be felt by all Arcane-sensitive people. It is a way to alert others of danger, also an involuntary result of a massive injury to the Veins.

Runician –n.c. a profession of Magi whose focus is on language, and the writing and recording of arcane language. They are functionally the scribes of the Arcane.

Shema –n.c. the 7th day of the week (Saturday).

Shiek – n.c. title of the male in charge of certain desert countries.

Sing-Wing River – n. river south of the Ashen Mountains that leads into the Reservwyre and continues on below the falls to where it connects into the Singing Bay. Named for the waterfalls by which Reservwyre was first created.

Soul temptation – n.c. If a deceased or disembodied soul is fed a dab of the Vein's arcana, they become content. It is the best way to hold onto a soul.

Skeleton Key – n.c. it is the title of the master of the Keyhall. Aethir-appointed leader of the Order of the Vein.

Slop boy/ girl – n.c. title of whatever male/female has the odorous task of emptying slop buckets/ chamber pots.

Stinging bluebells – n.c. a type of blue flower whose thistles sting painfully and that reek of manure.

A Summons – n.c. an official count of 50 Magi. Each graduating class of the past several hundred years have been measured as a Summons.

The Age of Arcana – n.c. The Age of Arcana is the time since the creation of the first adaptations to life. Osaizi, known in history as The Blessor, yet whose actual name is forgotten, was captured, though legends say that he disappeared into lands and dimensions far away. At the start of the 12 Cataclysms, it is the 1765 year.

The Bough – n.u. (formal) the official seat for the Skeleton Key of the Order of the Vein.

The Dreamscape – n. one of the nine Realms connected by the Innervein. This is a dimension of unrealistic or hallucinatory properties, where concept becomes reality and flash and potential are liabilities, where creativity and imagination flourish.

The Honeycomb – n. a representative understanding of how the Realm of Capo looks.

The Keyhall – n. created as a pun on the concept of a "keyhole in the dimensional walls between realms," The Keyhall is the main hall of the Order of the Vein

The Seven Gods – n. Aulis, Candra, Ellehad, Kibosh, Cradall, Laon, and Teiid are the seven deities of the KAT LECC. Popular in certain desert or western-continental regions. The seven months of a year are unilaterally named for them.

The Singing Bay – n. bay that juts out from Reservwyresport, named for the immense sandstone towers in the bay that have eroded and which blow a series of songs during particularly windy days.

The Validation – n.u. the name for the trial period where an apprentice magus is judged for his second level of Efficiency in the Order of the Vein.

The Wizard's Cleanse – n. (historic period) – a time when the city of Oprahca outlawed the use of Arcana in all forms, and in the ensuing chaos, managed to infiltrate the Innervein and attack the magi of the Order of the Vein.

The Zeu'yan Valley – n. a quasi-mystical region in Traumanfang where the Tinker originated. Supposedly surrounded on all sides by high mountainous peaks and walled off from the rest of the world. Supposedly, an endless variety of mecha constructs exist within. According to legend, it has been cursed so that none may find it.

Three Heavens – n.c. Four of the nine Realms that make up the World Tree that is connected by the Innervein. These are the Blue Realm, Lamytal and Capo.

Traumanfang – n. one of the nine Realms. This is the

realm of man and Blessed, where the story of the Twelve Cataclysms takes place.

Vein - n.c. ley lines spread throughout the Nine Realms. Among those found on Traumanfang are: Gho, Re, Cha, Dei, Wn, among many others.

Veinway - n.c. paths of thin dimensional barriers. It is through these that Ventagists travel.

Ventagist - n.c. one of the professions of magi, whose adepts focus on "ventigation" both along the Veins of Traumanfang and from Realm to Realm.

Ventigation - v.t/i. to transport by Veinway. What another might call teleportation.

Wizard - n. (colloquial) unlearned term for magus. Not an insult, just incorrect terminology, mistakenly used by a politician several hundred years ago. Still accidently used.

Yom - n.c. 6th day of the week (Friday)

Beasts

Bogeymen - Live under beds and pilfer hairs from nose. Nobody is quite sure why they do this.

Chimera - Bizarre creature whose arcana allows it to switch heads/ polymorph between a goat, a wolf, a snake, crab, and vulture

Gergia sand snake - massive sand snake that leaves dunes in its wake. Drills through sand via its oscillating layers of teeth, which it ejects as waste. Can move quickly if necessary, though are generally pretty slow.

Gryphon - also known as an eagle-lion. Head and wings of an eagle, body of a lion.

Kremsek - jovial little creatures who love making mischief and spreading fire. They exist as beings of energy. Hail from the Realm of Lamytal

Maigre - a spidery creature inhabiting the Dark Realm. 4 clawed, 4 eyes, a swollen sack for a body, black in color, servant to the Master.

Ostrore – two-legged horse that can sprint for short periods of time at speeds of 70 leagues per hour. Carnivorous.

pelican-hawk – A massive sea-soaring carnivore. Very common around Reservwyresport for the sandstone pillars growing out in the deeper parts of the bay.

Rava – large war cat, tamable but nonetheless very dangerous.

Techichi – small yelpy dog with small pointy ears.

thunder-lizards – massive belly-crawling lizards that roar at enemies. Carnivorous.

tiger-oxen – tigers that have the cloven hooves, four stomachs and tusks of oxen. Carnivorous.

Vulphon goose – goose with golden down feathers. While their eggs are golden in color, these are not made of solid gold as legends would have you believe.

walking fish – fish with either one pair or two pairs of legs that crawl/walk on land. They have both gills and noses. There are 74 counted varieties so far.

Wyvern – called "lesser dragons" because while they are scaled, flying animals; they also sport fur on their backs and buckled noses. Not really actual Dragons, especially as these originate in Traumanfang. Additionally, they are only about the size of a full-grown human.

Spells and Literature

* Books are written in italics. All varieties of spell maintain normal writing.

The Adventures of Heimdall Lei – novel.

Armageddon in the Palm of You Hand – Mo-Chai. Historical journal.

Ask Your Captain for That Raze – a how-to book

.

Buh Nohr Bible – bible to the Buh Nor people.

Choker of Sorrow – spell. Creates total servitude in the person it is cast on. Virtually unbreakable, unless countered with greater magic, but as this is dependent on force of will, only those with powerful wills even dare to use it.

Coulculations – guide-book/ historical journal. Misspelled title. "Idiotic author" according to one magus.

Curtain of ephemeral silence – spell. Protective ward that dampens nearby arcana "noise."

Dewballs – spell. Balls of dew. Often used as an anesthesia.

Flight cloud – spell. A summoned semi-tangible cloud that allows flight.

Friendly Chitter – spell. It is euphoria that is often used by medical magi, but also employed by many as a means of distraction.

A Gout – spell. Literally, a gout of water, air or any other material that the caster chooses to employ.

Holy Hail – spell. A rainstorm-led spell that rains hail down on an area. Very potent natural summoning spell.

Hound – Mystical doodad. An arcane sphere with the ability to track an arcane "scent" across the ley of the Veins.

Irony – spell. A powerful chaos spell which creates ironic instability in an area. Very disruptive of everything. Highly unpredictable.

Lovelorn Lord – novel. Romance.

Mullet's Cloak – spell. Snaking containment field that muffles and smothers sounds, heat and other things.

A Murder of Crows – spell. Summons a flock of ethereal crow spirits purify certain spells/ corruption.

Mutt – spell/relic. A silver relic mecha with the ability to sniff our specific scents, much like a bloodhound. It grows to the size of a small Dalmation, whines and lies down upon failure or attacks upon victory, unless otherwise commanded by its master.

Necrocommunique - book. Banned from arcane libraries across the world. In its pages is the Soam Ule, a potent spell that can imprison souls or summon them.

Osaizi's Cant - cant. Osaizi's Cant is a curse more than anything, for it calls upon super-dimensional powers for fuel. Curses all involved in it. With its actual *name* being the method for banning the cant, it has generally been forgotten to the extent that its name prevents the learning of even the more simplistic aspects of the spell. Part of its words sound thus: "All Hell's wrath I call to bear/ The devils' wrath, I will not fear/ A child's life gone with a tear/ But these binds shalt you wear,"

Ouaja - spell. Ouaja is a soul trap which enables communication with a soul.

Peacott Eggplant - spell. a containment spell that suffuses the localized casting area with a quieting smoke.

Rum in the Cellar and Other Stories - Cycka Moe. Short story collection.

Sheer's Blight - curse/ spell. A long-lasting spell that causes a number of ailments upon its target, from rust in iron to verdigris in copper, to flu-like symptoms in living things.

Smoker's Shield - spell. It draws smoke to create a protective shell. Also used to cleanse an area of a stench.

Soam Ule - spell. A spirit summoning spell which is highly dangerous in the uncertainty of the spirit that it calls down. Found in the *Necrocommunique*.

A Soul's Eclipse - spell. The total subversion of a soul for the sake of possession. Also; a type of possession that allows experience through the target but prevents control. Highly brutalized.

Splitting Worlds: An Exploration Outside Dimensions – Aler the Omega. Covers one man's experiences with super-Realm travel.

Switch of Luna – spell. Summons facsimile of moon to create an intense white light.

Tactile Recall – spell. The ability to learn the history of an object through touch. Can be used to connect with an item's memory of people and places it has encountered during its existence.

The Ten Suitors of Dinah Bezar – novel

Threads of Ignity – spell. A binding agent that captures strangers to the Innervein, among other uses. One of the many defenses that protect the Innervein from intruders.

A Thunderclap – spell. A clap of thunder. Also recognized as a means of super-Realm travel.

Treatise on Shellacking – book.

Whispering Wail – spell. A messenger spell that can connect two people over great distance.

Will Container – spell. A transparent sphere of green energy.

Yolanda Witherspoon – novel that follows the misadventures of a Blessed. Social satire.

About the Author

ROBERT'S CREATION WAS UNREMARKABLE: EACH OF THE GODS cut from themselves their most prized piece of flesh, which the great spirits of the universe bound in their own essence. This mass was then encased in pure diamond and thrown into the great volcano, to be forged and tempered in the writhing molten sea for a millennium. Then, with a great crack of lightning, the mountain was split open, and into the world stepped the Robert. A fairly typical beginning for such a storied being.

Yet, despite the Robert's humble origins, he went on to perform many great feats like travel the world and write the book you just finished.